Promised
LAND

Promised
LAND

John Culea

Chariot Victor Publishing
A Division of Cook Communications

Chariot Victor Publishing,
A division of Cook Communications, Colorado Springs, Colorado 80918
Cook Communications, Paris, Ontario
Kingsway Communications, Eastbourne, England

Editors: Gloria Kempton, Barbara Williams
Design: Bill Gray
Cover Illustration: Frank Ordaz

1 2 3 4 5 6 7 8 9 10 Printing/Year 02 01 00 99 98

Library of Congress Cataloging-in-Publication Data

Culea, John.
      Promised land/John Culea.
           p.   cm.
      Includes bibliographical references.
      ISBN 1-56476-722-1
      I. Title.
PS3553.U48495P76   1998
813'.54--dc21   98-17112
                                                                      CIP

To Patti
You are my love and you understand why I write.

Special Thanks

Loving editing from the intellectual beauty in our family, my wonderful daughter Heidi.

Faithful support from the bubbly promoter in our family, my precious daughter Janet.

Brilliant insight and a masterful touch from editor Gloria Kempton, who was a vital part of my first book, *Light the Night.*

Encouragement and key suggestions from Chariot Victor managing editor, Julie Smith.

Computer help from Gavin Cutshall, a microchip off his father's (Ben) block.

"Truth Is Truth" (Joel Weldon Hendrickson, Rob Bryceson) New Release on BEST PICKS 1994 OASIS MUSIC, 1989 Little Peach Music, BMI. (With great affection for the man who sings this song as no other, the best gospel-country singer and fastest guitar player in the world, Dennis Agajanian.)

Gritty guidance from Lieutenant Glenn Breitenstein, Homicide Department, and Dave Cohen, Public Affairs, San Diego Police Department.

And special treatment from Julie Clark of the Jack Ranch Cafe, a few strides from the James Dean Memorial on Highway 46.

"No change of circumstances can repair a defect of character."
Ralph Waldo Emerson, Essays, Second Series: Character

More than forty-two million Americans will move this year.
Source: Bureau of the Census

Introduction

Promised Land is the story of Braxton, a small town in coastal central California. If you travel to Highway 46 and search for Braxton, you won't find it. No town, no people, no dot on the map—only a few ravines, scruffy pastures on rolling hills, and prime vineyards. Braxton is a fictional town, but it may be the real-life secret destination of millions of people obsessed with finding that illusive greener grass.

I've lived in or visited sixteen foreign countries and most of the states in America. After packing and unpacking more times than I can remember, I have become convinced that life's best move is not in discovering the perfect place, but in knowing the perfect Person. That perfect Person is the God-man, Jesus Christ.

Promised Land tells the story of an imperfect town caught in a web of deception that presses them to seek the perfect Person.

CHAPTER 1

Braxton, California
Wednesday April 28, 3:25 P.M.

"Any second thoughts?"

Lance Milburn's voice on the other end of the line sounded like that of a movie star's and sent a long distance chill through Shelly Hinson, where she stood in her dingy studio apartment. She felt her knees begin to quiver. The closest support was a rickety folding chair, and she eased into it.

"I said, any second thoughts?"

"Everything is in place," she murmured.

Shelly's mind filled with the image of Lance in his New York City office. Then she frowned. He was using a speaker phone, and it spoiled the sound of his voice. Lance was the most intriguing hunk she'd ever met. She pictured his perfectly styled jet black hair, steely blue eyes, and the deep cleft in his chin complemented by matching dimples. When she had first seen his cheekbones, she thought they were just high enough to suggest Native American somewhere in his family tree.

"When do we pull the trigger?"

"Tonight. The wire services get excerpts of the story, and your people have scheduled a satellite video news release. Radio and TV stations will eat this thing up. Most newspapers too."

"Everyone likes to hear about the American dream," Lance said.

"And we've created it."

"You did a super job on this, Shelly."

She felt goose bumps cover her arms. "Thanks, you were my

biggest supporter." Would he think she was kissing up to him? She hoped not. She truly meant it.

Lance's voice softened. "It was a great idea. You did all the dirty work and wrote the story. If we pull it off, you get the glory, and who knows, maybe a shelf full of awards. Columbia University, George Polk . . ."

Shelly's heart skipped a beat at the mere mention of honors that were as coveted by magazines as Pulitzers were by newspapers. She felt herself blushing and nervously put her hand to her mouth as Lance continued.

"But, if it bombs . . ."

Shelly bit her lip and waited for him to itemize the potential consequences. Instead, she could almost hear him shrug as he said, "Hey, if it bombs, we'll probably get more attention."

She wasn't sure if that was good or bad. All she knew right now was that, as usual, Lance was stirring strong emotions in her. Perhaps she'd been simply overwhelmed by the big city when she'd first gone to New York to talk with him about the project. Still, she couldn't help wondering if something more than business was growing between them. The two times they'd gone out alone for lunch, she was certain he had noticed many of the other men in the restaurant watching her. And once, their eyes met with a smile when she caught him admiring her silk blouse; she'd purposely left the top button undone. At 5'2" and 110 pounds, she knew she had a good figure. She pulled at her short, dark hair now and scrunched up her button nose. She was ready to compete with a million other women in big cities or small towns, single or otherwise.

Lance's ability to take risks filled Shelly with exhilaration. She respected his vision. Still, she feared the unknown and wondered what would happen if their confidential plan backfired. Would Lance Milburn, publisher of *Destination* magazine, be as charming and understanding? Did they have a future together? Or was he just using her? A year from now, she'd find out. She'd been given a twelve-month contract to work undercover.

"You're one writer in a thousand," Lance went on. It sounded like he was grinning.

"Don't remind me. I've lived on Spaghetti O's and Kraft Macaroni and Cheese for too long." Lance laughed.

Shelly was twenty-nine, single, and a struggling reporter for a weekly hick town newspaper. She was also a free-lance writer, whose occasional magazine articles for obscure publications supplemented her meager salary. That outside income was often the difference between paying her rent and eviction. But two months ago she had bucked the odds and turned a query letter into a soon-to-be released national magazine cover story. "It's going to work, Lance, I know it."

Lance paused and Shelly heard what sounded like his leather chair squeaking as he leaned back. "OK, my secret weapon, let's see what happens. Keep me informed. Any suspicions out there, especially from your editor?"

"None that I know of."

"Good. Call me Saturday morning."

"Will do."

"And give my best to *Bernardo*," he teased. "I like his writing."

"Yeah, right."

"No, seriously. That phony article you wrote about Braxton was great, but the name you picked for the writer, Bernardo Javier, was perfect. It's so, so innocent sounding—almost like a Franciscan monk."

Shelly's spirits soared. "I'll be sure to tell him when I drop by the mission."

Lance howled with laughter. "Congratulations, Shelly, you two have just created the lead story out there. Have fun watching the news."

"I will, but Bernardo won't see it. The mission doesn't have a TV."

Lance roared over the speaker phone again. "Later."

As Shelly replaced the receiver, she closed her eyes, took a quick breath, and blew it out of her mouth. There was nothing to do now except wait for the eleven o'clock news.

Braxton
11:00 P.M.

"Good evening. Our top story tonight, a national honor, right in our own backyard." The young man speaking was a boyish looking news anchor for KSBY-TV, Channel 6 in nearby San Luis Obispo, NBC's affiliate in the nation's 112th largest market. "Braxton has been chosen as the best small town in America."

Shelly stared at the tiny TV set, picked up for twenty bucks at a garage sale. Rabbit ears and a wire clothes hanger did little to improve the picture. Curled up on her tattered sofa, she nervously jammed three barbecue-flavored potato chips in the direction of her mouth. One broke off and fell in her lap. The newsman's co-anchor suddenly appeared on a two-shot with him. She was a dark-haired beauty with sorority-like features, and Shelly liked the way her mouth moved when she spoke. "The award was announced tonight and is the cover story of *Destination* magazine," the young woman said. "Braxton Mayor Roger Carter told Channel 6 News that the honor, while unexpected, is a tribute to the people of Braxton and the town's leadership."

The male anchor's toothy grin showed off gleaming white teeth. His curly red hair was sprayed into a brittle mop that looked like a Brillo pad. "Here are more of the mayor's comments."

Carter, a chubby-faced man in his late thirties, had only memories of a full head of hair. He stood on a sidewalk in what appeared to be a downtown area. "Friendly people, safe streets." His grin grew wider as he took in an exaggerated breath of air. "Clean air, good schools, low housing costs, and a thriving economy. What's the big surprise? We've known this for years. Was there any other choice?"

Video of a tree-lined street flashed on the screen with a graphic that read "Courtesy: *Destination* magazine." People with smiling faces strolled on sidewalks in front of neatly kept shops. The woman news anchor began reading over the video. "As we know, Braxton is in our wine region, nestled along Highway 46. Retailing, tourism, vineyards, wineries, and a revitalized downtown have helped the town prosper." The screen now showed a park set in a wooded area, then what looked like a community swimming pool. Shelly heard the sounds of children in the background, squealing with delight as they splashed water on each other. "According to *Destination*, Braxton's crime rate is low and its student test scores are high." The video showed a residential neighborhood of ranch-style one- and two-story homes on large lots. "Housing is still considered affordable for this community of 15,000 people."

The video ended, and the two news anchors appeared on the set together. "Whew!" the young man exclaimed. "This kind of caught us off guard. I understand the magazine hits the newsstands Friday."

"I wonder how our friends in Braxton will handle the attention."

He smiled. "We'll soon find out. We plan to have our cameras there to follow the story in the days to come. In other news . . ."

The TV anchorman's mouth continued to move, but no words could be heard. A military jet fighter appeared over his left shoulder, and a graphic read "F-18 Crash," but Shelly had zapped the news reader silent with her remote control. She felt a shiver of excitement, then a sense of foreboding. Alone in her Braxton apartment, she looked at the television screen, then absentmindedly poked some stuffing back into the armrest of the sofa. It had really happened. The story was out. She longed to share her moment of triumph with someone, anyone, especially those in her hometown who doubted she'd amount to anything. But for now that was impossible.

"I did it!" she screamed, pumping a fist into the air. Startled by the sound of her own voice, she covered her mouth with her right hand and hoped the other residents in her seedy apartment complex hadn't heard her. Shelly reached for the paper on the coffee table and read again what had been sent to the Associated Press and media outlets across the country.

> Feature Print Advisory (with Best Small Town story)
> (The following advance is an excerpt from *Destination* magazine.)
> BRAXTON IS BEST
> Small town shows big is not better
> By Bernardo Javier
> Reprinted by permission

> Along California's Central Coast
> Dawn's first rays peek over the Sierra Nevada and bring light to the agricultural valley of the Santa Lucia Mountains. I am up early, driving north from San Luis Obispo to Braxton, California.
> Off to the right, on the valley's floor, is a dusty gully that gushes angry brown water during the rainy month of January. The rest of the year, the Salinas River is a zipcode for lizards, snakes and whatever else creeps, crawls, but doesn't swim. Next to it are scrub trees that hide the riverbed and bend in the direction where most of the Santa Ana winds blow, east to west.
> Railroad tracks that cut through the valley look like a long surgical scar. The tracks strain under the weight of loaded freight trains, and barely notice half-empty Amtrak trains that run *clickity-clack* north and south. Every once in

a while, the tracks veer close to Route 101 and follow the same direction as the four-lane highway on which I'm traveling.

Shelly took a sip of her Diet Coke. It had lost most of its fizz, but she felt positively bubbly. "Bernardo, you are one terrific writer." She giggled. "I think we're going to have a wonderful future together." She continued reading.

Miles of vineyards on both sides of the highway lead to the Paso Robles wine country. Signs invite the traveler to leave the highway, enjoy some rural atmosphere, and sample the ambience of small wineries that dot the oak-lined hills. I plan on having a taste or two.

Wine-making and grape-growing in this region began in 1797 at Mission San Miguel Archangel. Today, more than twenty-five wineries and one hundred vineyards grow premium wine grapes on rolling hills that vary from 700 to 1,900 feet in elevation. The truth is, despite award-winning claims for Chardonnay, Zinfandel, Cabernet Franc, Pinot Noir, Merzin, and Cigare Volant, the area plays second fiddle to the wines of Napa Valley to the north. And the people who live here say they couldn't be happier.

Shelly let out a dissenting sniff. Not her. She wanted out, and the article in her hands was certainly her passport to riches and fame. She loved the next part.

However, from San Miguel to Santa Margarita, from Whitley Gardens to Templeton, the sun rises and the sun sets on what people here consider the best-kept secret in

America. And they don't want that to change. The asphalt jungles and freeway-choked parking lots of Los Angeles are 200 miles south, while quake-prone San Francisco and its liberal lifestyle are out of sight and out of mind, 200 miles north. Central California's inland coast is where people have room to live and be left alone. Tourists are welcome, but as the slogan goes: *Buy our wine, and when you leave, that's just fine.* Nowhere is that felt stronger than in Braxton.

As they turn off State Route 101 to Highway 46, motorists come upon a yellow flashing light at the bottom of the off-ramp. It hangs over the intersection and blinks every second of the day in order to slow traffic. A bird of some kind is perched on top as I pull up. I turn left, pass under the freeway, and head west on Highway 46, a two-lane asphalt road, with few hints that a town is ahead.

The drive along the winding road is peaceful. Lines of coastal live oaks top the hillside ridges, and cattle are scattered on nearly barren slopes. I wonder if anything on the ground is worth biting into. Some in the herd are grazing, others seem to be dozing. Patches of wet fog cling to ravines, a hawk circles overhead, and a road sign warns of deer in the area.

My attention shifts to road signs that beckon me to the next town. A sign informs me that the next two miles of highway are litter-free because of the Golden State Classic Car Club. Another stretch of litter pickup was paid for by Roger Carter, Mayor of Braxton.

"Mayor phony-baloney," Shelly scoffed aloud. She drained the last of her Diet Coke and tossed the can toward a wastebasket. It bounced off the wall, splattered onto the faded wallpaper, and settled into the basket. She continued reading her article.

> Travelers are promised they'll find fast food restaurants, service stations, a Ford dealer, a Motel 6, and a Wal-Mart ahead. But my question is, so what? Is this line on the map any different from other black veins between *who-cares* destinations?
>
> I spot a sign that reads "Braxton, next two exits," and flash my turn signal as the ramp approaches. Steering my car off the highway, I soon reach the bottom of the ramp. I am about to discover why this town of 15,000 people cherishes its privacy so much. Soon we will all know the secret of what makes Braxton the best small town in America.
>
> (More excerpts of article to follow)
>
> AP/4-28/2330EST

―――――

Shelly wasn't surprised that the local television newscast's coverage of her story was a no-brainer. Her concern was that it would be ignored altogether. After all, if it wasn't a big deal in the viewing area of Coastal Central California, it wouldn't even make the newscasts in other cities across the country. But it did, and later Shelly learned how it played at 11:27 P.M. that night in Los Angeles, the nation's second largest market.

―――――

"Finally, tonight, a story from our 'American Dream' department." The news anchors were bringing KCBS-TV, Channel 2's local news to an end. "For those of you looking for the perfect place to live, *Destination* magazine has chosen Braxton, California as the best small town in America," the woman said.

Her partner, a distinguished looking black man in his early fifties, turned to his blonde co-anchor, a woman twenty years his junior, and said, "Vicki, the editors of the magazine say it wasn't even close. They compared Braxton with a hundred other small towns for such things as housing, environment, education, and the crime rate. Braxton came out on top by a wide margin."

Video of the town appeared on the screen once more. The same tape had been sent by satellite to stations around the country. "Braxton, population 15,000, is about 120 miles north of us," she said. "It's near Paso Robles, on Highway 46, in San Luis Obispo County. There are a number of wineries in the area. With this honor, I imagine the town will have a lot of curious people coming their way—not only to taste the wine, but to sample the good life."

"I haven't heard that much about Braxton," said the man honestly, "but I'm sure life is about to change for the townspeople who now find themselves in the national spotlight."

The two newscasters appeared together on the set. "We're out of time," the woman said. "Thank you so much for looking our way."

"Good night, and have a great tomorrow," her partner added. The music began to play as the closing credits rolled across the screen.

CHAPTER 2

Braxton
Thursday April 29, 4:46 A.M.

Shelly watched through the window as a car made its way through the darkness, its driver tapping the brake lightly as he stopped in front of house after house. It was the one good thing about her apartment—she had a terrific view of those who lived behind her. She would never admit it to anyone, but Shelly secretly enjoyed spying on people and keeping track of their private lives. Now, at just about every house, newspapers wrapped in plastic bags sailed out of the car's passenger side window. Each paper whirled like a helicopter blade, hitting a driveway or porch with a *plop*, then skidding a few feet. Most of the hometown folk were asleep, but when awakened, they would find a frontpage editorial in the weekly *Braxton Banner*.

Shelly couldn't sleep. She'd tiptoed outside a few moments before to get her copy of the newspaper in the mail rack. It now lay on the table next to a steaming mug of coffee. She'd crunched the last of her cheap coffee beans and turned them into just enough grounds for two weak cups of java. How nice it would be to share this simple pleasure with a man. She expected it to happen someday, but better a man of means in New York than a country bumpkin in Braxton.

Shelly chuckled to herself, remembering how the Associated Press story about Braxton had caused a last minute panic at the *Banner*. When Shelly's editor, Marty Cavitt, had called her at home the day before, she feigned surprise when told about it. Her boss, a low-key, scholarly man in his mid-thirties, had joined the paper two years before. The publisher had brought Marty in, and Shelly resented that he had been promoted over her.

Marty was her opposite. She was a Stanford journalism grad, while he had a degree in English from Northern Arizona University in Flagstaff. She passionately longed for the excitement of a big city newspaper, and Marty disdained that kind of atmosphere with equal fervor. He delighted in the little stories of everyday life that, when added up, was what mattered most to people. Actually, Shelly had to admit he wasn't a bad guy and after the initial friction, the two of them had begun to work well together. She considered herself a better storyteller, but Marty knew Braxton and was a genius at editing each story so that it was a true reflection of their small town. She had expected him to be skeptical about the national honor, and he was.

"I don't have a good feeling about this," he had told her. "I'd like to see the whole article."

"Well, why not Braxton?" Shelly asked. "Just the other day you were talking about how things are a lot better than when you first arrived."

"No, something's fishy here. A magazine just doesn't pick us out of the blue. They never talked with me or the mayor."

"Maybe the reporter was here while you were on vacation," Shelly suggested.

Silence. "Well, I guess that could have happened. Were you contacted by anyone?"

"I don't know . . . a lot of people come into the paper asking questions. I just think they came in unannounced and formed their own opinion. You think they'd get an honest answer from the mayor?"

"Probably not. OK, it's late, and I've got to write something for tomorrow. Talk with you in the morning."

The front page had been redone immediately, and Shelly smiled now as she read Marty's editorial:

Unexpected Honor

Uh, oh, Braxtonians, the world is about to learn some of what we've tried to keep quiet. Our little secret is out. *Destination* magazine has chosen Braxton the best small town in America.

With the announcement comes a rush of civic pride, but it should also be tempered with a dose of restraint. We were not notified that the award existed or that Braxton was in the running. It seems someone from *Destination* slipped in and out of our town without being detected. But that may be the beauty of the honor. We don't need to put on a show to impress outsiders. What you see here is what you get. Braxton is far from perfect, but we can be proud that *Destination* liked what they saw.

Destination hits the newsstands tomorrow. We have much to be proud of. The story of Braxton, mentioned briefly last night, will be detailed on local and national television tonight, and printed in newspapers across the country. We'll look and sound pretty inviting. Today, and during the next few weeks, if your ears begin to itch, it may be from the thousands of people talking about the *Best Small Town in America*. Those of us who live here know that we've arrived, and we're glad to be here. Now the questions are: How many people are headed our way? Who are they, why are they coming, what will they bring, when will they arrive, and how will we change?

———·•·———

Braxton Town Council Chamber
10:36 A.M.

For a small town, Braxton's council chamber had a big-city look:

cedar-paneled walls, cushioned theater seats for the audience, and rose-colored plush pile carpet. The only stain to be found was on the stained-glass windows that reflected light through colorful scenes of the Paso Robles wine country. Off to one side, directly in front of the council chambers, at a table reserved for the news media, sat Shelly. One of her beats for the *Braxton Banner* was to cover City Hall, and as she looked at the council members in front of her, she knew the reason for the room's relative splendor. It was Mayor Roger Carter and he was now in control.

"The motion is to authorize an emergency expenditure from our cash reserve," the mayor said with a look that communicated it was a done-deal. "A thousand dollars for two signs at the town limits, and $20,000 for miscellaneous expenses. Do I hear a—"

"I second the motion, Mr. Mayor!"

"Please, Phil," chided the mayor, "let me finish. Do I hear a second?"

"Sorry," the man said with a grin. "I got a little carried away." He then bellowed, "I second the motion!"

Mayor Carter shifted his girth and moved forward in his chair. "OK, all those in favor, say—"

"Wait a minute," demanded a council member seated to the mayor's left. "What about discussion?"

Shelly sighed. Once again, Calvin "Cal" Spencer wasn't about to rubber-stamp Mayor Carter's wishes.

"We've been discussing this all morning!" whined a woman in the back of the room.

"I agree," said the mayor. "All those in—"

"You're out of order, Mayor Carter!" Cal interrupted. "It's crazy, spending money we don't have just because some magazine back East decides they like our town."

Audible groans rose up from members of the town staff. Cal was the lone voice of dissent on an emergency agenda item that seemed ready for approval.

Shelly looked up from her notes, her eyes on the second district councilman. Cal Spencer, the brooding middle school teacher, had been known to explode in fits of anger. Now he stroked his black beard and mustache in an obvious effort to keep his temper in check. The beard was a seasonal thing, grown during the school year and shaved off on the first day of summer vacation. Shelly had no idea why he did that. He was a bit of a mystery, always returning her phone calls and available for interviews, yet distant. Since his arrival in Braxton, Cal had taken Shelly out to dinner and to the movies a few times, but she never sensed the teacher-councilman had any long-term, romantic interest in her. Long-term? She chuckled to herself. She'd settle for short-term and go from there.

"We've tried for years to put Braxton on the map, Mr. Spencer," the mayor said in a strained voice. "Now, in one day, a national magazine has done it for us."

"Fine, it's done. We're on the map. Big deal. I just want to know where in the budget we are going to find $21,000 for two signs and what did you call it—miscellaneous expenses?"

"For cryin' out loud, Spencer!" Phil Prescott, the fourth district councilman, leaned toward his microphone. "Uh, Mr. Mayor, may I be heard?"

"Certainly," Carter said eagerly, obviously glad to get Cal off his back. "The Chair recognizes the gentleman from the fourth district."

Shelly knew that Prescott was Carter's strongest ally. The two men were former college classmates at San Jose State.

"Councilman Spencer, you've fought growth ever since you came on this council. You love being the town rebel—leading your little band of anti-everything, bleeding liberals—"

"Shut up!" Cal yelled. "You've lined your pockets with—"

The mayor pounded his gavel. "Knock it off!" he shouted.

"I'm sorry," Prescott apologized. "I just can't understand why he wants to throw a bucket of cold water on our success."

Cal glared at Prescott. "Better check the water if it was drawn from Sheepcamp Creek, Phil. The last time I looked, your cabinet shop was dumping toxic waste in the creek."

"Ancient history, Spencer," Prescott snapped. "That's not what we're discussing."

"I will not vote to spend money for the mayor's boondoggle."

"It's an investment," the mayor argued. "Once visitors start coming, we'll get the money back in sales taxes."

"Ha! You think one magazine article is going to start a boom?"

"Absolutely. It sounds better than if we wrote it ourselves. I think we're going to be swamped this weekend, and we've got two days to get ready."

"And how do we do that?" Cal asked.

The mayor looked at Cal as if he were the adult explaining the obvious to a child. "I'll try to make it simple for you, Mr. Spencer. We spruce up the town with paint, fill in some potholes—"

"We haven't even seen the article!" Cal protested. "And don't patronize me!"

"Who needs to see the article?" Prescott waved a hand. "All that matters is that the whole country thinks we're the best."

"Hear, hear." the mayor said, nodding.

"Aren't you a friend of this town?" Prescott asked.

"That's a cheap shot, Phil. I was elected to give leadership to my district. Who spoke to this magazine? Who gave them their information? It surely wasn't Marty Cavitt over at the *Banner.* He told me this came out of left field."

"I'm sure they contacted the right people in *right field.*" The mayor chuckled. "Perhaps even someone who knows *everything* about

Braxton, like you. How long have you lived in this town?"

"Five years."

"My, my, I'm honored to be in the presence of one of our founding fathers," the mayor mocked. Prescott guffawed loudly. "The Chair appreciates the concern from the *junior* member of the council, Mr. Spencer," Carter went on with a smile at his adversary. "We'll soon be able to see the magazine article and judge for ourselves."

"So why not wait until then before we vote to spend the money? This is nuts!"

Shelly was seeing another side of Cal. He was often stubborn in his frequent battles with the majority, but she couldn't remember him being this demonstrative before. She felt a stirring inside; actually, his spark of energy was quite attractive. Perhaps she was getting a glimpse of what Cal was like before he came to Braxton, a hint of what they had only heard about. Rumors about Cal's past ranged from his being a soldier of fortune in Africa to a defrocked Roman Catholic priest.

The other council members looked on with glazed eyes. An older man with a bulbous shaped nose blinked twice, then shouted, "Question!"

Next to him, a woman council member, on the verge of falling asleep, sat upright. "Question!" she blurted in a screechy voice.

The mayor looked tired. "We're just repeating what's been covered before—"

"No, we're not!" Cal protested. "I think we should table the motion and have the town staff come back with a report."

"There's a motion on the floor," Prescott argued. "Let's vote."

The mayor nodded. "Mr. Prescott's right. If it fails, you can make your motion, Mr. Spencer. Madam Clerk, repeat the motion, and call the roll."

The town clerk, a thin, wiry woman in her sixties, adjusted her bifocals. "The motion is to authorize the expenditure of $1,000 to build and display two signs at each end of the Braxton town limits that will read *Welcome to Braxton, Best Small Town in America*. Also, the council will provide an additional $20,000 for immediate miscellaneous expenses, as submitted by the Public Works Department. Your vote, Mr. McKnight?"

"Yes."

"Mrs. Drew?"

"Yes."

"Mr. Spencer?"

"No!" he barked.

"Mr. Prescott?"

"Yes!"

"The motion passes three to one, with no need for Mayor Carter to cast a vote."

"Thank you all very much," the mayor said. "This is a thrilling moment in our town's history. I believe we're on the verge of tremendous growth and prosperity."

Shelly closed her notebook, rose from her chair, and quietly left the room through a side door.

CHAPTER 3

Braxton
Friday April 30, 7:55 A.M.

Shelly Hinson tapped her fingers in a staccato rhythm against the icy cold steering wheel. To her right, an aluminum thermos of coffee sat in a console. She removed it and took a sip through the small hole on top. A few drops dribbled off her chin and fell on the letters of her cardinal red sweatshirt; a small brown stain slowly spread across the n and f in *STANFORD*.

She had parked her car along the curb on Main Street a few moments earlier to watch a young man unload his semi-truck trailer and deliver what she and the townsfolk of Braxton had been waiting for. Across the street, on the sidewalk outside Roxy's Drugstore, stood a line of people. They were huddled against the storefronts in an effort to keep out of the cold, damp wind blowing from the west. Shelly counted roughly fifty people from the corner of Jefferson and Main to the store. Those closest to the door were peering inside, waiting for the store to open. She picked up a spiral notebook from the passenger seat and wrote down her observations so far, then opened her car door.

Well, here we go, Shelly thought, as she climbed out of her car and began walking across the street to the store. *Will they believe it? Did I do the right thing?* These people were her neighbors, her friends. They trusted her. She paid close attention to the facial expressions of those in line, as she leaned against a stucco wall near the front entrance. Edging closer, Shelly nodded to a few of her friends, then looked in the window. Her mood brightened when she saw councilman Cal Spencer inside. But to her dismay, Mayor Carter stood beside him, a person Shelly considered entirely too pompous. They were standing near a pile of magazines, reading her article. Correction: Bernardo Javier's article. She figured the store's owner, councilwoman Roxanne Drew, had let them in through the back. Drew was now at the front door, and Shelly watched as she turned the dead bolt.

"It's the old double standard, huh, Roxy?" yelled a man near the front of the line.

"Yeah, you let your council buddies in early," said another.

"Nice way to freeze your customers," one woman complained.

"Come on now, be nice." The store owner pushed the door open, causing a small metal bell above the doorjamb to jingle. The old-fashioned sound fit the small town. The door was only half open when the crowd surged forward into the woman, causing her to stagger. "Whoa! No need to run me over! There are plenty of magazines for everyone." She stepped aside, and a buzz of excited comments could be heard as the crowd pushed their way inside the store. Some were laughing, while others made snide comments about having to wait in line.

Shelly cut in front of one man and ducked into the store.

"Hey, who do you think you are?" a woman called out. "You think you're someone special? Wait in the cold like the rest of us!" Then for emphasis, she threw a curse at Shelly.

"Sorry," Shelly said. "I'm doing a story for the newspaper." She had recognized the angry voice. She had gone to high school with the woman, and the two had never enjoyed one minute of friendship.

On the floor near the cash register, Shelly counted at least ten stacks of magazines. A stock boy was cutting a plastic binding strap from one of the piles, and as his knife cut through the strap, she heard a snapping sound, and the pile collapsed to the right. Copies of *Destination* magazine spilled out over the floor like a thick deck of cards.

One by one, copies of the magazine were snatched up. Roxanne Drew would collect the money later—reading the article came first. Customers continued to arrive, and by now at least a hundred were jammed inside. But the room was strangely quiet. Shelly could hear pages turning and once in a while a muffled voice; the place felt more like a library than a drugstore at the moment. She watched as smiles and looks of pride spread across faces around the room. She spotted Cal and the mayor again, but this time they were talking in hushed tones. She moved over near them, opened her notebook, and began writing.

"Well, what do you think now, Mr. Negative?" The mayor thrust the magazine in Cal's direction. "Have you seen enough of the article to admit you were wrong?"

"Save your jabs for the council meeting, *Mr. Mayor*." Cal thumbed through the article. "It's a great story. I just wonder what town this guy is writing about."

"You still don't get it, do you?" Carter pointed to the magazine. "If you had to make a real living in this town, you'd understand."

"What's that supposed to mean?" Cal asked with a puzzled look.

"Well, Professor, you live off of public money, right? You get your salary, no matter what."

Cal's eyes narrowed in anger. "When was the last time you returned your paycheck as mayor?"

"I'm not talking about what we get on the council. That's peanuts." The mayor pointed to himself. "I earn my money in business," he said, then jabbed a finger into Cal's chest. "You're paid by the school district."

Cal slapped the mayor's hand away. "Well, excuse me, but that's how the system works."

The men's voices had risen several notches, and Shelly saw that others were now listening in on the argument.

The mayor moved closer to Cal, so that their faces were just inches apart. "You really are a piece of work, Spencer. The system, as you call it, only works if we have money to support you. Property taxes and school taxes don't just happen. We need new people, new business. Without that, your job and your precious classroom shrivel up."

"What's your point, oh, great benevolent leader?"

"Braxton needs growth, and this magazine article is going to do it. Just don't stand in the way, or you'll get run over."

An elderly woman stepped forward. "Cal, you sound like you're against our town."

"Don't you think we deserve this?" one man asked.

"Times haven't been easy for a lot of us, Cal," another woman added. "You ought to back the mayor on this one."

Cal looked around and raised his hands, as if warding off an attack. "Listen, don't get me wrong. I'm all for what's best for Braxton. It's just that I'd like to know who wrote this story. Who is this guy Bernardo Javier anyway, and where did he get his facts?"

Shelly shifted nervously on her feet, avoiding the mayor's eyes when he glanced her way. "Hey, Shelly," he called out, "you're the star reporter for *The Banner*. Did you know anything about this?"

She had to make this sound convincing. "Uh, no, not at all. I'm as surprised as anyone. Nobody at the paper, from the editor on down, knew this was coming."

The mayor laughed. "Well, it looks like you missed the biggest story this town has ever had."

Several people nearby began to chuckle, including the woman who'd cursed at Shelly when she entered the store. "That's no surprise, Mayor," the woman said through a face caked with makeup. "When Shelly-too-good-for-the-rest-of-us graduated from *Stanford*, her nose never came out of the clouds. Trouble is, no one would hire her at a big paper. The only job she could get was with our local fish wrap." Two men near Shelly guffawed.

Shelly felt a surge of anger. She wanted to slap the woman, but instead, she hoped she looked sufficiently embarrassed. "What can I say? I got scooped in my own backyard."

"Are you saying that no one from the magazine contacted you?" Cal asked in a shocked tone.

Hiding the truth from the town was uncomfortable, but with Cal, someone she respected and wanted to know better, it was almost painful. Shelly quickly reminded herself that what she was doing was for the good of the town. She shrugged. "Yesterday, when the story hit the wires, it was the first any of us at the paper had heard about it. Didn't you read our editorial this morning?"

Cal shook his head. "It just doesn't make—"

"Spencer, would you give it up?" the mayor roared. "I haven't the slightest idea who wrote the article, or whom he talked with. All I know is that I love the story."

Shelly breathed a sigh of relief, thankful the mayor had shifted attention from her. She closed her notebook and turned to leave. Just as she reached the front door, she heard the mayor say, "Councilman Spencer can rain on his own parade. I say Braxton had better stock up. People are coming our way."

Out on the sidewalk, Shelly heard a resounding cheer from inside. She was jostled then, as several people leaving the store bumped into her. They didn't even apologize. She watched as the crowd inside of the store began to disperse, hurry to their cars, and drive away. A loud and long screech caught her attention, and she turned in the direction of the noise. A block away, at Main and Lincoln, two of the cars made a hard left at the traffic signal, cutting in front of a pickup. She held her breath as the driver of the truck slammed on his brakes to avoid a collision. She walked toward Lincoln then and turned left at the corner, where she saw a line of cars backed up to the parking lot of Food Right, Braxton's only supermarket. *Something weird is going on*, she marveled.

Shelly approached the parking lot to see a number of people outside the supermarket grabbing shopping carts and pushing them toward the store's front entrance. Two shoppers, each rushing to get inside before the other, collided broadside at the door with their carts.

Shelly walked into the store and found herself confused as she saw people hurrying up and down the aisles, loading their carts with many of the same items. There was an eeriness to it all.

Then she realized what it was. The place was completely silent. No one talked to anyone else. It was every person for him or herself.

For the rest of the day and well into the night, Shelly watched how her hometown dealt with its newfound fame. She walked the sidewalks and entered businesses. Most of the time, she felt invisible; everyone around her seemed to be concentrating so much on the moment at hand, they didn't even see her. Once again, Shelly noted her observations in her notebook. A story seemed to be growing within its pages, a story of a town taking on a new identity.

Rather than return to her studio apartment, Shelly drove to the neighborhood where she had grown up. She parked across the street from the small house her parents had rented before she was even born. It now belonged to a Hispanic family. As curious as she was about things, she had no desire to see inside the home. She wanted to remember things as they were when she was a child. Thankfully, the outside of the house hadn't changed that much, although her father would not appreciate the pea-green paint that now adorned the exterior. Shelly smiled to herself. Her daddy had hated peas. She punched in an oldies station on the radio, tilted her car seat back, and turned her mind from the present to the past.

Shelly was born in Braxton and knew from an early age that she wanted to write. It may have started the moment she took a black crayon and scrawled "See Spot run" on her bedroom wallpaper. The thrill of seeing those words she had written all by herself was remembered long after her hiney stopped throbbing. As soon as her mother saw what she did, she gave Shelly a thrashing with her father's belt. It was to be one of Shelly's most significant memories, because moments later her mom returned to her bedroom carrying a dish containing two large scoops of chocolate ice cream. Her mother then handed her a bright red notebook. "Write as much as you want in this," she told Shelly, "and when you fill it up, I'll give you another one."

That would be the first of many journals and diaries Shelly kept, the secret thoughts of a bright, shy, awkward little girl who grew up between lines of paper. She wrote at least a sentence every day, but sometimes she poured her heart out for hours. Shelly was the sole judge of her life; her words declared what was good, exciting, scary, and impossible. The sights, sounds, and smells were always more vivid when she wrote them on paper, and best of all, they could be relived over and over again. One night she would warn of hideous shadows that lurked in her room, another she would plot the painful death of a neighborhood bully. And then, the very next night, she might describe, in tender detail, a secret boyfriend she saw in the clouds. She wrote about animals, movie stars, grown-ups, school friends. Using elaborate description, she wrote of her love for long-distance running, the weird changes she felt in her body, and a prince who would one day appear in Braxton and take her away, perhaps to a place like nearby Hearst Castle. She wrote of fantastic dreams, about the things that made her happy, and those that made her sad. Shelly decided what was fair and what was not. The words came freely, with emotion, passion, and reckless abandon. She lived for those moments she could enter the world of her journal.

Then, in December of her senior year in high school, something happened that was so painful, so personal, she stopped writing. It was the first time in her life that she couldn't put words on paper, and she remained paralyzed like that for months.

It was a rainy Saturday night, and her father, mother, brother, and sister were returning home after watching Shelly compete in her school's cross country finals in Fresno. Shelly was at least ten minutes behind them, having decided at the last minute to take the team bus. Witnesses said the Hinsons were westbound on Highway 46 when a thirty-foot motor home crossed into oncoming traffic and struck them head-on. A pickup then hit the Hinsons' car from behind. All three vehicles, entangled in a pile of twisted metal, burst into flames. The accident killed the motor home's driver, the driver of the pickup, and Shelly's father, mother, and eight-year-old brother. Miraculously, Shelly's twelve-year-old sister was pulled to safety by another motorist. Shelly and her teammates arrived at the crash scene fifteen minutes later and found the wreckage still in flames and three bodies on the highway covered with sheets.

Six years later she finally found the strength to write about the accident in detail and its impact on her. It had been part of her master's thesis in journalism at Stanford: *After the Tragedy: the Unreported Story.*

Shelly was never able to put aside the memory of that accident. The crash was one of many that earned Highway 46 the title of "Blood Alley." The memory haunted her every time she opened a notebook, typed a paper, or sat in front of a computer keyboard. Frank Hinson was a hugely popular English teacher at Braxton High School, and Helen Hinson was principal of Braxton Middle School. Their lives were dedicated to their family and the town they loved. Yes, Shelly felt responsible for the death of her parents and brother. Had they not driven to Fresno to see her run, they would be alive today. Worst of all, she carried tremendous guilt for not being with them when they died.

Was that what had motivated the *Destination* project? To somehow please her parents by making their hometown famous? Shelly didn't know, but she now had two chances to find out. She had two jobs, and two paychecks. Before taxes, the first job with *The Banner*, at $313.26 a week, barely covered her rent, food, and car payment. After taxes, she had nothing left over, which meant from the time she joined *The Banner* three years before, she'd been slowly sinking in debt.

Returning to a weekly newspaper in her hometown was not the career path she'd charted when she left Palo Alto. But reality set in when she got tired of counting form letter rejections. Newspaper editors from Maine to California, from Minnesota to Louisiana, had no room for a hotshot Stanford grad. It was weird, as if some force (was it God?) wanted to keep her in Braxton. For years, she wondered if she were fooling herself. She was a writer and longed to write for someone other than herself. No one had wanted her, but now, in what she considered justice long overdue, she was being paid twice for work on the same story. And in a stroke of irony, her take-home salary each week from *The Banner* was almost identical to the taxes deducted from her paycheck at *Destination*.

The money from *Destination* was automatically deposited for Shelly every other Friday at New York's CITIBANK. She was encouraged to not make a drastic change in her standard of living, which she followed, although the extra income would pay off her many creditors.

Shelly's first article for next Thursday's Braxton *Banner* would be a benign, rah-rah, "how-about-that" kind of report. She would chronicle the basics of the magazine award and report the townsfolks' surface reaction. She was saving the good stuff for the project Lance was paying her to do. *You get what you pay for*, Shelly reasoned.

Lance Milburn and the editorial team at *Destination* had given Shelly a timetable. He wanted a major cover story for the following June, an in-depth progress report detailing what had happened in Braxton since the award was given. Until then, she was to keep the magazine editors informed of her findings and hire free-lance photographers as needed. A staff photographer would be assigned at a later date to shoot a photo layout.

The original magazine article byline carried the pen name of

Bernardo Javier, but in the final story, Shelly would reveal herself and explain that she had written the entire project. It was something that still troubled her. She recalled her conversation with Lance at his New York office when the idea was first approved. "How do you want me to get around the problem that we're—that I'm basically not telling the truth?" she had asked him.

Lance had held his hands in front of his face and tapped his fingers together. "Never use those words."

"What do we say then?"

"From the start, we make it clear that this was a *study*, not a *story*. It was a quantum leap in journalism—a sociological experiment that used traditional news-gathering techniques to show the truth."

"Let me play the devil's advocate," Shelly said. "People will say we lied."

Lance got up from his desk chair and looked at the skyline. He was silent for a few moments, then spoke in precise words. "If your idea is as good as you say, and as good as I think it can be—it's up to you to write something so powerful, people will forget how we got it."

Shelly searched for the right reply. "I just want you to know the risk."

"Let me worry about the risk. Your job is to get the story." He paused for a moment. "This is breakthrough stuff we're talking about, national recognition and awards."

She hadn't forgotten those words, and sometimes at night, she used them to help her drift off to sleep in the cramped spaces of the dump in which she lived. She would dream of living in a luxury apartment, of being on the staff of *Destination*, working out of places like New York, Los Angeles, London, Paris, Rome—living the life of a star correspondent. At least, that was what she hoped would happen.

She had completed part one of the project; the magazine article was in the hands of the people of Braxton. The story had also been played out in newspapers across the country, and on television and radio. Shelly's assignment now was to record the events in Braxton, watch the people who lived there, and keep an eye on newcomers to the town.

Already, there was much to report. After she left the chaotic scene at Food Right supermarket, Shelly made the following entry in her notebook:

> It is noon, and most of the shelves at Braxton's supermarket are stripped of their supplies. You'd think a tornado was coming. In a way, maybe it is. Merchants have driven to Paso Robles, Atascadero, and San Luis Obispo. Restaurant owners are stocking up and loading their cars and trucks with steaks, chicken, ribs, hot dogs, hamburger, cases of beer, soda pop, boxes of produce, potato and tortilla chips, and cans of beans. Townspeople are buying souvenirs, sun screen, and maps of the surrounding area—anything that can be resold to tourists. The cellars of local wineries are fast being depleted.

Shelly learned about calls being made to silk screen T-shirt makers. She watched business owners and employees prepare for the anticipated wave of visitors, touching up paint here and there and filling balloons with helium. The sidewalks of Main Street, usually rolled up by eight o'clock, were jammed with people. Shelly knew they were high on the anticipation, but something different had taken hold. People spoke to each other, but not with the enthusiasm of the past. Now, there was an edge to the greetings, a halfhearted wish for success.

Another entry in her journal noted this:

> The town is ready to ring in a new era of prosperity. In years past, the thoughts of these people would have been on

the collective good for all of Braxton. Resources would be pooled, ideas shared, and a universal plan of success devised for the community. The magazine article may have changed all that. People seem to be asking themselves, "Whose cash register will ring most often and most loudly?" A word that has been foreign to Braxton's way of life now dominates the actions of business owners. That word is "greed." At two restaurants in town, and at the local burger joint, the owners have added a dollar to each main item on their menus. Gasoline prices have gone up ten cents a gallon, motel room rates are now thirty dollars higher, and grocery stock boys have begun changing the prices on all the shelves to reflect a ten-percent increase. The rush is on. Merchants believe Braxton is now "on the map."

All during the night, Shelly watched as cars and trucks arrived back in town. The store owners and managers unloaded huge crates of supplies and carried them inside their stores. The atmosphere suggested a nighttime military logistic mission. Their assignment was to find supplies, buy them, and get them back into town, away from the watchful eye of enemy competitors. Normally friendly people, who had lived in a spirit of small town togetherness, now stayed in the shadows, shying away from each other. Muffled voices whispered under the stars.

In the darkness, Shelly watched one of those people move quickly. Keeping to herself, avoiding eye contact with her neighbors, she was a person who normally did just the opposite. She thrived on public contact; it had gotten her elected twice. The woman was Roxanne Drew, owner of Roxy's Drugstore, and a member of Braxton's town council. But on this night, Drew walked with her head down. She was pushing a dolly down the sidewalk.

Shelly stepped out under a street light to meet her. "Hi, Roxy."

"Who's that?" Roxy said in a startled voice.

"Shelly Hinson. Need some help?"

Roxy continued wheeling the dolly into the street. She stopped behind a dark blue Cadillac, then opened the trunk. "Ah, no thanks, I can handle this myself."

Shelly walked to the car and saw that the backseat was loaded with cardboard boxes. "Are you sure? Those look pretty heavy. What's inside?"

"Uh, stuff for my store. Really, Shelly, I don't need any help." Roxy brought the lid of the trunk down just enough to conceal what was inside.

"If it's for your store, then it'll soon be for sale. What's the big secret?"

Roxy sighed and lifted the trunk lid again. "Well, if you must know, I've got five hundred silkscreen T-shirts." She grunted as she struggled to remove the first box and load it on her dolly.

"T-shirts? I didn't know you were in the clothing business." Shelly lifted the flap of the box on the dolly while Roxy strained with another. She took a T-shirt out, held it up, and smiled. "Well, how about this?" She read the words stamped on the front. "'Braxton: Best Small Town in the U.S.A.' Boy, you got the jump on your competition. Where did you get it done so fast?"

"Get your grubby hands off that!" Roxy ordered, grabbing the shirt from Shelly's hands. She stuffed it back into the box. "Where I got this, and who did it, is none of your business."

Shelly spotted the company's name on the box; it was the only maker of T-shirts in the area. During her coverage at the town hall, she remembered the owner was involved with Braxton's council. Didn't the guy have a zoning dispute with the town? Maybe the "honorable" council member Drew had arranged an exclusive T-shirt agreement in return for the swing vote on the zoning matter.

"Did you hear what I said?" Roxy demanded. "I've got to get my store ready, and don't need you snooping around."

The town, it is a-changing, Shelly thought. "Sure, Roxy—just trying to be neighborly." She began to walk away.

"Neighborly is one thing, nosey is another," sniped Roxy.

"That's the life of a reporter."

———————

Shelly watched the people of Braxton work well past midnight. She found open doors everywhere, and dropped in, seemingly covering the story for *The Banner*, visiting with old friends, and offering help. But when she spoke to merchants, she encountered eyes that failed to see her. No one seemed interested in what Shelly had to say, unless it was about money. Only then did they talk about wish lists that included new homes, cars, pickups, boats, vacations, big screen televisions, new wardrobes, jewelry, and college educations for their children. Anything was possible, she was told, once tourists and new residents began rolling into Braxton.

Sunrise couldn't come fast enough. Eyes would be fixed on the road in from Highway 46, waiting for the string of headlights the people were sure was coming their way. Excitement was building; soon the sun would arch over the Santa Lucia Mountain range.

CHAPTER 4

Braxton
Saturday May 1, 6:01 A.M.

The first thing Shelly heard was his cough. That alone was enough to send a pleasant shiver all through her body. He coughed again. "Hello?"

"Hi, Lance, this is Shelly. Are you OK?" She could hear the sound of birds chirping in the background. *He must be on the back patio*, she thought, *probably on the redwood deck*. She tried to guess which lounge chair he was sitting in.

"Oh, yeah, I'm fine, just catching my breath after a little run."

Shelly laughed to herself. She knew a "little run" for Lance was at least five miles in the woods surrounding his palatial Connecticut estate. He'd invited her there just once, but one visit was all it took; she knew she could be very comfortable there if it were ever her permanent address.

"Kind of early out there, isn't it?"

"Oh, I guess it is," she said, then switched the spotlight back to him. "How'd you do?"

"Personal best," he said in a tone that sounded a little matter-of-fact and a little like bragging. "How's our project doing?"

"You would have loved last night. It was unbelievable." Shelly giggled.

"What's the town doing now?" Lance asked. Shelly heard the tinkle of ice against a glass. She could almost taste the freshly squeezed orange juice Lance might be sipping.

"Lance, Braxton is stocked to the gills. You were right. These people are convinced an invasion is coming. Half the shop owners went back to their stores before the sun came up."

"Plenty to write about?"

"If the first two days are a sign of things to come, I'll be able to write a book."

Lance laughed. "Better to have too much material than not enough."

"You sure you want to wait until next year?" Shelly asked.

"The plan stays the same. Call me tonight."

"It may be late . . ."

"Don't worry. I'll be up until midnight."

—•—•—

Braxton
One hour later

Shelly parked her car on Main Street and waited. A hot thermos of coffee sat in the console, and she held a notebook in her hand. Seven o'clock came and went. She hadn't slept well. The last thing she remembered was looking at her alarm clock and seeing that it was 3:38. At 5:30, her alarm had jolted her awake, and then at six, she'd called Lance Milburn. *Me and my big mouth*, she thought. She winced as she replayed her conversation with him. *If the first two days are a sign of things to come, I'll be able to write a book.* She looked down the street now. If there was going to be an invasion of visitors, the first wave was a little late. Downtown Braxton today was like any other Saturday morning, perhaps even quieter than normal.

Eight o'clock passed, then nine. Shelly was puzzled. She hadn't expected throngs of people to storm the town, but she thought at least a few visitors might show up. By now, she had driven around town four times. Hers was one of the few cars on the street.

Ten o'clock came and went. Some of the shop owners, obviously nervous and tired of waiting inside their stores, began to drift outside. Some pretended to sweep the sidewalk, wash a front window, or wipe off tables and chairs, as if nothing was wrong. They would sneak quick glances left and right, then across the street. Necks strained to see if cars were approaching on Main Street. Shelly had overheard someone say the night before that the sun reflecting off the line of windshields would be so bright, Braxton would be blinded by success. But so far, only the locals could be seen doing business in town, regular Saturday stuff, maybe even fewer people than normal.

Shelly opened her notebook and made the following entry:

> Lunchtime in Braxton. Food is prepared and is being kept warm, kegs of beer are chilling, and extra bags of ice are stored in freezers. Tables are set, and I've noticed there's not a piece of silverware in town with a water spot on it. Additional waitresses have been hired for the expected rush. I saw them adjusting their aprons and making sure they have new order books.
>
> Young people from Braxton's Community Bible Church are walking along Main Street, prepared to hand out fliers to visitors. They told me that a barbecue and potluck are planned at the church tonight to get the first crack at would-be members. All of this anticipation has created a kind of holy war; dressed in white shirts and ties, Mormons and Jehovah's Witnesses are staked out on their own corners. They had boxes of *Watchtower* magazines and the *Book of Mormon* shipped in overnight.

Shelly saw Mayor Carter in her rearview mirror now, walking with his head down. A half block in front of her, she saw councilman Cal

Spencer approaching, his eyes straight ahead. *This should be good*, she thought. She got out of her car and stood, looking over the roof, as the two men neared one another. Carter, still looking down, hadn't seen Cal. Just then, he glanced up, spotted Cal, and angled toward the street, apparently trying to avoid him.

"Hey, Roger," Cal called out. "Be careful. I wouldn't be jaywalking if I were you. You might get run over." Carter, decked out in Levis and a rust-colored long-sleeved cowboy shirt, now stood in the middle of Main Street. There wasn't a car coming in either direction. Cal laughed. "Man, that big invasion you promised has sure caused a monster traffic jam, huh?"

The mayor whirled. "I told you to get out of the way of progress," he said in a tone that sounded both confident and anxious. "They'll be here, and you'll be the one who gets run over." His words echoed in the empty street.

—————◦•◦—————

High noon on Saturday passed. Braxton's police force, on standby for traffic control, returned to normal duty. Main Street remained empty. Shelly watched store owners with overextended credit lines look nervously at what they hoped to sell. Many of the businesses had more merchandise on hand now than they would for the entire Christmas season. Bells over doors that rang announcing customers were silent. Electric eyes, used to alert shopkeepers when people entered their stores, never blinked. And so, one by one, merchants threw in the towel, flipped signs over to read, "Sorry, We're Closed," and went home. Shelly watched as they passed each other on the streets, looking sheepishly at friends whom they had tried to avoid the night before and mumbling something about crowds that would surely be there the next day.

Shelly remembered the young people she'd met on the street corner and drove to Braxton Community Bible Church on the east side of town. Once there, she was offered all the food she could eat. Church members were confused, discouraged, and some admitted they were angry. Here they were, prepared to feed a multitude of new friends and, hopefully, new converts. *In what order?* Shelly wondered. Instead, they were face-to-face with a mountain of barbecued ribs, chicken, hamburgers, and hot dogs. Desperate pleas went out to the townsfolk to join them, but no one was in the mood for what some called a last supper. The outsiders had ignored them, and so it seemed that most Braxton residents had lost their appetites. Saturday evening would be spent at home, in silence, stewing over money that never came in, praying that Sunday would be different. The downtown area was virtually deserted, except for an occasional car full of teenagers halfheartedly cruising Main Street. Her notebook in hand, Shelly had recorded it all. She returned to her apartment.

8:50 P.M.

Shelly had put it off too long. Time was running out. She knew she needed to make the call, but she had no idea what she was going to tell Lance. She glanced at her wristwatch; his day was almost over.

After seeing what had happened in Braxton since they'd spoken this morning Shelly wondered if this was the beginning of the end for her career. What was she feeling? Panic? How stupid could she be? The only reason Lance was interested in her was because of the story. She felt stupid for believing it was ever anything more than that. What if the story never got off the ground? Frantic thoughts raced through her head as she listened to the phone ring once, then twice, then, "Hello?"

A chill raced from her spine to her legs. "Lance, this is Shelly," she answered, barely whispering her name.

"What's the verdict?" He sounded upbeat.

"Ah, the jury's still out," Shelly replied, hoping her answer would buy her some time.

Lance was quiet for a moment. "Oh?" he said finally.

Her mind went blank. "Yeah. Ah, how can I say this?" She paused. "Lance, nothing happened."

"What do you mean?" he said tensely.

Shelly fought to hold back tears. "Everyone was ready. The stores were stocked, the cops were on alert—and no one showed up—just the regular folks . . ."

Silence.

"Lance?"

"I'm here. Let me think for a second." He paused. "OK, make it part of your story. It's early."

"But no one is coming."

"How do you know?"

"Well, I—ah—" Shelly stammered, "everything I thought would happen never did. It was no different from any other Saturday."

"Stay with the story, Shelly—it's not over."

She wasn't so sure. "I thought this would help Braxton out, be good for business, bring a little fun, but it flopped, Lance. These people here are really down. They haven't even had their fifteen minutes of fame."

"Don't count on it," he said. "Give it another week, then call me again."

CHAPTER 5

Braxton
Sunday May 2

Shelly stirred in her bed and opened one eye to see what numbers had formed on her digital clock. In fuzzy red, she saw that it was seven-something. The numbers on the clock were large, perhaps two inches high. She needed all the help she could get without her contact lenses. She rolled over on her side. A crack of sunlight peeked through the drawn-down patched-up shade. *Can't blame the weather if people don't come today,* she told herself.

Shelly swung her legs over the side of her bed, stood to her feet, and immediately felt the warmth of the wool throw rug underneath her bare feet. It was time to get up and get moving on this dreaded day. As much as she hated the thought, Shelly had to go to church today. Not just one church, but as many as she could visit in three hours. It was part of her story; she had to report what was happening inside Braxton's places of worship. She would make the rounds quickly, slipping in and out of as many churches as she could, hopefully without being noticed.

Shelly knew the normal routine for most families in Braxton on Sunday mornings. They got ready for church. Some took time for breakfast. Others did well just to get their children dressed, their hair combed and, Bibles tucked under their arms, not be late for Sunday School. To miss church was unthinkable. It was the place to be seen, and in which to meet the right people. Church was an event in Braxton, to be celebrated weekly and cherished forever.

It took Shelly less time to choose what to wear for church than for a normal workday. In minutes, she was out the door and into her terminally ill 1992 black Ford Escort. On this particular day she would not have complained if the engine had decided not to start, but it turned over on the first try.

As she chugged through her apartment's parking lot and on to the street, Shelly thought of the people she had grown up with. To them, God, country, mother, and apple pie were the things that held their hometown together. Not for the Hinson family. In one way, they were considered outsiders. Ever since she could remember, Shelly had heard the gossip, seen the raised eyebrows, and wondered about the low voices. "That Frank Hinson," Shelly remembered them saying, "such a good, kind, and intelligent man, so popular with his students, such a community-minded man. But you know, he's a godless pagan." Shelly hadn't known what *pagan* meant, but she knew it wasn't good.

As she passed a row of houses now, Shelly saw two men talking on the sidewalk. It reminded her—the only time she ever saw her father lose his temper was when someone tried to talk with him about religion. She walked out of the front door once just in time to see him knock a neighbor out cold—punched him right in the mouth when he tried to convert her dad to, what was it, Mormonism, Christianity, Jehovah's Witness? It didn't matter. To Frank Hinson, Sundays were for rest and relaxation, not to be wasted on what he called Bible baloney. Religion was a closed door in Shelly's family, not to be opened for any reason. This was why Shelly had insisted the funeral be held at the high school gymnasium, anywhere except a church. She was sure her father would have wanted it that way.

And so, a subject that was taboo in her childhood was eventually pushed to the back of her mind. However, there were times, albeit rare, when Shelly yearned to know more about the mystery of God (or whatever His name really was). Shelly was aware of a void in her life, but always figured it would be filled once she was married and had children. Occasionally, she wondered if church might be a place where she could find the kind of man who would be a good husband and father. But that meant buying into some kind of religion, and she just couldn't see herself doing that. Any kind of relationship with a man had to begin with honesty. The thought of faking an interest in God repulsed her. Besides, how could she ever forgive God (if he or she existed at all) for robbing her of her father, mother, and brother?

At nine o'clock, church bells pealed their reminders from steeples, but one look at Braxton's streets told Shelly the sound was falling on deaf ears. As she drove down Main Street and then circled around town, she noticed that several stores which were normally closed on Sundays were now open. A few of these were owned by people who openly condemned anyone who worked on "the Lord's Day."

The first church she visited was Gothic-looking Saint Paul's Lutheran. It was half empty. Those who were there fought sleep or fidgeted in their pews. They didn't seem to have their heart in either singing the hymns or listening to the message. She slipped out early and walked down the street to Braxton's newest house of worship, the United Methodist church. But an usher at the door told her that attendance was way down there too. Shelly only stayed for a few minutes. She wanted to see what was happening at Our Lady of Guadalupe Catholic Church. Maybe the Catholics would have their act together. The setting was different, but the atmosphere seemed about he same. She couldn't help wondering if it was God on their minds today. How many thoughts were on the almighty dollar that was supposed to be coming in on Highway 46? At each church, it seemed that people eagerly waited to hear the final *Amen*.

In reality, Shelly learned that the benediction had already been spoken for the entire town. Sunday in Braxton passed without notice. It was as if the town had been quarantined. Wherever Shelly went, she found business people who were shocked and angry. Most of Braxton was in a funk. The town had been snubbed and feelings were hurt.

The only ones not disappointed were those who had been nervous about the town's new fame, mostly Braxton's old-timers. They breathed sighs of relief, pleased that what made their town special was not going to change.

CHAPTER 6

San Diego
Monday May 3, 4:30 P.M.

Leona Kyle's grade book was littered with "F's." She'd stayed after school to check papers and meet six students who wanted extra help. She was thankful the kids were trying to learn their lessons, but she was also discouraged. The second-year English teacher at Santiago Junior High in San Diego ran her finger down the list of names in her grade book. She shook her head wearily. Students—what a joke! Many were children of illegal aliens from Mexico—here one month and gone the next. Some of the American kids refused to do any work, a few were already hard core gang members, and the rest were so lacking in fundamental skills, Leona felt she might as well be teaching third-graders. She sighed. At least a few were trying, and as long as they kept trying, she wouldn't give up on them.

Two years earlier, with a double major in English and Spanish, Leona had graduated with honors from Penn State. She'd grown up in Southern California and had planned to return there and teach junior high students. She was quickly disappointed to find that teaching positions were scarce, interviews were rare, and job offers were nearly nonexistent.

The one exception was in the San Diego Unified School District. There were several openings for bilingual teachers in what was quaintly referred to as the *barrio*, or neighborhood. When she arrived for her appointment at district headquarters, she sensed a feeling of desperation in those who interviewed her; only five minutes after the interview began, she was asked when she could start. She took the job on the spot without even visiting the area where she would be working.

Two months later, Leona loaded every one of her earthly possessions into a sputtering beige Toyota Corolla, and drove to San Diego. She was bubbling with enthusiasm, nervous about working in the inner city, but filled with idealistic determination. However, she soon learned the schools were located in gang-infested, graffiti covered, crime-plagued ghettos. Those students who decided to show up had to walk through metal detectors. For some, it was just one more test to fail. Knives were concealed in ink pens, shoes, and notebooks. Some weapons were confiscated, most were not. Still, she was certain things were not as bad as they appeared, or fellow teachers lamented.

Then, on a Tuesday night in October, Leona had to face reality. At an open house, one of her students, a bright, twelve-year-old boy was struck by a bullet during a drive-by shooting. A teacher in the classroom next door was also hit. She died on the way to the hospital, while the boy's unsuccessful fight for life lasted six days. Police detectives called the incident "gang-related," and no arrests were ever made.

After this tragic beginning to Leona's teaching career, she struggled daily not to give up on her students or herself. Still, by Christmas she was ready to quit. Most of her students were failing, and she blamed herself. She could count on one hand the students she felt were prepared to enter high school and handle academic work.

In spite of it all, Leona returned for the second semester. She was discouraged to see that there was still no change in her students' classroom performance, and she found herself becoming increasingly concerned for her personal safety. Twice, she was threatened by students in her classroom, and once on the playground a student pulled a knife on her.

Leona put down her grade book and looked out a dirty cracked window that was laced with spider webs. She could see basketball backboards, but no children played on the court. As soon as classes were over for the day, Santiago teachers rushed to their cars and drove home. Earlier in the school year, a few teachers had tried to stay late and supervise after school sports, but found it useless. The basketballs in the equipment room were flat, and the rims on the backboards had been ripped off or bent grotesquely out of shape. But airless basketballs and rimless backboards weren't the reasons teachers stayed away from the schoolyard. When the final bell rang, drug dealers, gang bangers, and pimps moved in.

Leona's thoughts stopped suddenly. At first, it felt like an insect bite on the back of her neck, but then she heard a mean-sounding voice. "Don't turn around—or I cut your head off, you hear?" It was a young male voice, one that was trying to sound deeper. "I want your money."

She was being robbed in her own classroom! She couldn't believe this was happening. On the playground, in the parking lot, on the street—but not in her own classroom! "Don't hurt me—I'll give you my money."

Leona felt something sharp break her skin, then moisture on her back. But no pain. Was she in shock? Was that blood running down her neck?

"Where's the money?"

"In my purse, under the desk." She started to reach toward the floor, then winced as the knife poked another hole in her neck. "Owww!" This one hurt.

"Don't move!"

An arm snaked under the desk and grabbed hold of her purse. Leona caught a glimpse of the face. It was not a young man, but a boy. He was a former student, one of many who'd failed ninth grade, and dropped out of school.

"Just keep lookin' straight ahead."

She waited as the boy rummaged through her purse. He wouldn't find anything of value except her wallet. Finally, she heard a thump as her purse was tossed aside. "Take the money, Vi—" she stopped before saying his name, "but, please, don't hurt me."

"Shut up!" he ordered, without disguising his voice this time.

The room was silent for a moment. She felt the blood on her back sticking to her blouse.

"Seven lousy bucks! That all you got?"

"I'm sorry." She slid her watch off her wrist. "Here's my watch."

As he took it, Leona felt a paper bag being pulled over her head. It made a low crumbling sound in her ears, and then all she saw was brown. The bag smelled like sawdust. "Please don't hurt me."

"Put your hands behind your back!"

She did, and then her wrists were bound with some kind of rope or twine and secured to her chair. When the last knot was finally tied, she heard the squeak of basketball shoes running in the direction of the door.

* * *

Phoenix
Monday May 3, 6:30 P.M.

The only sound the Reverend Nick Martinez heard when he walked into the room was the drone of the air conditioning. So far, it was winning in the battle against the outside Arizona desert where the late afternoon temperature had only cooled down to 101 degrees. Nick wore a white short-sleeve, button-down dress shirt and a blue-and-gold-striped necktie, loosened at the collar. No one in the Valley of the Sun ever wore a coat once Easter had passed, except preachers. Nick had left his in his church study. He closed the door, stopped, and looked at the twenty men seated around four tables arranged in a square.

Nick surveyed the room and was relieved to see three men in particular sitting apart from the others, men who had been an encouragement to him. But when he nodded in their direction, they looked away. The rest of the men wore blank expressions.

The silence was finally broken by a man dressed in jeans and a golf shirt. He flashed a toothy smile at Martinez and motioned to an empty chair beside him. "Thanks for waiting in the other room, Nick. Have a seat."

Nick was senior pastor at Northeast Phoenix Community Church. He studied Dr. Brad Felix's face now. The older man was the chairman of the church's board of elders. An enormously popular man in the community, he had been a board member at the church for seventeen years.

"I didn't think we would take this long," Felix said as Nick sat down beside him. "Did you get enough to eat?"

"I'm fine."

The room smelled greasy to Nick. In front of the men were spread out cartons of pizza scraps, stripped chicken bones, empty soft drink cans, and containers of coleslaw, baked beans, and soggy looking French fries. It had been a working dinner, obviously, with an overdose of cholesterol, saturated fat and, Nick was certain, no shortage of ill will.

"Is Karen still here, or did she go home?" the chairman asked.

"She went home."

"With a baby on the way, we've got to take care of her, right?" He looked at Nick, and when the pastor didn't answer, he coughed, and fumbled with some papers. "Well, of course." He turned toward Nick. "We've taken our vote, Nick."

Nick detected a tone of regret in Felix's voice. "What's the jury's verdict?" he asked. "Guilty or not guilty?"

Several men at the table lowered their gaze.

"Nick," Felix went on, "this is the most difficult decision we've ever made. I've prayed, fasted, and done everything I could to avoid it."

Nick bit his tongue to keep from calling the chairman a liar.

"The rest of the members have wrestled with this too." Felix paused, then looked directly into Nick's eyes. The air-conditioning system kicked into high with a loud *thunk*, and four of the elders jumped in their seats. "We've voted and I'm sorry, but we're going to recommend to the congregation that you step down as senior pastor."

Nick felt his throat tighten, but he fought back his anger.

"According to our bylaws, the church will vote on this two Sundays from today." The chairman's muffled words sounded as if they were spoken in a fog.

The pastor's eyes swept the silent room, stopping for a look at each man. Before the meeting, he'd known he was in trouble. In recent weeks he'd lost his temper with several board members. He tried to swallow, but couldn't. This decision was so final. He wasn't prepared for such a final decision. Just like that, *boom*, he'd lost his job. "I—I don't know what to say. Was the vote unanimous?"

"It was enough. More than two-thirds of the lay elders voted in favor, satisfying the constitution. But you'll be getting six weeks severance pay, three times the normal amount." The board chairman looked at Nick with compassion, paused, then said, "I insisted on it."

Nick sighed and looked back at Felix. "Brad, is this what you wanted?"

Felix reached out and put his arm around Nick's shoulders. "It's not what I wanted, Nick—it's what's best for our ministry here. Jesus was able to relate to people on their terms. He was a seeker. We think a change in leadership will help us do that."

"Don't you mean someone who can *market* the church?" the pastor asked. "Isn't that what we're talking about?"

"You wouldn't change, Nick—there were many chances," the chairman said as he doodled on the yellow legal pad in front of him. He had written *Salary for pastor, $65,000 +benefits*. Then, under the amount, he had scribbled a number of lines that got progressively smaller. He drew an "X" over the salary now and looked up. "You disappointed us, Nick. We paid you a generous salary and gave clear direction for what we expected."

"And what was that, Brad?"

"Make three thousand church members happy. And keep the church's four-million-dollar budget healthy. Simple as that."

The room fell silent, while the two men stared at each other. Nick wiped beads of sweat off his upper lip.

"Nick, surely you can't be completely surprised by this," Felix said gently. "The board went more than halfway with you. We brought you in five years ago over guys with a lot more experience. You were barely thirty when we hired you. You'd never had your own church before. We hoped you could help bring change. But you fought us every step of the way."

"All I wanted to do was preach the Gospel, Brad, nothing more and nothing less."

"That's wonderful, commendable—but not enough these days, Nick."

"And what would have been enough to satisfy you?"

"To be honest, we were never on the same page from day one."

"As in page one in the hymnal?" Nick asked with a weak, but knowing grin.

The chairman sighed. "You know it was a lot more than that, but your choice of music was a factor. People today don't know the old hymns."

"Right, because we don't sing them anymore." Nick heard the edge in his own voice.

"We've had complaints," the music minister spoke up. "One woman asked me if this was a blood bank."

Nick stared at him. "Blood bank?"

"Yeah, washed in the blood, power in the blood, a fountain of blood—the hymns you wanted sung after your sermons."

"That's exactly what I'm talking about," the board chairman said with a nod. "We can't automatically assume that what worked in the past is good now."

"And what's the magic formula today?" Nick felt the sarcasm creep into his voice. "If this board has created the perfect church, please reveal your divine secret."

The board chairman ignored the dig. "Our ministry is to create an atmosphere of worship that doesn't scare away visitors. We need music that's positive and full of praise. There are plenty of songs like that."

"Was that my job, not to offend people?"

"Your job was to preach sermons that would make people, especially young families, want to join and be financial partners with our church," Felix answered. "I've never told you this before, Nick, but it has always puzzled me that your main appeal was to older folk. That's not good. The last two years, our growth has been flat. You know why?"

"You seem to have all the answers. Tell me."

"Too much doctrine and not enough pizzazz."

Nick struggled to remain calm. "Doctrine should be the heart of our ministry, not pop psychology."

"It's over, Nick. You couldn't or wouldn't change."

"What's wrong with the old Gospel?" The voice came from the far side of the room. Nick was surprised to see the one newcomer on the board, a high school principal, supporting him. "Nick, I'm sickened with this—"

"You're out of order, Alex," Felix barked.

"No, Mr. Chairman, you're out of your mind!" Alex was a large man, well over six feet tall and close to 220 pounds. He'd played college football for Arizona State and now looked ready to get up and paste the chairman to the wall.

"All right, go ahead, Alex," Felix said reluctantly.

"Nick is a young man who had the courage to stand firm against a group of men whose spines have turned to Jell-O. I'm grieved with the direction this board is taking." He glared at the board chairman. "But more than that, I'm outraged at how we're abandoning the truth our church was built on." He scanned the room. "Once Brad Felix and his majority get Pastor Martinez out of the pulpit, this church will belong to the Devil."

"I resent that," whined a wiry-looking elder. "We're—I agree with our chairman. Show people that we're more tolerant—not dogmatic—we need to be inclusive. That's how we can add new members."

"Ken's right," another board member agreed. "Offerings are way down, the budget is in trouble. We need someone who preaches shorter sermons. Nick's messages were too long, too negative—too much—how can I say it? Just too much Bible."

"Too much *Bible?*" roared Nick's backer. The former football player ran both of his hands through his hair and turned to the wiry man. "How can we ever have too much of the Gospel?"

"The vote's been taken," the chairman said, cutting the debate short. "He's out, case closed. Sayonara, adios."

"Yes, he's out," Alex said in a low voice. "You've got the votes here and in the congregation. But I won't be part of this. I'm resigning from the board and this church."

"Well, Alex, I don't think something as drastic as that is necessary, but if that's what you want to do . . ."

Nick stood. He looked at his ally. "Thanks, Alex." Then he turned to the board chairman. "Brad, no need for the congregation to vote. You'll have my letter of resignation within the hour."

Miami

Monday May 3, 10:13 P.M.

Sultry and alluring, she walked under the light and turned sideways, sending her message silent and clear. She wore a red skintight, leather miniskirt, three-inch spiked high heels, and a white figure-clinging, rayon blouse. She carried a small black handbag over her right shoulder.

The Florida night was hot and muggy, and the middle-aged man driving the late model maroon Buick Ambassador had just returned for another look. As he cruised by, she gave a coy wave. His brake lights immediately flashed red. The driver shifted into reverse, and his tires made an *eek* sound as the car lurched backward.

He stopped parallel to the woman, and the passenger side window slid down. She walked closer, leaned over, and stared across the seat at him. "Hi," she cooed in a low-pitched voice. "Lookin' for a date?"

His gaze moved from her blouse to her heavily made-up face, and his mouth opened slightly in surprise. She glanced at her full lips in the car's side mirror. Almost as if she were outside of herself, she saw the black mascara-caked eyelashes and her dark brown combed-up hair. He stared for several seconds, then blurted, "Can we—do you, uh, are you, would you—"

"Calm down, honey. What do you want?"

When he made a sexually explicit proposition, she didn't bat a false eyelash. "How much you gonna pay for that, big fella?"

"How much do you charge?"

"Fifty bucks."

"Fifty dollars! I'll give you thirty."

"Okay, darlin.' I'm in a bargain giving mood." She pointed to her right. "Drive around the corner—there's a parking lot."

The woman watched the car turn into the vacant parking lot of the boarded-up, blackened restaurant. A burned sign spelled out the irony: LEW'S FLAME-BROILED STEAKHOUSE.

When the car rolled to a stop, she approached. But then the sound of tires squealed nearby. She saw the man glance quickly into his rearview mirror, while one car skidded to a stop behind him and another roared up in front, boxing him in.

"Miami police!" The "hooker" looked in his window and flashed a badge. "You're under arrest for soliciting prostitution."

On the other side of the car, a man tapped hard on the rolled-up window and showed his badge. "OK, lover-boy, open up and get out." The driver began to cry. Both officers stood up straight and looked at each other over the roof of the car. "Another weeper," said one officer, shaking his head.

"They're all sorry when they get caught."

Bang! The two men immediately looked back into the car. The driver was slumped over in his seat. Blood was spattered on the window, and he held a pistol in one hand.

———•———

Fifteen minutes later, Miami Police Vice decoy Gina Wells was seated in the back seat of an unmarked police car, a clipboard in her hand. She'd learned the dead man was a prominent local citizen. In one desperate moment, his orderly and respectable public life had careened out of control.

Over the sound of the car's air conditioning, Gina heard a rapping on the window. She pushed the switch, and the window came down.

"Hey, Gina, I guess that guy figured life wasn't worth living if he couldn't have you," the large man said, leering at her chest. She clutched her blouse closer.

"Shut up, *Officer* Harris. Try your tired act on someone else."

Harris lumbered away, while Gina turned back to the crime report in her hands and thought about her life. She didn't like either one. Now thirty-four years old and never married, she'd fulfilled her lifelong dream to become a law enforcement officer in her hometown. She was close to making sergeant, and had been told she was on track to one day become assistant chief, maybe even the city's first female police chief. Her personnel file was filled with special commendations, citations for bravery, and letters of appreciation. It had not come without a price, however. During her eleven years with the department, the last four in vice, she'd been involved in three shooting incidents. The most harrowing one had happened four years earlier when, as a backup, she was called to an armed robbery at a liquor store near the Orange Bowl. She immediately spotted the suspect, who was ready to ambush a fellow officer. When she yelled a warning, he turned and fired at her, the bullet striking her just under her right arm. Gina returned the fire, a single shot that hit the gunman between the eyes. She had suffered two shattered ribs and a collapsed lung, but three months later, she was back on patrol.

What did all of this mean in the broader scheme of things? Very little. Crime and violence were worse now than ten years ago. She looked at the name on the crime report: Berkeley J. Melton. Blew his brains out in a parking lot. Who would tell his wife, his family? *Hello, Mrs. Melton, I'm Officer Wells, Miami Police. Your husband wanted to have sex with me, but when he found out he was about to be arrested, he put a gun in his mouth and pulled the trigger. Sorry about that, just doing my job. Good night. You and the girls have a nice rest of your lives, OK?*

To her right she saw members of the coroner's office removing the victim's body from his car. She called them ankle grabbers—people who picked up what was left of victims and hauled them away to a refrigerated slab.

All of this had taken place two blocks from the American Police Hall of Fame and Museum. The irony wasn't lost on Gina. She knew she'd done her job well. But she also knew she felt dirty. Something had to change.

⎯⎯•◆•⎯⎯

Norfolk, Virginia
Monday May 3, Midnight

Benny Green's lips made a flapping sound as he blew a tired sigh of relief out of his mouth. He shut down his computer and waited for the disk to eject. "Let's go home," he said to the woman behind him. Then he moaned, "I've got to be back in seven hours." Benny felt soft hands on his shoulders, tenderly rubbing his muscular neck. He reached back to pat her fingers, then closed his eyes. "You have a magic touch, Maggie." The heavyset man grimaced when she located a knot and began to massage it loose.

"You're a hard working man, Benny. You've given me a good life, but this place is killing both of us."

When a person wanted authentic Mexican food in Norfolk, Virginia they went to Casa de Benito at The Waterside. There was always a wait, but once inside, few people were ever disappointed. First-timers were usually surprised to learn that Benito was really Benjamin Green, a man in his early forties, and that he was black, not Hispanic.

Ten years earlier, Benny had served a four-year hitch as a sergeant at Kirtland Air Force Base near Albuquerque, New Mexico. It was there that he had three life-changing experiences; he met his wife, Maggie, he discovered true Mexican food, and he learned how to re-create the cuisine he loved to sample in local restaurants. When Benny and his wife moved back to his hometown of Norfolk, they used all their savings to open Casa de Benito, a lunch time, ten-table taco shop.

This east coast Navy seaport was known for its honky tonk bars and burger joints, not its cantinas and burritos, and Benny nearly lost his XXL-sized shirt. But friends told friends, and those who found their way to the little taco shop eventually became regulars. They asked for more choices on the menu and more room to eat. A year later, Benny had to move to a new building. Six months after that, walls were knocked out, and a second floor was added. Soon Casa de Benito was Norfolk's most successful restaurant. It opened at eleven in the morning, except on Christmas, and stayed open until eleven at night. On some days, a thousand meals were served, and Benny Green was usually there to greet every person who munched on his tortilla chips and dipped into his secret salsa.

"How many times has someone tried to buy this place, Maggie?" Benny asked as he stuffed a wad of cash into a safety drop box.

"Five or six, I think."

Benny put the computer disk in his desk drawer and locked it.

"What did we do today?" she asked.

He spun around in his chair and looked at her. "Thursdays are never great, but we still took in $5,500. And that's with half the fleet out."

"Benny Green, if you don't slow down, they're going to take you out and bury you at sea."

Benny knew his wife was right. He breathed deeply, and felt a dull pain in his chest. When he glanced down at his waist, he saw a bulge that hung over his belt; his ample belly had popped the last button on his shirt. He never had any time to exercise. He was under a doctor's care now for high blood pressure and had been told to cut back on his work schedule.

"What's the order, boss?"

"Sell the place, Benny."

Benny knew there was no use arguing. His wife rarely insisted on having her way, but when she did, it was usually the right thing to do.

Wilmette, Illinois
Tuesday May 5, 3:04 A.M.

A distant sound invaded the man's darkened world at a wretched hour. What was it? Two, three rings. *Shut up!* It was a familiar sound and it wouldn't stop. He reached out and banged his hand against the side of the night stand, then groped for his alarm clock. No, it wasn't the alarm. Four, five, six rings. Telephone! Pete Stanley felt for the lamp, and knocked it off the stand. The porcelain base shattered on the hardwood floor. He cursed under his breath. "Stupid lamp!" he declared.

"Get the *phone*, Pete," his groggy wife pleaded. She found the light switch on her own night stand lamp, and turned it on.

Pete picked up the receiver, but the telephone answering machine downstairs was already dutifully playing its recorded message. He listened to himself in the parody of a baseball stadium announcer. "He once batted fourth for the Chicago Cubs, number 15, Pete Stanley, third base. Thanks for calling. I'm away from the dugout. Please leave a message, and we'll—

"Hello?" Pete called over the message as it continued:, "'—get back to you.' Hello, hello?"

"Is this Pete Stanley?"

Pete ran a hand through his thinning hair. "Yes." He recognized the voice. "Is this who I think it is?"

"I'm afraid it is. Sergeant Ross, Wilmette Police Department."

"Is it Brian again?" he asked, as beside him, his wife sat up straight.

"Yes, sir," the police officer said, then paused for a moment. "Mr. Stanley," he continued, "uh, you know how big a Cubs fan I am—followed you from your rookie year to the Hall of Fame."

"Thanks, but what's my son done this time?" Pete braced himself for what was coming.

"Let me put it this way, sir. I gave your son a break the first time. You know, boys will be boys, a couple of six packs, that kind of thing. Then two weeks ago, because he was your son—Hall of Famer and all that—we kind of overlooked the drinking again. We got the charges dropped when you agreed to pay for the broken windshields. Remember?"

His wife touched his shoulder. "Is Brian OK?" Pete waved at her to be quiet.

"You've been very kind, Sergeant. I really appreciate—"

"Your son is drunk." The officer's voice was no longer that of a base-ball fan, but a lawman. "He and two of his friends were arrested for criminal property damage and indecent exposure."

Pete closed his eyes and shook his head, then asked for details. The words of Sergeant Ross stabbed at his heart. "At approximately 0100, officers responding to an anonymous 911 call found juveniles Brian Carlton Stanley, age sixteen, Eric Conrad Fortunato, age seventeen, and Walter Raymond Patterson, age fifteen, standing on the front hood of a BMW convertible owned by Alphonse Muscatelli of Wilmette. The con-vertible top was down, and the three juveniles were . . ." He hesitated. ". . . relieving themselves on the front seat of the car."

"Oh, no."

"Oh, yes. But let me tell you, Mr. Stanley, you're a lucky man. Muscatelli is an even bigger fan of yours than I am. He says if you pay for the damage, he won't press charges."

"What about the indecent exposure charges?"

Pete's wife groaned and grabbed hold of his arm.

"We'll talk about that when you get down here," the sergeant answered.

"Thank you. Can I bring you an autographed bat?"

"No thank you."

"I'll be there in fifteen minutes." Pete hung up the phone, then turned to his sobbing wife. "He's out of control, Beatrice."

He jumped out of bed and began to get dressed. Despite the kind of home most would consider a mansion, three luxury cars in the garage, membership in the Indian Hills Country Club, and invitations to play golf anywhere else, Pete knew his life was crumbling. He was tired of the banquets, speaking appearances, and glad-handing required for his business interests. He had once thought this was the lifestyle he wanted after his baseball career and induction into the Hall of Fame. It wasn't. Pete had assumed that once he left baseball, his retirement would bring about a closer relationship with his family. It hadn't. He felt like a phony, but more importantly, he considered himself a failure as a husband and father. Brian was not only in trouble with the police, he was failing half of his classes in high school, and their fourteen-year-old daughter, Nicole, was asking about birth control pills. As for Pete's relationship with his wife, they seldom shared a tender moment anymore. Pete Stanley knew their lives must move in a different direction.

CHAPTER 7

Braxton
Friday May 7, 2:03 P.M.

A week after *Destination* hit the newsstands, a thousand extra copies of the weekly *Braxton Banner* were printed and distributed in town. Shelly learned that the paper's editor, who objected to the special run, had caved in to pressure from Mayor Carter, who threatened to withdraw advertising for the businesses he owned.

The paper usually came out on Thursday, but an extra day was needed for the special edition. At fifty-five pages, it was triple the normal size. Major businesses had bought full-page layouts, congratulating the town for its honor, and smaller ads were sprinkled throughout the paper. Shelly had heard that the townsfolk were pressured to be part of this historic edition. Advertising rates for the issue had doubled.

The additional papers were printed for those subscribers who wanted to mail issues to relatives and friends. But the bulk of them was sent to major corporations with a letter from Mayor Carter inviting them to consider Braxton for future expansion.

Shelly's article was spread across the front page. She'd rewritten it five times. Her first draft, completed the day the award was announced, was upbeat and hopeful. The second draft reflected the shock most of the residents felt after the weekend had turned into a financial flop. The townsfolk had spent thousands of dollars and gone all out for visitors who never showed up. But with each passing day, Shelly sensed an even deeper collective disappointment among Braxtonians (as they called themselves). It wasn't just the monetary loss; the town had suffered a hard psychological blow. Few people expected the coming weekend to be any different. Shelly's fifth and final draft of the story barely made it to press before the deadline.

It was mid-afternoon now as Shelly opened the door to Roxy's drugstore and heard the familiar jingle of the bell. The place was deserted, except for Roxy, who was straightening bottles of shampoo in an aisle underneath a sign that read "Hair care." The woman turned with a smile, but when she saw who it was, she returned to her work without a word.

All the warmth of the iceberg that sank the Titanic, Shelly thought. "Hi, Roxy."

"What do you want?" Roxy demanded without looking up.

"I'm wondering how many of those Braxton #1 T-shirts you've sold. You had five hundred made, right?"

"It's none of your business," Roxy snapped, and walked away from Shelly.

"I've only seen twenty or thirty around town," Shelly said, following her to the store's checkout line. "Maybe if I mentioned something in next week's story, you'd sell some more."

Roxy stopped and eyed Shelly with a look of contempt. "Oh, you're a big help!" she said, pointing to a stack of newspapers by the cash register. "I read your article in today's paper. I didn't appreciate the nasty innuendo about the T-shirts."

"Were the facts wrong?"

"The way you wrote it, people will think I made a deal under the table with the silk screener."

"Come on, Roxy. All I said was that you knew where to go to beat the competition."

"Well, you made it sound illegal."

"Was it?"

"Shelly, you wouldn't know the truth if it hit you in the face."

Just then, tires screeched to a stop outside the store. Shelly grimaced and hunched her shoulders, waiting for the crash. Instead, a horn began to honk. The two women ran to the front door. Main Street was filled with cars.

———————

And so it began—an invasion of people and vehicles the likes that Shelly and others could not remember. A line of cars and trucks stretched down Main Street all the way north to Highway 46. They came from the west off Highway 1, and from the east, past miles of vineyards off Highway 101. Hundreds of people were looking for California State Highway 46. Shelly heard that some were taking the scenic route from the south, weaving their way past White Rock Reservoir on bumpy Old Creek Road. They traveled by car, truck, bus, and motorcycle. Some even pedaled in on bicycles. The cars would drive to the edge of town, then turn around, and cruise by on the other side of the street. It was easy to spot the visitors—they craned their necks from inside their cars, gawking at both sides of the street. Shelly's heart pounded with delight as she watched many of them park their cars and emerge with copies of *Destination* magazine in their hands. Last week's despair and defeat now became Shelly's vindication and victory. She was convinced the story in *Destination* had brought immediate fortune to Braxton and future fame for herself. The previous weekend had been a bust. Shop owners figured they were stuck with food and merchandise they'd never sell, but as it turned out, Shelly knew they should have bought even more.

Who were these people? Shelly began walking the streets, picking strangers at random. She would identify herself as a reporter for the local paper and then start firing questions. The first visitors she spoke to were Joe and Christie, a married couple in their early thirties from smog-infested Pomona. Shelly knew it to be a drab cookie-cutter suburb east of Los Angeles. Joe told her he worked two jobs, one as a men's clothing salesman at Penney's, the other as a newspaper delivery supervisor for the *Los Angeles Times*. His wife was a dental hygienist, and they had three children, a boy, nine, and two girls, twelve and six.

"Why did you come to Braxton?" Shelly asked.

He held a rolled-up copy of *Destination* magazine in his hand. "Christie and I have been looking to get out," he said, pointing to the magazine. "Once we read this, we had to see the place for ourselves."

"Our home has been broken into three times," Christie said. "It's a miracle we haven't been killed. Then, after what happened to Joe last week . . ."

"Tell me," Shelly prodded.

"I got held up at knife-point while delivering papers."

"That's awful," Shelly said, trying to sound sincere.

"No, what's awful is that we just found out our son is mixed up with a street gang."

"Your *nine*-year-old?" Shelly asked in disbelief.

"Yeah." Joe shook his head. "Now you know why we want out."

They told Shelly they both called in sick to their jobs after Joe delivered his papers. Then they left their children with Joe's parents and drove straight through to Braxton.

"We want a new life," Christie said. "Maybe we'll find it this weekend."

Next, Shelly interviewed a couple who came from the north. They were happy living in San Jose, but curious about a town they'd heard about on the local news. The casual, but smartly dressed man was a successful computer programmer, while his wife worked in residential real estate. Their two children were in college, and they told Shelly they wanted a simpler life.

"Do you think this is the place?" Shelly asked.

"Well, not many things live up to the hype." The man looked up and down Main Street. "We haven't seen much of Braxton yet. Ask me tomorrow, OK?"

As the couple moved down the sidewalk, Shelly heard something that caused the hair on her neck to stand up. Few sounds could provoke the raw, almost sensual thrill that now filled her. It began as a low rumble in the direction of the highway, and gradually grew louder as it moved down Main Street. There was no explaining her love for it—it actually scared her to death. Shelly's father once told her that if he ever caught her on one, she would regret the day she was born.

As she snapped her head to the right, she saw the chrome on the motorcycle. But this wasn't just any bike. No, this was a hog, a Harley-Davidson, rolling in from heaven. She strained to see who it belonged to, and felt a pang of disappointment when she saw the rider. What a runt. He pulled his blue Harley to a stop in front of Shelly and gunned the engine. The handlebars shook under the rumble of the bike. The rider took off his helmet and their eyes met. Then he surveyed the rest of her body. *Creep*, she thought.

When his eyes moved back to her face, he turned the engine off and grinned. "If you're here to welcome me, I'm glad I came."

"Dream on. The only thing you've got going for you is your hog."

He shrugged. "It wouldn't be the first time. But when ladies like you get to know me, they forget the Harley."

Anger shot through Shelly. "Even though your feet barely reach the ground?"

The rider hung his helmet on his bike, revealing his short, black curly hair. He dismounted and put the kickstand down. He wore black boots that had forgotten their last shine, dirty Levis, and a tattered leather jacket. "Don't judge a gift by the size of the package," he said with a grin.

"Or what it's wrapped in, that's for sure," Shelly said, motioning to his clothes.

He glanced at the notebook in her hand. "What's with the pad? You want my autograph?"

"I didn't know bikers could *write*."

The rider chuckled. "Well now, after reading and hearing about this place, if you're like the rest of the people here, I'd hate to see the worst small town in America."

"I didn't know bikers could *read*," she countered. The guy was a punk, but Shelly was kind of enjoying his quick retorts.

The biker removed his backpack and walked toward her. He stood about three inches above her. "OK, *Miss Unwelcome Wagon*, after hearing about your town in a bar while passing through Yuma, I was a little curious. I'm like that, you know."

"So what's your name? Johnny Yuma, the rebel?"

"Cute," he replied. "Johnny Cash sang that, didn't he?" Shelly didn't answer, and he smiled. "Name is Rick, Rick Aguilara. I'm twenty-six, single, from Winslow, Arizona—kicks on Route 66 and all that stuff, OK?" He pointed to his motorcycle. "Just me and my ten-year-old Harley."

"You have, like, a *job*?" Shelly wondered.

Rick looked at Shelly's notebook and winked. "Nothing like being a reporter for a big-time newspaper."

The dig ticked Shelly off. "So you just drift from town to town? That's really impressive."

Rick seemed amused by Shelly's slam. "Let's just say I manage," he said softly. "I do some construction work, and I'm a pretty good short-order cook." He smiled. "Could I build you an omelette?"

Shelly's mouth fell open, and before she could close it, Rick was walking away.

———— ◆ ————

Shelly wasn't sure how long Rick the biker would stay, but she met others who came to Braxton with no intention of leaving. At one point, late in the afternoon Shelly watched as a maroon (at least that's what appeared to be the original color) beat-up minivan slowly approached the curb. Steam was escaping out of the front hood, while boiling water squirted out from under the van. The cracked windshield had what looked like a growing fault line stretching from the passenger's side to the driver's. Two brown, battered suitcases and a black steamer trunk were strapped to the luggage rack on the roof. Campaign bumper stickers were plastered on the side of the trunk; Mondale-Ferraro, Dukakis-Bentsen, Jesse Jackson, and Clinton-Gore. The cases were held together with gaffers' tape, and the trunk could have been fifty years old.

When the motor stopped running, Shelly approached the van. But a second later, the engine coughed and sputtered three times, the van shook once, then was still. The driver's door opened with a crunching sound that suggested the van had endured at least one accident. Shelly could hear two children crying inside the van.

"Hi, glad you made it," she said, greeting the driver with a smile.

The driver's return smile revealed gaps where at least two teeth once took up space. "Thanks," he said. "Been a long drive."

Shelly peered inside the van; it was jammed with boxes and loose clothing. She heard the other door open, but couldn't get a good look at the woman, or the children with her. "I'm Shelly Hinson, a reporter with the local paper. Where you from?"

"Texas." He nodded to his right. "This here is the missus."

The woman held a young girl in one arm and gripped the hand of her small son in the other. The children had stopped crying, but both had runny, dirt-caked noses.

"Looks like you've got two, tired travelers," Shelly said.

The woman nodded slightly and made a half-audible sound.

Shelly wasn't sure how old the woman was; there were traces of beauty on her face that age couldn't conceal. But Shelly guessed it wasn't the age that betrayed her good looks—it was the mileage. "Where did you live in Texas?" she asked.

In a voice as flat as the Lone Star State, but with a drawl that was learned deeper in the South, the woman said, "El Paso."

"What brought you here?"

"That magazine article," the woman answered, a tiny sign of life in her eyes. The toddler in her arms began to cry.

Shelly stared at the loaded van and felt a stab of guilt. "You came from El Paso, sight unseen?"

"Yep." The man spit a stream of chewing tobacco that splattered off his left front tire. "Packed up everything and drove straight through. We're here to stay."

The woman nodded. "After reading that magazine, this place has got to be a hundred times better than where we've been."

"What are you going to do?" Shelly asked in a shaky voice.

The man leaned against the side of the van. "Shouldn't be a problem. The magazine says you got plenty of jobs around here."

"Did you call or check it out?"

He shrugged. "Nah, didn't have the money for no long distance call. I figured the quicker we got here, the better the chances of finding work. We been down on our luck a long time." He looked around. "Yes ma'am, this place is gonna solve our problems."

Shelly felt sick to her stomach. This was incredulous. "Well, I—I hope everything—" She searched for the right words. "I hope this is the best move for you." Stunned, Shelly moved away. She had started something that was going terribly wrong.

———— • • ————

"Hey, Spencer!"

Shelly jumped. The voice was like a rifle shot. She glanced across the street at the beaming face of Mayor Carter. He was shouting at Cal

Spencer, his arch rival on the council.

"How about this traffic?" The mayor pointed to a line of cars in the street that stretched for three blocks. "Got any wisecracks, now?"

Cal didn't answer. The mayor stepped off the curb and walked into the street. Traffic had stopped, so he eased in front of a pickup and stood at the center line. "In the words of Yogi Berra, 'It's déjà vu all over again,'" he said with a laugh. "I'm in the middle of the street, just like last week, but the invasion you said would never happen is here!"

Shelly felt sorry for Cal and saw his jaw tighten. "Congratulations. If you step into traffic, your next campaign slogan will be 'Tread on Me.'"

Shelly laughed. The mayor glanced at her, then he dismissed Cal with a backhanded wave. Shelly watched as Carter greeted people in their cars and pointed in various directions, obviously relishing his role as the town's VIP. Traffic moved slowly, but whenever it stopped for a moment, he reached inside cars and shook the drivers' hands, welcoming them to Braxton.

———◆———

It was six o'clock, and Shelly was hungry. She didn't want to return to her apartment, so she headed to the west side of town. Mexican food at LoLo's #2 didn't excite her, but it beat cooking for herself. Besides, she wanted to look over her notebook. At last count, in nearly four hours, she'd interviewed fifty-eight people. Most had told her they were visitors, there to enjoy a weekend outing and see the town for themselves. They said they hadn't been disappointed so far, although they had expected a bit more than the article implied. The majority expressed amazement at how the locals made them feel at home.

Lolo's #2 was a converted Spanish-style home with red rounded tile slats on the roof and white plaster archways. Shelly found a line of people outside, waiting to be seated. She couldn't remember ever seeing that before, even on a Friday night. After adding her name to the list, she looked for a place to sit in the outside patio. Two strangers, seated on a bench near a purple bougainvillea, slid over and made room for her.

"Thanks," she said to the woman. "Where are you from?"

"Bakersfield. How about you?"

Shelly guessed the woman to be in her early forties, Hispanic with black hair pulled tight and covered with a yellow silk head scarf. "I live here. Shelly's my name. What's yours?"

"Carmen." She pointed to the man next to her whose face was built around a thick, black moustache. "This is my husband, Roberto."

"Is it always crowded like this?" he asked in a thick Spanish accent. "We drove over for a quiet weekend." He gestured to the crowd of people seated around them, waiting to get into the restaurant. "This is ridiculous. We've been here an hour."

"It surprised everybody," Shelly told him. "Last weekend no one showed up, and now the place is practically a mob scene."

"Sandoval, party of two?" A woman's voice over a loudspeaker announced the end of the couple's wait.

"At last!" the man said, getting up.

His wife stood too. "I would think as a local, you'd get special treatment."

Shelly laughed. "Are you kidding? They want you back. I live here."

———————

For the rest of the evening, Shelly watched as her hometown struggled with its newfound fame. Clearly overwhelmed and ill-prepared for so many visitors, Braxton's only lodging, a forty-room Motel 6, turned on its *Sorry, No Vacancy* sign for the first time that Shelly could remember. Disappointed tourists had to travel to nearby Paso Robles and San Luis Obispo to spend the night. Others would sleep in their cars.

At midnight, Shelly finally returned to her apartment. Her scheme was in motion. She had plenty to write about, but she had no idea how the story would end.

CHAPTER 8

Monday May 10, 6:33 A.M.

Braxton police officer Blake Hesterman, back on duty after only four hours sleep, was cruising deserted Main Street in his black-and-white squad car. He was covering the patrol shift of another officer injured in a barroom melee the night before. The aftereffects of the weekend invasion were clear now that the sun had risen over Braxton. The town looked, felt, and smelled like an environmental hangover. Trash cans overflowed with half-eaten food, and flies, hornets, and lines of marching ants swarmed around them. Hesterman frowned then at the scene before him. At the corner of Lincoln and Main, two cars, a white Pontiac Grand Prix, and a fruity looking metallic violet Geo Metro two door, had collided and knocked over a street light—yesterday. He'd been on the scene. Now both cars were still blocking the sidewalk in front of Willard Snerdley's True Value Hardware Store.

"Unit one to base," the officer spoke into his two-way radio.

"Go ahead, unit one," a female police dispatcher replied.

"This is Sergeant Hesterman. What's the status on the car wreck at Main and Lincoln?"

"Not sure what you mean."

Idiot, he thought. "Well, maybe I can explain what I mean," he said in a condescending tone. "Last night, two cars went *boom-boom*. I was on the scene. The people in the cars suffered multiple *owies*. After they were taken to the hospital, I called for two tow trucks."

The dispatcher was quiet for a moment, then, "Continue, unit one."

Hesterman rolled his eyes, and looked with amazement at the

microphone in his hand. "Betty, if the cars are still on the sidewalk, obviously, the tow trucks never came."

"Must have been some kind of mix-up, Sergeant. I'll put in another call."

"Ten-four," he said, and angrily jammed his microphone into a clip on the dashboard.

Saturday and Sunday had been nightmares for Hesterman and his fellow police officers and paramedics. No one could say for certain, but rough estimates put the number of visitors who jammed the town's streets on Saturday at more than two thousand. Most newcomers mingled with the locals, asking about real estate, schools, and churches. And at first, Hesterman thought all would be peaceful. However, things quickly began to unravel, and the car crash Sunday night ended the weekend on what Hesterman believed was a symbolic note.

Braxton General Hospital had been like a M*A*S*H unit. Patients began arriving at the emergency room by late Saturday morning—a seemingly endless string of broken arms, bee stings, sun strokes, sprained ankles, cut fingers, and bruised ribs. Visitors may have come with peaceful intentions, but by early evening, a number of people had suffered injuries from fistfights and there was even one minor stab wound. One police officer had a beer bottle broken over his head at the Hometown U.S.A. Bar and Grill. For the first time in two years, all three holding cells at the Braxton jail were occupied at the same time.

Hesterman, his fellow officers, and a number of security guards were needed at the local Wal-Mart for crowd control. The store stayed open an hour longer on Saturday night.

Then a fistfight broke out just before midnight at the local ARCO station. Motorists became upset when the station ran out of gasoline, and a near riot occurred. Police Chief Trevor Talbot ordered the gas station closed, but Hesterman didn't get home until two in the morning. He was back at work four hours later.

Sunday was an eighteen-hour work day. Tempers may have cooled, but hundreds more tourists found their way into America's best small town. There was a brief, morning respite, when visitors packed Braxton's churches, but it didn't last long.

That afternoon, the town was filled with noisy, sometimes rowdy newcomers. In his eight years on the police force, Hesterman had never seen anything like this. The town merchants were giddy with excitement, not seeming to mind people acting up as long as they kept spending their money. But as the afternoon turned into early evening, Braxton found itself short of supplies.

The first to go was beer—it ran out at four. Braxton's last liquor bottle was drained at five, and the final bottle of wine was uncorked at six. At about the same time, both restaurants in town and the burger joint stopped serving meals when food supplies were exhausted. So, when the visitors could find nothing more to eat or drink, and no more souvenirs to buy, those who hadn't planned on staying returned to their cars and trucks, and headed back to where they came from. The car wreck in front of Snerdley's Hardware Store brought Braxton's forty-eight hours to a crashing close.

Hesterman cruised down Washington Street now. As he looked to his right, he spotted a body, partially covered with a blanket, lying in a store entryway. He pulled alongside the curb, turned on his flashing blue and red bar lights, and spoke into his two-way radio microphone. "Unit one to base."

"Go ahead, unit one."

"I'm going to be out of my car. Checking a guy on the ground outside Aunt Willie's Florist Shop."

"Ten-four."

Hesterman hadn't seen the body move. Was he dead? He approached slowly and pulled back a green threadbare Army blanket. The man was lying on his back. He had a long unkempt beard, and it was impossible to tell his age. A strong odor, suggesting a long time between showers, offended Hesterman's senses. He looked down at the transient's boots: they were minus a left heel, and both soles had gaping holes in them. The man wore a tattered long-sleeve red plaid shirt, and underneath, a soiled crew neck T-shirt. His Levis were a grimy brownish blue, and his fly was unbuttoned. Hesterman nudged the man's shoulder with his shoe. "Hey, wake up. Are you OK?"

The transient opened his left eye slightly and squinted through bushy eyebrows at Hesterman. He blinked his brown bloodshot eyes. "Good morning, your honor. J. Oswald Theodore the Third, representing himself."

"Get yourself up, old man." Hesterman was reluctant to touch the vagrant. "Let's take a trip to the police station."

"I'll wave my Miranda rights," the man replied, struggling to his feet, "and plead guilty to obstructing the entrance to this business establishment."

Hesterman found the old man a little intriguing. Then, on the way to the police station, Theodore revealed a capsule history of himself. He was a former criminal defense attorney from San Francisco, who fifteen years before had specialized in representing drug dealers. "I laundered one too many Ben Franklins for a Mexican drug cartel," he admitted.

"Your first offense?" Hesterman asked.

"Yes. But it didn't matter. I was made an example of." He paused, sighed, then continued. "I was indicted, convicted, disbarred, then sent to prison."

Hesterman looked in the rearview mirror at his passenger. "That's a long fall."

"And without a parachute too."

"Are you still falling?"

Theodore looked out the window. "I don't know. What's the name of this town again?"

"Braxton. Braxton, California. Best small town in America, or so they say."

Theodore wrinkled his brow. "Maybe this is where I'm supposed to land."

CHAPTER 9

Burbank, California
9:37 A.M.

"Any of you hear about that small town up the coast? The one bombarded over the weekend by tourists?" Harvey Golden, NBC bureau chief, leaned against the wall and squinted through smoke rising from the cigarette that dangled on his lips. He eyed the fifteen people seated around the rectangular oak table littered with Styrofoam coffee cups, a half-empty box of donuts, and strewn newspapers. No one answered him. "New York wants us to do a closer on it for tomorrow," he told them.

"Oh, come on, Harvey, not another one of those." Rosie Pender-Atkins scowled at Harvey's puffy face. As the Los Angeles-based correspondent for NBC News, she felt herself being backed into a corner. "I know where you're headed," she carped. "Another feature on small-town America, pushed by the idiots in New York."

"This one sounds different, Rosie." Harvey reached for the magazine on the table in front of him. "*Destination* picked it as best small town in America." He held up two pages of wire copy. "From the sound of this, the place was overrun. New York wants to see—"

"I know what they want," Rosie snapped. "Tell them to watch reruns of Andy Griffith. Mayberry, U.S.A. doesn't exist anymore." She usually did hard news stories, but she knew the other bureau correspondent, who was more comfortable with features, was on vacation. "I'm not doing the story," she said, and crossed her arms defiantly.

Harvey looked up at the ceiling, then at her. "Well, Braxton is a real town, and I want you to go there, do the story, and do it right."

Rosie slid down in her chair. She knew what would happen if she did the story. It would be outstanding—the network would love it. But she feared it would take her further away from hard news stories, the stuff of crime, corruption, and politics. She hated features. "I thought you wanted the piece on gay and lesbian discrimination in the L.A. Fire Department," she countered.

"That'll have to wait. New York wants this badly." Harvey rolled the sleeves of his white shirt up to his elbows and tucked in his shirttail. He reached up to loosen his coffee-stained red and blue polka dot necktie. "Now, Finley will be your photog," he ordered. "It'll take you a while to drive there. Work on the piece this afternoon and tomorrow morning, then take it to San Luis Obispo. KSBY will uplink the tape by satellite to us. We'll edit the piece, then feed it to New York."

Rosie scooped up the papers in front of her and stuffed them into a large black leather briefcase next to her chair. "Small town, America— this stinks," she mumbled to herself, but loud enough for all to hear. She hated the story she was about to cover and despised people outside of big cities. Narrow-minded, bigoted, polluting, anti-abortion, homo-phobic, Christian, conservative, gun freak Republicans, she fumed to herself. Just like good old Mom and Dad in Franklin, Tennessee. "Where are you going to put us up? I can imagine the wonderful accommodations they have in—what's the name of the town?"

"Braxton," Harvey said. "We have two rooms for you at the Motel 6." He seemed to be trying to hide a smile.

"Oh, terrific! That's the one that leaves the light on for you, right? Do we need to bring our own cockroach spray?" Rosie glanced at a photo on the wall next to Harvey—a framed shot of Chet Huntley and David Brinkley, the first and most famous anchor tandem of the early seventies, a moment frozen in time. Talking to the photo, as if Huntley and Brinkley could hear, she said, "So this is the legacy you left, huh, guys?" Then to Harvey she offered a final blast. "Harvey, this is a ridiculous story, but you know the sick part about this?"

"No, Rosie, suppose you tell me."

"As bad as you are at your job, when you send my stories back to New York, you end up getting all the glory."

Harvey glared at her. "Rosie, you're good at what you do, but you're also a pain in the rear. You are, without a doubt, the most disagreeable person I've ever known."

"I don't care what any of you think of me personally," she shot back, as she threw a cold glance around the room, "just get what I do right. Harvey, you're wrong when you say I'm *good* at what I do. Always remember, I'm the *best*."

CHAPTER 10

The white Ford Astrostar turned right off of Highway 46 at the east exit to Braxton. News photographer Mario Cedeno of KSBY-TV News 6 was at the wheel. He didn't have to look at his passenger to know she was conked out; Heather Landis had been snoring ever since she stopped yakking about herself over an hour ago. That was when Cedeno had turned off Highway 101 from San Luis Obispo.

Cedeno's morning assignment was this trip with the newsroom's prima donna. Heather Landis had made it clear that Channel 6 was a minor pit stop in what she expected to be a quick trip to the network. It was her first job out of Washington State University, and she considered her field reporting assignments useful only in helping her land a permanent spot on the anchor desk. She'd given herself six months to a year in San Luis Obispo; after that she expected her career to skyrocket. Phoenix, Boston, Los Angeles, New York? Maybe straight from central California to the Big Apple—at least that's what she'd boasted to Cedeno. He'd heard it a hundred times. He glanced her way now and wished his camera were rolling. *Here she is, America, the next Barbara Walters*—as she liked to present herself to everyone. Heather sat with her head tilted sideways, resting against the window, and her mouth wide open. She inhaled, snorting the air in, then exhaled, coughing, sputtering, and blowing it back out. Not a pretty sight, even from a beautiful woman. Cedeno covered his mouth with one hand to muffle a laugh as he entertained a brief fantasy—Heather Landis snoring right in the middle of one of her reports.

Cedeno decided to give her a personalized wake-up call. He scouted ahead for something suitable on the road. There it was—a large jagged pothole. Cedeno sped up and deftly scored a direct hit: the car's right front tire slammed into the hole, jarring Heather awake. Her head bounced off the side window.

"Owwww!" she cried out in surprise. She touched her head, then pulled down the visor and studied herself in the mirror. "Mario, you dummy—that messed up my hair."

"Sorry, *Network*. What time are we due at the mayor's office?"

"Nine-thirty." Heather began to try to repair the damage to the mound of clay-colored hair that had fallen over her face. Cedeno marveled at her beauty. Heather was striking; a full-figured brunette, about 5'6", with perfect teeth, flawless, creamy skin, and winter-green eyes. The young reporter was a dream to look at, but once Cedeno had learned what made her tick, he decided Heather Landis was a cuckoo clock.

Cedeno turned left at Main and Grape. The town hall was a block away.

"Hey, Mario, look!" Heather shouted. "There's a TV news crew! Wait a second—" She leaned forward, putting her hands on the dashboard. "That's—yeah, that's Rosie Pender-Atkins!" She looked at Cedeno, then gawked out her side window. "I've never seen a network news correspondent in person before. Slow down." Cedeno watched as she sized up her competition, now just a few feet away. Her eyes narrowed. "I've seen her stuff on the air—for what she's paid, it's nothin' special." As they drove past the other woman, Heather rolled down her window. She stuck her head out to get a better look at Pender-Atkins. Her hair, flying in the wind, was now more of a mess than before the pothole. "She doesn't look so hot," she announced, flopping back in her seat and crossing her arms. "I want to know what she's doing in *my* territory?"

Cedeno laughed. He wondered how many reporters in the business were like Heather Landis. He wouldn't know; only twenty-five years old himself, this was his first TV news job.

He maneuvered the car into a small parking lot next to a Spanish style, one-story building. The sign on the lush, green lawn read *Braxton Town Hall*. Purple bougainvillea, perfectly trimmed, clung to a trellis, and a well of yellow chrysanthemums bloomed under three fan palm trees.

Cedeno looked for a place to park. "Since this is your *territory*, do you have a parking spot with your name on it?"

"Shut up, Mario. One day, when I'm in New York, you'll be telling people you worked with me."

As Cedeno opened the trunk and unloaded his camera equipment and portable lights, he saw Pender-Atkins and her photographer enter the parking lot and drive to the front of the town hall. He watched as she got out of her car and walked to a pay phone next to the building. "Hey, *Network*," Cedeno called to Landis, "check who just invaded your territory?"

Landis was still inside the car, listening to the radio, painting on a fresh coat of lipstick, powdering away some shine, and playing kissy-poo with herself in the visor mirror. Cedeno ducked his head into the driver's side and took the keys out of the ignition, cutting off her rock concert. She began to protest, but he nodded and said, "Look over there, Network. NBC is here to get some pointers from you."

———————

Rosie and her photographer had reached Braxton late the previous afternoon and were told they had missed most of the cleanup on Main Street. The trash was gone and the wrecked cars were towed away. They'd immediately called KSBY, their nearest NBC affiliate, and to their dismay, discovered the station had not sent a news crew to Braxton over the weekend. All that was left to videotape now was merchants replenishing their stores. In other words, the story was visually as close to a zero as it could get.

Rosie was in a foul mood. After interviewing councilman Cal Spencer, the lone voice of dissent in town, she learned of the stormy council meeting the week before. But again, she had no video of the meeting for her report, so she got on the phone to Los Angeles, demanding another day to develop the story. "I have no pictures, Harvey," she whined. "I need more time to snoop around."

"You don't have it," he said.

"I'll tell you what I don't have, Harvey, and that's a story."

"Rosie, the answer is no. New York wants the piece at the end of the newscast tonight."

"You spineless puppet! Can't you tell them I have no video from the weekend? Our local station didn't shoot *squat*."

"Save your breath. I've heard your tirades before. Just do the story. New York wants a light feature, not an exposé."

"But—"

"Call when you're ready to send it by satellite." *Click*. It was the first time Harvey had ever hung up on her.

Rosie slammed the receiver down, then looked up to see a young woman running toward her. *My worst nightmare*, Rosie thought, when she saw who it was. The local TV news queen. Following behind the advancing beauty was a stocky young man, struggling with a portable light, extension cord, tripod, and a news camera.

"Hurry up, Mario!" the woman shouted. "I want to see what they're doing here."

"*Si, senorita, el burro* is coming," the man said. "It would help if you took some of these."

"They're too heavy," she said without looking back. "They break my nails and get my blouse dirty. Hurry up!"

The woman, dressed in skintight fire-engine-red pants and a silky white blouse, walked purposefully across the parking lot toward Rosie. The tight-lipped expression on her face hinted of things to come.

It was 9:25, the coastal fog had lifted, and bright sunshine had begun to cook the morning humidity into a scorcher. But Rosie knew something else was about to boil over and that her photographer had seen it too.

"Hey, Rosie," her photographer called. "Some gorgeous young trouble is headed your way."

"Yeah, but she's no different from a hundred others," Rosie replied.

The photographer whistled softly and slowly shook his head. "None of them ever looked like that."

Rosie agreed, but she'd played a part in similar showdowns in other cities. The scene was usually the same, whether in Glen Dive, Montana or New York City. When network people came into town, the home folk usually resented their presence, believing they could cover the story better. Now Rosie felt a classic brouhaha unfolding.

"I'm Heather Landis, KSBY-TV, News 6." She didn't offer her hand, and she met Rosie's gaze steadily.

Rosie felt a twinge of jealousy. How could anyone be that beautiful? "OK, Heather, thanks for telling me. So what?"

"Well, I was just wondering what y'all are doing in Braxton?"

Rosie looked her up and down. "Who'd you say *y'all* were?"

"Heather Landis, NBC, in San Luis Obispo."

"I didn't know the network had a bureau there," she replied with icy sarcasm.

The cut went over Heather's head. "Oh, they don't—I work for the NBC affiliate." Then she quickly added, "But I'll be moving to a larger market really soon."

Rosie was in no mood to make idle conversation with a news babe from the toolies. "I'm sure you will. Listen, nice to meet you, but we're very busy. We have an interview with the mayor at 9:30." She started to walk away, but Heather grabbed her arm.

"Wait a second—he's supposed to meet *me* at 9:30."

"Excuse me, Miss NBC, I have work to do." Rosie extracted her arm from Heather's grip. "Have a nice life *y'all*," she said as she headed toward the town's administrative building.

"Oh, no, you don't," Heather said, pushing past her to get to the door first. She reached the mayor's office, a cedar-paneled reception area with thick rose-colored carpeting. She bolted past Mayor Carter's secretary, a kindly looking woman in her fifties, seated at a computer.

"Excuse me, you can't go in there!" the startled woman sputtered, but Rosie and the two photographers were already charging past.

Rosie's ankles wobbled slightly as her shoes sank into the plush carpet. The local reporter pounded twice on the closed door, then burst into the room. His honor was leaning back in his chair, his feet propped on the desk.

Heather Landis stood in the doorway, her hands on her hips. "Mayor Carter, what's all this garbage about?" His mouth dropped open, but she continued, "Your appointment is with *me*, not the network."

CHAPTER 11

San Luis Obispo
6:00 P.M.

Rosie Pender-Atkins sat in a darkened booth watching a newscast on a television set that hung from the ceiling. She frowned at the half-eaten, disassembled cheeseburger and soggy french fries on the plate in front of her: the middle of the meat patty was too pink, and the fries were too thick.

She looked up just in time to see a young anchorman smiling into the camera. He began to read rolling words from his TelePrompTer. "Good evening. Our top story at six tonight is life under the national spotlight for the town of Braxton. Last month, it was selected best small town in America."

She looked at her photographer and nodded to the TV. "Pay attention," she sneered, "we're going to see how we should have covered the story." He gave her a tired look in return.

Rosie sighed. She had just finished watching her report on the network news that aired at 5:30 P.M. in San Luis Obispo. Braxton's new-found fame was the closing story. Twelve million people watched as she revealed a community on the verge of major change. Most of those interviewed were happy their hometown had been discovered. They looked forward to growth and prosperity with Mayor Roger Carter as their head cheerleader. Included in Rosie's report, of course, was a dissenting viewpoint from Councilman Cal Spencer.

Rosie cited "reliable sources," who questioned the claims made in *Destination* magazine about Braxton. However, there was no time to follow up, as Rosie had asked for. Instead, her photographer's spectacular video, with its panoramic shots and close-up faces of people in small-town America, dominated the report. Rosie knew she had given the brass in New York what they wanted: a soft feel-good feature that tucked the nation in bed, and assured them that the world was not such a bad place after all.

The anchorman and his female co-anchor were now on a two-shot. She looked at her partner. "For a week or so," she said, "things were pretty normal in Braxton, but that certainly has changed."

A wide shot of the news set now showed a familiar face. Heather Landis looked even more glamorous to Rosie now than when she had first seen her.

"We sent News 6's Heather *Braxton* to *Landis*," the anchor man said in a jumble of words. Heather let out a giggle, then held her hand to her mouth, obviously trying to suppress her laughter. Noticeably flustered, the young man corrected himself. "I mean, we sent Heather *Landis* to *Braxton* to see how the people there are coping. Heather?"

"Thanks, Artie and Kim." Heather turned to a camera that showed her in close up. She shifted nervously in her chair, then settled herself. "In all my time in TV news, I can't remember a story quite like this," she said with a serious look. She then gave the camera her brightest smile. "It was my first visit to Braxton, and here's what I found."

The first video showed a ringing telephone. A graphic on the lower third of the screen read *Braxton, California News 6 Today.* "Area code 805 has never been busier," Heather began "ever since the news media reported the article in *Destination* magazine, naming Braxton as the best small town in America."

A young woman appeared then to answer the phone. "Good morning. Braxton Chamber of Commerce."

Heather's report continued over shots of other people on telephones. "No matter where you go in this town of fifteen thousand, about thirty miles north of San Luis Obispo, the phone circuits to Braxton have been jammed. And where are the calls coming from?"

The next person on the report was Mayor Roger Carter. "Big cities, small towns—you name it, they've called," he said. "Teachers, computer workers, business people, retired folk—they all want to know more about Braxton—and we're trying to tell them."

A heavily made up woman spoke next. A graphic identified her as the president of Braxton's Chamber of Commerce. "The response has been amazing," she said. "I've heard from two companies back East interested in moving here, just about sight unseen."

Heather's narration resumed over shots of the community. "Until now, the rest of the country had never heard of Braxton, but the word is out. So what do the people who live here think of their newfound fame?"

"I'm worried," an older woman spoke into the camera.

"I've lived here fifteen years, it makes me sick," an older man complained.

"I think it's neat," said a smiling young man. "It'll be good for business."

Heather stood next to the town limits sign and concluded her report. "This sign," Heather said, and then pointed to the sign, "says the population is fifteen thousand." Rosie let out a laugh because Heather's hand movement was out of sync with her words. "The question now is," the reporter went on, "how many more people will be arriving here on Main Street?" Her motion to the street, again, was a beat too late. "Heather Landis, News 6, reporting from Braxton."

Rosie shook her head, closed her eyes, and leaned back in the booth. "I didn't think anything could be worse than our piece, but I just saw it."

Her photographer simply motioned to their waitress and pointed to his empty glass. "Another, please," he said, then turned to Rosie.

"Forget the story. It's over. We did what they wanted."

"She never mentioned housing. What about police and fire protection, traffic congestion, or medical services?"

He shrugged. "So what?"

"What about the school system? Can it handle a flood of new students? Are there enough jobs for people who come looking?"

"You didn't have that, either," he countered.

"I didn't have time to dig deeper, bonehead. She's supposed to be a local reporter. What a laugh. She doesn't have the talent to break a sweat, let alone a story."

"Yeah, but you got to admit, she was nice to look at."

Rosie rolled her eyes.

The waitress brought the photographer's drink, then looked at Rosie. "Something for you, ma'am?"

"Triple Scotch on the rocks."

"*Triple?*"

"*Hable Inglesia?*" Rosie snapped.

The waitress glared at Rosie. "*Si. Tres* Scotch on la rock—oh, la-pronto."

Rosie's photographer took a long swig of his drink, wiped his mouth, then put the glass on the table. "Hey, forget our story, OK?"

Rosie struck the table with her fist, causing his glass to wobble. He reached to steady it. "Look," she said, "we put three minutes and five seconds of unmitigated puke on the air. You may not care, but I do. It's my name, face, and reputation that just stunk up twelve million homes."

CHAPTER 12

Wilmette, Illinois
Seven months later, December 2

"You're puttin' me on." Brian Stanley's eyes were wide and his voice was shaky.

Pete didn't respond to his son. He simply sighed and moved to the corner of the family room, near the French windows, where he stared at the ten-foot-tall blue spruce Christmas tree, decorated with hanging memories of happier family holidays.

The teenager turned to his mother. "Come on, Mom, this has got to be a joke, right?"

But Beatrice Stanley was silent also.

"It's true," Pete said.

Brian's mouth drooped, and he sagged against the wall. All color drained from his acne-covered face as he stared down at his tennis shoes. Then, with a toss of his head, he flicked a clump of curly, red hair out of his eyes, and glared at his father. Millions of sports fans still idolized Pete Stanley, ex-Chicago Cubs' third baseman and Hall of Famer, but he knew his sixteen-year-old son hated his guts.

"I told you about this—now it's time to do it. We already bought a house out there. End of discussion." Pete studied his son's face and felt both pride and regret. Physically, Brian was a spitting image of Pete at that same age: the curly, red hair (although Brian's was a lot longer than Pete would have ever dreamed of wearing his), the same ready smile (although he didn't seem to smile as much as he moved deeper into his teens), and the same sparkle in his eyes. He had his father's athletic physique, but to Pete's silent disappointment, his son had no interest in organized sports, especially baseball. The few times Pete had seen his son play baseball informally, he was astounded at Brian's raw talent. But as far as what was going on inside his son's head, Pete had no clue. The teenager spent hours locked in his bedroom, never talked about girls (unlike his father at that age), and would likely have to repeat his sophomore year of high school. Pete hated the earsplitting noise that Brian called music, was shocked at the grotesquely violent posters that hung in his bedroom, and considered his son's friends lowlifes. Other than the times Brian got in trouble, Pete rarely spoke with his son anymore. He couldn't trace the moment he and his son had lost their closeness—it might have happened at the same time his marriage had lost its spark. But right now, he felt like he didn't even know this young person who stood before him.

"I'm not going with you!" Brian announced.

Pete took a deep breath. He wasn't surprised at this reaction, but he was uncertain what to do next. He walked over to a barstool in the kitchen and sat down. The two stared at each other over the kitchen counter. Pete's gaze moved for a moment to the mounted silver bat hanging on the wall just over the boy's left shoulder—a symbol of Pete's third National League batting championship. Most people were fascinated with the baseball memorabilia that filled the room. Pete knew his son found it dumb and boring.

"Brian, our house is sold. We've found a new place to live. You can start the new semester out there. The move will be good for you."

"What about my friends?" Anger and desperation gave Brian's voice a slight quiver.

"Your *friends* are part of the reason we're doing this. We all need to get away from some people and things that have been destructive."

"You don't know my friends! At least they have time for me."

Brian had scored a direct hit. "You're right," Pete admitted.

"Baseball, the Hall of Fame," he motioned to the house, "a big place to live—it all came before you. And that was wrong."

"Spare me the sob story."

Pete took the shot much like a fast ball to the ribs in his playing days. He winced, but tried not to show the pain. "Braxton will give us all a fresh start. New town, new neighbors, new friends—"

"Right. Bush town, hick neighbors, and a bunch of country rubes." Brian plopped down on a black leather sofa. "I'm not going."

Pete got up from the stool and sat down on the opposite end of the couch. "I wasn't going to tell you this, thought I might surprise you when we got there, but the high school in Braxton wants me to be their baseball coach—on a volunteer arrangement."

"Why would I care about that?"

"They could use a good third baseman who hits with power. Despite what you say, I think I'm looking at him."

"Me?" Brian asked in disbelief. "And you as my coach? Yeah, right."

"Well, it was just an idea." Pete reached in his pocket and pulled out a set of car keys. He laid them on the coffee table, then pushed them toward Brian.

"What's that?" Brian looked at his father with a suspicious frown, then at the keys, then back to his father. "Are those for me?"

"Yeah."

"What for?"

"To help make the move a little easier." His father nodded toward the kitchen window. "Look outside in the driveway."

Brian sauntered over to the window near the kitchen sink and peered outside. His eyes widened, and his mouth opened when he saw the new silver Porsche convertible. "Rad' car."

"Yes, it is. You probably know the specs, just by looking at it."

With his eyes glued on the car, Brian said, "'99 Boxster model, mid-engine, two-seater, Spyder design. Who does it belong to?"

"It's yours—if, and I emphasize the word, *if* you come to Braxton with us." His son's face contorted in disbelief. He ran back into the family room, picked up the keys, grabbed his red jacket, and sprinted out the door.

Beatrice followed Pete to the kitchen window. They looked out to see Brian seated behind the steering wheel, revving the engine, an excited grin on his face.

"How much?" Beatrice asked with a tone of resignation.

"You'll think I'm nuts . . . just under a hundred grand." When he received no immediate response, Pete braced for an explosion.

"Do I think you're nuts?" she returned calmly. "No, you're not crazy, Pete, just stupid if you think you can buy his love."

He wished she had yelled at him. "But look at him, honey. When's the last time you saw him grinning like that?"

"Oh, try two weeks ago when he came home drunk," she answered coldly. "Pete, he's so messed up, I wonder . . ." Then she just shrugged.

Pete gazed at his wife—a gentle woman, with porcelain doll-like features. She was a private person; many thought she was ill-suited to be the wife of a professional baseball player, especially one who would achieve so much fame. The two had met during Pete's rookie year in the minor leagues. She was a preacher's daughter, swept off her feet by the gifted young athlete. Pete had no interest in religion, especially the personal relationship with God that Beatrice's father spoke about. Her mother and father had told them they were against the marriage. But she had insisted there would be a spiritual change in Pete after the "I do's." He knew nothing would happen, and it didn't. Soon, much to Pete's relief, Beatrice stopped talking about religion and drifted away from the church.

"You know what I see in that car?" she asked now.

"Tell me."

"I remember Brian's first steps, his first tooth, the first words, and the first day of kindergarten. I knew that little boy."

"They can't stay that way forever."

"I know, but when did he become a stranger?" They were silent for a moment, then, "Do you think Brian will come with us?"

Pete put his arm around her shoulder. "Yeah, I don't think he can turn down the car. We'll leave on the seventeenth."

Beatrice eyed their Christmas tree. "Not much of a holiday for us."

Pete grunted. "You think Brian and Nicole were about to hang around here with us for a good old-fashioned celebration?"

She shook her head. "Probably not. But do you think it's wise to pull them out of school early?"

"At this point, with their grades, it won't make a difference." He looked out the window and saw his son returning to the house. "There's one other thing that should seal the deal with him."

"What's that?"

"You'll think it's weird, but you know that movie poster he has on his bedroom door? James Dean with the cigarette dangling from his mouth?"

"Uh huh."

"We're going to be living close to where his hero got killed. I figure that might impress him."

Brian entered the kitchen then. He dangled the car keys in front of his parents. "The car is mine if I go with you, right?" he asked in a suspicious tone. "No strings attached?"

"That's the deal," Pete said. "Plus there's a bonus."

"Oh? What?"

"Braxton is near where your hero, James Dean, was killed. You'll get to drive by the spot any time you want." Brian's eyes lit up and a smile turned his face into the first civil look Pete had seen in a year. "What do you think about that?"

"Cool," Brian said, then turned toward the door. "Later. I'm outta here." And he ran back out to his car.

Beatrice sighed deeply. "We've spoiled him rotten."

"Yeah, I know."

"He's a troubled kid, Pete."

"Maybe he'll leave his problems behind," Pete said, wanting desperately to believe his own words.

CHAPTER 13

Braxton
Thursday December 15, 8:15 A.M.

Benny Green figured just about everything was in place for his grand opening the following day. He knew his restaurant was a curiouis addition to Braxton. It was located only two blocks from Lolo's #2, the most popular eating spot this side of Paso Robles, where the original Lolo's also thrived. His new restaurant, Casa de Benny's, had practically come to life overnight: less than three months had passed since they'd signed the lease, installed the kitchen equipment, and had remodeled the building.

Benny and his wife had had little time to socialize with the locals since they'd moved to Braxton five months before. But, then, not many people had gone out of their way to get close to them, either. That was fine. Benny and Maggie were in no hurry to push themselves on the small town, especially since few blacks lived in the community. Benny's remodelers had told him that the word around town on the Greens was that they were friendly, private people, who wanted a slower pace of life. Long-time residents were taking a wait-and-see attitude toward the newcomers.

Benny heard a tapping sound at the restaurant's front door now. He wiped his hands on his Levis and tucked in his red golf shirt, then moved toward the door. He opened it and gave the young woman a wide grin. "*Buenos dias, senorita de la prensa,*" he said with a sly grin. "*Como se llama?*" She was there to write a story on the restaurant owner for the local newspaper.

The woman returned his grin. "I think you just said 'Good morning, Miss-of the press.' And to answer your question, my name is Shelly Hinson."

Benny laughed. "My Mexican food is better than my Spanish—come on in. Can I get you some coffee?"

"Sure, I'd like that," she said, walking to a nearby table.

As Benny closed the door, his wife, Maggie, entered the room, carrying a tray with three steaming cups of coffee. He chuckled and looked back at Shelly. "This is what happens when you've been married as long as we have. Maggie not only knows what I'm going to say before I say it, she reads my mind."

Maggie responded with a knowing grin. "You'll find cream and sugar on the table, Shelly," she said, giving the first cup to Shelly, the second to Benny, and the third to herself.

"Nice place," Shelly said, "but kind of risky, isn't it? You know, two other restaurants tried to take on LoLo's here and went belly-up within six months."

Benny moved around the room, checking the twenty tables, ten booths, and more than a hundred chairs he hoped would soon be filled with customers. The tables were set with colorful pottery plates from Mexico, ornate silverware, and heavy drinking glasses with origami-like white paper napkins tucked inside. "So I've been told. We think there's room for competition."

"Tell me, when did you first hear about Braxton and what made you move?"

"We'd wanted to get out of Norfolk for a long time." Benny turned to Maggie. "You showed me the newspaper article first, didn't you?" She nodded. "After that, I went out and bought the magazine. We checked out the area—actually, we were more impressed with Paso Robles, but we took a chance and came here." He smiled. "The article was pretty convincing."

"Who does the cooking?" Shelly asked.

"You can have nice atmosphere, great service, but if the food is lousy—it's *adios*. I interviewed several guys. Only one of 'em came close, but he was not quite right."

"Short guy? Rides a Harley?"

"Yeah," Benny answered with a look of surprise. "How'd you know?"

"It's a long story. No, actually, it's a short story. Not worth   repeating."

Benny explained that this wasn't exactly his idea of a slower pace, but he knew if customers didn't like the food on the first visit, they wouldn't come back. No, if the restaurant were to succeed, he had to do the cooking. The tortilla chips had to be baked and his secret salsa mixed fresh for the lunch crowd.

Benny stood. "I've got to get started. We can talk in the kitchen— if you don't mind watching the owner at work."

Shelly agreed and followed Ben and Maggie into the kitchen. Benny slipped into an apron, then fired up the stove and heated the oven. As he reached for a skillet from an overhead rack, out of the corner of his eye, he saw Maggie shaking her head, a wry smile on her face. Now it was his turn to read her mind. "Don't say it, Maggie."

His wife chuckled.

"Say, what?" Shelly asked.

"She's thinking that my retirement lasted one month," Benny said. "Right?"

"Try one day," Maggie said with a laugh.

CHAPTER 14

Saturday December 17, 9:49 A.M.

"There they are!" Beatrice Stanley pointed ahead to a car on the shoulder of the road. A large sign beside it read, "Welcome to Braxton, Best Small Town in America." Brian was perched on the left front fender of the silver Porsche convertible and their daughter, Nicole, was in the passenger seat. She wore headphones, and her head bobbed—probably to some annoying rap song, Pete guessed. Brian's feet hung over the side of the fender, a cigarette hung from his mouth, and his red jacket was half open.

"Well, I see he brought those stupid Chesterfields," Pete grumbled. Of course: James Dean was puffing a Chesterfield the moment he took his last breath.

"And we know what's in his pocket," Beatrice said in disgust.

Pete nodded. "He would sooner go without eating than not having—what does he call it—his thirty-three-oh-three?"

"It's sick, Pete. The exact amount of money James Dean had on him the day he was killed?"

"That's our Brian." Pete couldn't help chuckling. His son's idiosyncrasies irritated and amused him at the same time. "Look at that pose. He should be in the movies."

His parents had seen it all before; the pained look on Brian's face, tousled hair, cigarette on his lips, white T-shirt, and red jacket.

"I wonder how long they've been here." They had last seen Brian and Nicole two hours earlier when both cars had refueled in Bakersfield.

Beatrice shrugged. "I just wonder how many speeding tickets he has in his glove compartment."

Tires crunching in the gravel and dirt, Pete pulled his white Lexus to a stop behind Brian's car. He turned to Beatrice. "Welcome to Braxton. Let's see what James Dean and his sister think of our new home."

The journey from Wilmette to Braxton had taken four days, but it felt like four weeks. Through snow and sleet, they'd logged more than two thousand miles, passed through eight states, stopped at twelve restaurants, slept in four hotels, fueled up in seven gas stations, and engaged in at least twenty arguments. Pete knew of at least four states in which Brian was stopped for speeding. The cross-country trip in separate cars was his son's idea. Pete had wanted to put his son's Porsche in the back of a moving van, but hadn't pushed when Brian threatened once again to stay behind. Nicole chose the lesser of two evils and rode most of the way with her brother. Now, at least, the trek was over.

"Well, you guys made pretty good time," Pete said, as he approached Brian. "Did you see the monument?"

Brian took a drag on his Chesterfield. "Yeah," he said, blowing smoke out of one corner of his mouth.

Forty minutes earlier, Pete and Beatrice had stopped along Highway 46 at the intersection of James Dean's accident in 1955. They were confused when they couldn't find a monument. They drove west then, and Beatrice spotted something on the north side of the highway. Nine hundred yards from the fateful intersection was a strip of stainless steel, wrapped around a scruffy-looking tree. At the base of the tree sat a bronze plaque that paid homage to the late movie idol.

"What did you think?" Pete asked his sulking son.

Brian looked down and mumbled, "I don't know."

A bad imitation of James Dean, Pete thought. "Isn't it ironic, Brian, that they have a traffic safety experiment and it starts right where James Dean was killed?" Pete hoped this might at least open up some kind of conversation.

"You mean the sign that says you gotta turn on your headlights for the next twenty-three miles?"

Pete felt his spirits lift. "Yeah. Of all places to have the experiment—it's almost spooky. Did you do it?" He was desperate to talk with his son.

But Brian just shook his head and sneered, "Me, drive with my lights on during the day? Sounds like the kind of lame idea the losers out here would dream up."

Pete chided himself for even mentioning it. "OK, I thought it was a little odd myself. But now that we've arrived, what do you think of the town?"

Brian took one last drag and flicked his cigarette onto the dirt. "It stinks."

"Not exactly a ringing endorsement, but a starting point." Pete congratulated himself for not losing his temper.

Just then, Nicole yanked the headphones off her head. "So, where's our house? I want to make some phone calls."

"You know some people in Braxton?" Pete asked with a smile.

"Yeah, right," Nicole snapped. "There's nobody in this town worth knowing. I promised Fernando I'd call him when we got here."

Pete took a deep breath, much like he used to before stepping into the batter's box against a tough pitcher. "OK, follow me. Our house is about five minutes from here."

CHAPTER 15

Sunday December 18, 12:14 P.M.

"Now to him who is able to keep you from stumbling, and to make you stand in the presence of his glory blameless with great joy . . ."

Nick Martinez began walking up the center aisle as his associate pastor gave the benediction to the eleven o'clock worship service.

". . . To the only God our Savior, through Jesus Christ our Lord, be glory, majesty, dominion and authority . . ."

As Nick reached the rear of the sanctuary, he noticed that a number of his church members were sneaking a peek at him as he passed.

". . . Before all time and now and forever."

Nick timed his move through the open doors on the final "Amen" and positioned himself in the foyer near the front entrance. As the organist played the first note of "A Mighty Fortress Is Our God," Nick prepared himself for the first wave of his congregation—the ones in a hurry to reach the parking lot, the ones who sat in the rear of the church. He sighed. Some had dozed during his message, and he was sure that others had their minds on the football game they were missing on television. *Must be in the third quarter now*, he thought. Stomachs were growling, and as all preachers know, when it gets past noon, church folk are ready to eat.

Nick had a theory. He believed those who sat in the back of the church were the least enthusiastic about his sermons. It grieved him that these were the ones who probably had the greatest need for the Gospel. And as he suspected, the first back-pew-Baptists barely greeted him as they filed past. Some gave him only a quick glance or a limp handshake, while others used their spouse as a shield and darted past, avoiding him altogether.

Nick was now into his second month as senior pastor of Braxton's First Baptist Church, and he was convinced today's sermon had been his worst. At least that's what he read in the glazed eyes of those church members who remained awake during his forty-five minute message. Nick had challenged his congregation to resist getting caught up in what he called a syndrome of success. He preached from the twelfth chapter of Luke—the parable of a successful man whose philosophy in life was to eat, drink, and be merry, but who turned out to be a fool in God's sight. Nick was only too aware that few in Braxton would want to hear this now that they were living in the "Best Small Town in America." From the skeptical looks he received during his sermon, he guessed these folks believed Bible parables were for little old ladies and Sunday School kids. The promise of prosperity had hit Braxton, and the town was ready for the good life.

Nick hadn't seen this attitude when he and his wife, Karen, had arrived in town for his one and only interview. On the contrary, he had sensed a spirit of togetherness in the community, an absence of jealousy and greed. Could he have been that wrong? Maybe he should have listened to Karen and waited longer before deciding to accept the call. Did he pray enough about his decision? Was he that desperate for a job that he had overlooked the obvious? Still, he had a family to support, Karen was pregnant, and they needed a paycheck.

The whole process had happened so quickly. A month after being asked to leave his church in Phoenix, a friend from seminary had told him about the opening in Braxton. The Baptist church of about three hundred members seemed a perfect fit. The leaders informed him that the last pastor had wavered in his preaching; they wanted someone who would hold true to the Gospel. The church elders made it clear they didn't want Nick to sugarcoat his sermons. Nick and Karen prayed about the opportunity, and two weeks later he accepted the call to be senior pastor.

It was shortly after they'd moved to Braxton that Nick began to see what he'd missed. Something dangerous was happening in the lives of the people he'd felt called to shepherd. Because of that, he sensed the Holy Spirit's leading to sound a biblical alarm. He had done that this morning. But unlike a blaring smoke detector or a ringing burglar alarm, his words seemed to have fizzled. He was ashamed of himself.

His flock continued to approach. Those who had sat closer to the front of the church were now reaching him, offering handshakes and general pleasantries.

"Are you all moved in now?" one young woman asked.

"Still have a few more boxes to unpack," Nick answered. "What's your name? I don't believe we've met."

"Jennifer Marcus. We heard you were new in town. Are your sermons always that long?" But she was gone before Nick could respond.

"Nice looking tie, Pastor," a young man commented.

"Thanks," Nick mumbled.

Then he spotted the editor of the *Braxton Banner*, Marty Cavitt and his wife Gini. "Food for thought, Pastor," Marty said.

That was it? Apparently so—the couple quickly filed out the door.

The generic greetings continued, with no mention of the sermon's content, a message that Nick had taken three days to prepare. Most of the previous night, he'd spent in front of his bedroom mirror practicing. He gazed into the friendly, but distant eyes of each person who walked past. He knew they'd heard his words, but was anyone listening?

The last person to leave was the owner of Braxton's hardware store. He was also a member of the board of elders. "Good intent," the older man said kindly. "But, remember, you came into town during the good times, not the tough ones."

Martinez nodded and smiled slightly. "Thanks for the counsel, Willard," he said as he watched him leave. Then he felt the stab of an inner voice. *Who do you think you are? Ha! Look at you. You failed in Phoenix and you're about to do the same here. Nobody wants to hear your message. You're a fool.*

Nick knew that Satan was at work.

CHAPTER 16

Sunday December 18, 11:50 P.M.

Leona Kyle's 1988 rust-infected beige Toyota Corolla had been a cranky and reluctant traveler from the moment the trip began. The two greeted each other before sunrise at Leona's apartment parking space. She'd packed the car to the gills. Inside, she'd left barely enough room to fit behind the steering wheel. The back seat was piled high with clothes, boxes of dishes, a television, bags of groceries, two house-plants, and a fan. The trunk was filled with her computer, a printer, a stereo, a few shoes, and some books. She couldn't have fit in one more book, maybe not even a bookmark. Then, just as she was ready to leave, she realized the car's left front tire was flat. It took another two hours to unload the trunk, change the tire, and reload the trunk. She was a mess, and she smelled terrible. But she couldn't clean up as she'd given her apartment key to the landlord the night before, then locked the door behind her.

That set the tone for the next eighteen hours; 275 miles of agony and frustration. There were stops in five cities, hours spent at six service stations, including a thirty-mile ride with an obnoxious, foul-mouthed tow truck driver. She listened to auto shop lectures from seven mechanics, only three of which turned out to know what they were doing. The Corolla needed and received four life-extending trans-plants: a new fuel pump, alternator, water pump, and fan belt. Her UNOCAL credit card was maxed-out. The car could live without a headlight, a left turn signal, and the muffler that fell off somewhere between Santa Barbara and San Luis Obispo.

A bad omen, however, was the ugly, black smoke screen that trailed her like an environmental nightmare. As she chugged along, often in the emergency lane, a number of drivers honked their horns or gave her dirty looks and dirtier gestures. A few pointed to the back of her car (as if she didn't know about the smoke). At her last stop for gas, she needed three quarts of oil to make a warning light go out.

It was a few minutes before midnight now, and Leona believed the Corolla was going to make it. Maybe. As the car coughed and coasted down the off-ramp of Highway 46 into Braxton, she knew this was the end of the line for her not-so-faithful four-wheeled companion. The lights on the dashboard were a virtual doomsday message board— warnings to check low brake fluid, oil pressure, and her dying battery. But it wasn't a matter of checking; she knew what the problem was. It was just that if she stopped the car, she was afraid it wouldn't start again. *Please, God, help me get into town.* Worst of all, like a plane about to crash, her engine system warning kept blinking, silently screaming at her to take the car to the nearest Toyota dealer before it exploded. The engine was making groaning sounds, and now, with the accelerator pushed all the way to the floor, the car was traveling at only about twenty miles an hour.

Leona spotted a Denny's restaurant a block away. *Lord, one more block, please.* She aimed her car for the parking lot and stepped on the brake, but the pedal collapsed to the floor. Frantically, she grabbed the emergency brake handle and looked for a fence, a tree, anything to run into. Suddenly she heard a loud *boom!* The hood flew open, white smoke poured out, and the car rolled a few more feet, then stopped, having reached the end of its life.

Leona scrambled to get out of her seat belt and escape. But then she realized her Corolla was no longer in danger of blowing up or catching fire. From the sound of its death rattle, she figured it was one tow away from the junkyard. She reached back into the car for her purse, grabbed her green leather flight jacket and San Diego Padres baseball cap, then began walking toward the restaurant. She was tired, disgusted, and wanted to be left alone.

Out of the corner of her eye, she spotted a bearded man and a woman leaving the restaurant. He wore green corduroy pants, hiking boots, and a Mexican-looking shirt with drawstrings on the collar. The woman was striking, a short brunette who wore a sage denim button-front shirt and a matching straight skirt. He looked kind, but his girl-friend or wife looked a bit unhappy, Leona thought. As frazzled as she felt, she was not unaware of the man's admiring glance as she walked closer to him. His face revealed that he had seen much of the world, and his eyes studied her with amused curiosity. The woman had locked her right arm in his.

"What did you think of my entrance?" Leona said.

His laugh was jolly, gentle and deep. "Not the most graceful, but it had a flare for the dramatic, certainly better than the movie we saw tonight." He extended his free hand. "My name is Cal Spencer, and this is Shelly Hinson. I don't think we've seen you before."

She shook his hand. "I'm sure everyone *heard* my arrival. I'm new in town. Leona Kyle's my name."

The woman tugged on Cal's arm. "Nice to meet you," she said quickly, "maybe we'll run into you again."

Cal shook his head and gently pulled his arm free. "Come on, Shelly, she needs our help."

"It's late, Cal."

Cal turned from Shelly to smile at her. "Where are you from and what brings you here?"

"I'm from San Diego. I'm the new English teacher at your high school."

Cal's smile broadened. "Well, we have at least one thing in common. I'm a teacher, too—at the middle school." He nodded toward his companion. "Shelly's a reporter for our town newspaper." Shelly rolled her eyes.

Leona looked at her. "Are you on a deadline?" she asked sarcastically, then instantly regretted her words.

"Yes," Shelly snapped, "hello and good-bye. Come on, Cal, take me home."

But Cal didn't move. "I think Leona could use some help," he said. Shelly shrugged.

"I'll be OK," Leona said, "you and your *girlfriend* go ahead and do whatever it is you need to do."

"Shelly and I are just friends," Cal assured her, but Shelly's eyes narrowed at that. "I'm on Braxton's town council," he continued, "and since I'm a public servant, the least I can do is help our high school's newest teacher. Right, Shelly?"

Shelly started to answer, but instead, looked away.

"Thanks, but I'll be fine," Leona said, and began walking toward the restaurant. She only wanted to get to a motel, clean up, then regroup after her disastrous trip. She had no idea what to do about a new car. "Tell me," she said, turning around, "does Braxton have a taxi that runs this late? I need to get to my motel."

"Unfortunately, the only cabbies are in Paso Robles," Cal said, "and I doubt they'll want to come into town for that short a fare." He smiled. "If you don't mind being seen with a politician, I'll be glad to drive you there. The motel is only a couple miles from here."

Leona figured if she could make it through two years in San Diego's barrio, and survive the death run of her Corolla, she could handle a two-mile ride with this man. "Yes, that's very kind of you." Her voice sounded a bit raspy after the long adventure.

"It's obvious you've had the mother-of-all-trips," Cal said with a knowing look. He nodded toward the restaurant. "I know it's after midnight, but before we go, let me buy you some breakfast." He quickly looked at Shelly. "You don't mind, do you?"

Shelly took a deep breath, glared first at Cal, then at Leona, and then back at Cal again. "Cal, I don't give a rip what you do." She turned to Leona. "Leona, *Councilman* Spencer is all yours. One advantage of living in a small town is that everything is within walking distance. Goodnight, Cal, I'll walk myself home." And she turned and left.

CHAPTER 17

Gina Wells' first impression of Braxton nearly caused her to turn around and head back out of town. Two months before, Gina had sent a letter to the town's chief of police telling him she'd read about Braxton in *Destination* magazine. She'd included a résumé and informed him of her plans to visit friends in Los Angeles. She wanted him to know of her interest in any command openings. To her surprise, she received a prompt reply—if she planned on being in the area, be sure to stop by for an interview.

It was a Friday in October, around two in the afternoon, when Gina turned off Highway 46 and headed her blue 1996 Mustang toward Main Street. The drive from Los Angeles had been grueling; she felt grubby and was eager to check into her room at the Motel 6 and freshen up. She began to search the streets and numbers, then came to a red light at the corner of Main and Lincoln. She glanced in her rearview mirror and saw a car approaching fast. It suddenly changed lanes, flashed its blue and red lights, briefly sounded its siren, then blew through the intersection. When the signal turned green, she drove to the next block and pulled alongside the squad car. She looked to her left and caught the officer's eye. His passenger side window was rolled down and he winked at her. "Hi there. Haven't seen you in town before."

"Maybe it's because something's wrong with your eyesight," she retorted.

"What do you mean?" He grinned slyly and rubbed his moustache with his right hand. "My eyes haven't had this kind of a treat in a long time."

"You ran that red light. Is there a separate set of rules for police in this town?"

His smile vanished, and his jaw hardened. "You got a problem?"

"No, but you need a few lessons in driving."

"Oh, excuse me. Are you some kind of police expert?"

"I know the difference between red and green."

The officer reached for his instrument panel. Red and blue lights began pulsating on the bar across the car's roof. "OK, Miss, what colors do you see."

Gina craned her neck, glanced at the car's roof, then looked back at him. "Blue like your eyes," she cooed.

He warmed at that and grinned. "Why, thank you, ma'am."

"And red, like your neck."

The traffic signal turned green, and a car behind them honked.

"Very funny." He pushed a button and tapped his horn. His siren sounded a brief bark. He pointed to the side of the road. "Pull your car over there against the curb."

Me and my big mouth, Gina chided herself, as she signaled a right turn. But her signal stuck after the first blink. *This cop looks like a character out of a B movie,* she thought, *the one who drives his car into a lake while the good old boy gets away.* The officer double parked on the street beside her, then approached her window. She saw that he had three stripes on the sleeve of his uniform.

"I see you're from Florida," he said, sucking in his gut. "Is there a separate set of rules for you?"

"What do you mean?"

"Well, Miss Disney World, your Mickey Mouse turn signal doesn't work, so I'm going to have to write you a little ticket. Let me see your driver's license and registration."

"What's your name, Officer?" she asked, as she handed them to him.

Seventeen

"Hesterman, Sergeant Blake Hesterman." He eyed her closely. "And if you forget the name, just remember I'm the guy with the blue eyes and red neck."

"Don't worry, I'll file it under 'JIK,'" she said.

"JIK?"

"Jerks I know."

The officer glared at her, then stepped back and walked behind her car. "Well, well, well, Miss *Wells*," he said, as he returned to her window. "The *jerk* you know has another surprise for you. Seems you have about a foot of your car parked in a little ole' red zone, which means smart mouth Gina Wells gets *two* tickets from officer JIK."

CHAPTER 18

Monday December 19, 1:30 P.M.

"Your résumé, experience, and references are very impressive, Gina." Braxton Chief of Police, Trevor Talbot, looked at the paper in his hand. "*Very* impressive."

Gina began to say something, then decided against it. She wanted him to move the conversation forward and helped only by returning a pleasant look.

Talbot looked perplexed. That morning and over lunch, he was up front with Gina about joining his police department. "You had more action in one day in Miami than we have in a year," he'd told her. "In fact, my career probably looks like a school crossing guard's compared with yours."

Gina knew Talbot was stretching the truth, but probably not by much. His most exciting days were most likely as an F.B.I. special agent in Dallas. She'd heard from others that he was a good lawman—tough, fair, and outstanding at his job. He didn't have the stereotype cop appearance—she couldn't figure out what he looked like. A navy captain? A park ranger? She didn't know. His hands were huge; their first handshake was memorable, but not painful. The chief's brown hair was uncharacteristically long for a police officer, especially an ex-F.B.I. agent, but she thought it suited him. His face was that of someone who enjoyed the outdoors. Did he hunt, fish, play golf? She didn't care. He wore a noncommittal expression. And she actually kind of liked him.

"If I'm right," she said, "I was a rookie in Miami when you became chief of police here. Correct?"

"If it was ten years ago—yes." A wry smile came to his face.

"Well, I would imagine you found things much different here than in the *mean* streets of Dallas."

Talbot nodded. "I had doubts when I first arrived in town, but the difference was part of the attraction."

"Obviously, it worked for you."

"I was older, and married, Gina. The first year was a major adjustment, especially for Courtney, the big city girl. She gave up a public relations job at a large company in Dallas."

"I'm not a teacher, Chief, I'm a cop."

Talbot rubbed his hand across his face and sighed. "It was easier for me. I was glad to escape Big D, but Courtney went nuts that first year."

"And now your wife is crazy about Braxton. Right, Chief?"

Talbot laughed, and his head bobbed in agreement. "Yup. Best journalism and speech teacher the high school has ever had. Wait 'til you see the school newspaper. It sometimes has better stories than our local paper, *The Banner*."

"Then you understand why I'm here," Gina said.

"Yes, I do," he admitted with a sigh. "I just don't want to bring you on board, and a month from now hear you say there isn't enough action."

"I had enough action in Miami to last a lifetime. But from what I understand, what was true in Braxton a year ago is no longer true."

"You're right. Ever since we got that best small town in America thing, we've had more people move here and serious crime is way up compared with a year ago. I need an assistant police chief who can take command of the department's investigations." Talbot leaned back in his desk chair. "OK, you've got the job if you want it."

Her eyes widened. "You bet I do. When can I start?"

"If you were already moved, right now. We could use you today."

Eighteen

He got out of his chair and walked to the door. "For now, I want you to meet the guy you'll be working with." Talbot opened the door and gestured to someone in the other room. "Come on in and meet our assistant chief of police, and your new boss."

When he entered the room, his mouth dropped open, the color drained from his face, and his gut sagged.

"Captain Wells," the chief said, "say hello to your right-hand man, Sergeant Blake Hesterman."

Gina hid her surprise better than Hesterman whose knees looked a little rubbery. She crossed the room to the officer, who tried to say something, but couldn't. "Hello, Blake," she said, extending her hand, and winking. "I got my turn signal fixed and my car is legally parked."

CHAPTER 19

Braxton Town Council Chambers
Tuesday December 20, 11:13 A.M.

"I'd hoped the vote would be unanimous, but despite Councilman Spencer's myopic objections, we're going forward." Mayor Roger Carter eyeballed the room. "Six days from now, the best small town in America is going to celebrate."

"This is a boondoggle!" Cal Spencer pointed a finger at the mayor. "You're the one with myopia. How can you spend $49,868.23 for a—" He shuffled the papers in front of him, found the one he was looking for, and waved it at Carter. "Look at this. Just one item—we're literally blowing up $10,000 for a fireworks show?"

"Two fireworks shows," another council member corrected. "One after the New Year's Eve concert and the other at midnight."

Shelly watched the exchange and took notes from the spot reserved for *The Braxton Banner*. It was good stuff, especially because of the person in the middle of it. Shelly still had her eye on Cal, even after being dumped for Leona Sunday night. His objections would play a prominent part in her story for Thursday's edition, but the material had far more value six months down the line—when she would use it in *Destination* magazine.

Cal stared at the council member who had corrected him. "Oh, excuse me, Phil—*two* fireworks shows, as if that makes it OK." He turned back to the mayor. "Seems to me, we haven't had the big bonanza you predicted, Mayor—and now we're spending money this town doesn't have for a week-long party?"

"You know very well it's more than a party." The mayor sounded a bit testy. "And I disagree with you. Since the article came out, we've seen some good people move here, a few new businesses started, and others expanded."

"What about all those who can't find work or the stores that have flopped?"

The mayor shrugged. "I wish everyone could have made it," he said in a condescending tone, "but life comes with no guarantees. The week celebrates success and also gets tourists here. Christmas is Sunday—we start our festival on Monday, which is a holiday."

"And the grand finale is Saturday," said Cal, "when we set off the fireworks, right?"

"It'll be a great New Year's Eve," the mayor predicted.

"Nice touch, Mayor, the town's skyrocketing debt and the rocket's *red* glare."

"Why are we even discussing this?" another council member whined. "The vote's been taken."

The mayor nodded. "You're right. The dissenting opinion from the junior council member is noted, and has been for the past three weeks." He yawned, then extended his hands, palms-up. "Mr. Spencer, would you like to change your vote and make it unanimous?"

The council members were seated at an elevated, horseshoe-shaped desk area. On the wall above them, an electronic tally board recorded their votes. Next to the names, Drew, McKnight, and Prescott, green lights were lit. Beside the name, Spencer, a red light glared at them.

"One last chance," the mayor offered.

Cal, in a sign of disgust, flipped his pen onto a stack of papers. "No. I have a question, though."

"What is it?" the mayor asked impatiently. "We're going to have free hot air balloon rides, correct?"

"Yes. The town will love it."

"I have a suggestion, then, on how to save money," Cal said seriously.

"And what would that be?"

"We won't need to pay for any fuel if you just plop yourself under the balloon and keep talking."

A number of spectators gasped, then laughed nervously, while council members struggled to keep a straight face.

"Very funny, Councilman Spencer," the mayor declared. "I've heard enough. Let's move ahead. You all have a copy of the week's schedule. I think it's pretty clever—we have a number of events that play off the word 'small.' Lets go over it, in case there are any questions."

———•••———

Shelly looked down at her copy of the festival schedule. She had to admit—it looked like a week of fun for both the residents and visitors. She followed along with the mayor as he read down the list.

THINK SMALL-BE BIG!
Braxton celebrates

Monday, December 26
9:30 A.M.—Opening ceremonies with hot air balloon
10:30 A.M.—Planting of time capsule in Town Square
All day—Free hot air balloon rides
Exchange of Christmas gifts (wanted and "unwanted"
      gifts along Main Street sidewalk)
All day and continuing through Sunday—Special discounts
      for small sizes of clothing

Tuesday, December 27—Main Street
10:00 A.M.—Small people parade (five feet tall and under)
Noon—Bonsai tree competition
 —Model railroad display
 —Doll and shadow box art exhibits

Wednesday, December 28—Town Square
10:00 A.M.—Miniature dog show
Noon—Compact vintage car show

Thursday, December 29—Town Square
10:00 A.M.—Kiddie beauty pageant
Noon—Small business-owner-of-the-year award
2:00 P.M.—High school short story competition awards

Friday, December 30
10:00 A.M. to 10:00 P.M. Sunday—Movie marathon
    "Honey, I Shrunk the Kids," "Little Women,"
    "Little Big Man," "Little Miss Big,"
    "Little Miss Marker,"
    "The Incredible Shrinking Man,"
    and other selected "shorts."
Noon —Short-order cook-off
2:00 P.M.—Pee Wee Football championship play-off game

Saturday, December 31—Main Street
10:00 A.M.—Street fair with music, food, games,
    and pony rides
Noon—Potluck of finger foods
8:30 P.M.—Special music—Little Richard in concert
    (at high school gymnasium)
10:00 P.M. (Or following concert)—Fireworks, followed by
    community singing on Main Street and in Town Square
Midnight—New Year's Eve fireworks finale

Sunday, January 1—First Baptist Church
10:00 A.M.—Finals for best musical rendition of
    "Church in the Wildwood"

"Well, there it is," the mayor said proudly. "Great job. Thanks to the town's staff and council members for all your ideas. We did this without a public relations firm. However . . ." He looked out to the audience. "Courtney, would you stand?

The police chief's wife smiled and rose from her seat in the first row. Attractive, dark-haired, with enormous dimples, she held a clipboard against her red Christmas-theme cardigan. Shelly liked Courtney and knew she was happy to be in the middle of this project.

"One of the keys to the success of this week is Courtney," the mayor said. "She will be handling media relations. As you know, that was her specialty in Dallas." He motioned to Courtney. "Tell us what you've got planned."

"Saturday morning, we'll set up our media tent," she told the group. "I'm hoping we'll have TV stations from L.A. and San Francisco." She glanced at Mario Cedeno and Heather Landis standing over against the wall. "And, of course, our friends from the local media will be there." Mario was operating a TV camera, and Heather looked stunning in her peach-colored miniskirt and white silk blouse. "Friday we should have the media kits printed," Courtney went on, "and Monday, at the opening ceremony, we'll have catered food in the tent. The best investment for a good story is to feed the media." Everyone laughed as Courtney took her seat.

"Food or no food, we always get a good story," the mayor gushed, "from the lovely Heather Landis." Heather blew a kiss at him, and he blushed. "I wish other TV stations had the good judgment to be here today for our festival announcement. It seems all they're interested in is bad news. Not so with Channel 6." Shelly cringed as Heather straightened up, pushed out her ample chest, and beamed at the council, then those in the audience.

"Mr. Mayor," Cal Spencer called out. "How much did it cost to book Little Richard? What are we paying him to sing 'Tutti Frutti?'"

"It's public record, Mr. Spencer," the mayor snapped.

"Then say it out loud! I want the whole town to hear it from your lips."

The mayor leaned into his microphone and over modulated his words. "All right, read my lips, Spencer. Fifteen thousand dollars!" Gasps could be heard all over the room.

"Good Golly, Miss Molly," Cal quipped, "sure know how to spend."

The room erupted in laughter.

"Yuck it up, Spencer," the mayor angrily shot back. "We're charging ten bucks a person. We'll see what you say after the town makes a pile of money on the concert."

Cal sat back and folded his arms. Shelly could read his body language loud and clear. His fight was over.

CHAPTER 20

Wednesday December 21, 8:15 A.M.

Shelly Hinson sensed that her hometown was at a major crossroads in its history. She felt responsible for placing it there and wondered what direction Braxton would take. She'd risen early this morning to drive and walk the streets she knew so well, looking for changes. What was different from six months ago? Some things were obvious; the most significant was the 137-unit housing development called Braxton Ranch, well underway on the south side of town. A sign identified the developer as r.c. Construction, offering three-, four-, and five-bedroom homes on estate-sized lots from the low 190s. Shelly had toured the homes and lots and decided that one's definition of "estate-size" depended on who was cutting up the tract. She knew who r.c. was: Mayor Roger Carter.

On the north side of town, next to Highway 46, a new 75-room Best Western motel was nearing completion. An on-site construction trailer showed this project to be the work of ARCEE builders, another company owned by the mayor. The motel was scheduled to open in early spring. Carter, obviously, was putting his money where his mouth was. But there was another change—something invisible, yet clearly felt on Braxton's streets. An outsider might have missed it. Shelly didn't, and it troubled her.

Shelly was bundled in a light green jacket, zipped to the neck. A delicate mist swirled in the air, half rain, half fog that was now lifting like a curtain. She heard herself walking, her footsteps moving along Main Street's red brick sidewalk. The town was decorated for Christmas with plastic holly wrapped around light poles, and strings of red and green bells looped across the street on every block. Someone forgot to turn the lights off the night before, or maybe the town preferred to leave them on constantly.

Many of the town's shops had canvas or plastic awnings that protected Shelly from the elements. Cars left overnight on the street were beaded with dew. The days of free parking were just about over; town workers were in the final stage of installing parking meters.

No one seemed to notice her as she occasionally stopped to jot impressions in a small notebook. She wrote that the town's water tower had a fresh look. A month earlier it was painted for the first time in fourteen years. The white tower displayed the words, B R A X T O N— Best Small Town in America, painted in John Deere green. She knew the water tower was still used, while a nearby grain elevator from the defunct Braxton Feed and Grain Company was not. The silo went up in the early '50s, but the surrounding land was used mostly for vineyards today, and so there was talk about bringing it down. It stood as a testament to the past, trying to retain its identity. Over the years the elements had taken their toll on the ten-story structure and the painted words at the eight-story mark. Several letters had flaked off, giving a comical touch.

The air was surprisingly cool. Then, to her delight, she caught a glorious whiff of freshly brewed coffee, and saw a kiosk just ahead. Gourmet coffee, bagels, and croissants on the streets of Braxton. Who would ever believe it?

"A large cup of your Panama blend, please," Shelly told the older man with the weathered face and bushy brown eyebrows. He was about to grind some coffee beans and didn't reply. "How's business since you started this—what has it been—two months now?" She waited for his answer.

The man pushed down on the grinder, seemingly lost in thought.

While holding the switch, he counted out loud, "Ten, eleven, twelve." He then gave her a studied expression. "I've seen you before, Miss Hinson. But for some reason, you always crossed the street, as if you were avoiding me." Shelly looked down, waiting for him to continue. "Don't feel badly, I'm used to that." He poured the coffee grounds into a chrome container. "In response to your inquiry, as you know, I'm not the entrepreneur. No, I'm just a salaried employee for the owner, Mr. Benjamin Green, a kind, trusting soul, with a new eating establishment down the street."

Shelly was amazed at the man's sensitivity. Yes, she'd seen him on the streets, and it was true that she always shied away from him. Was it because of his appearance? That someone told her he had been found sleeping on the street? Or was it that she thought he would smell? It could be; she had a thing about body odor. However, now, beneath his navy blue wool cap and hardened surface, she suspected here was a man she wanted to know more about.

"Where are you from originally?" She wondered how a well-spoken sixtyish man had wound up selling coffee on the streets of a rinky-dink town, probably for not much more than minimum wage.

"To answer your interrogatory, I am not a native of this fruited plain." He handed her a cup of steaming coffee. "Would you like a lid? It helps prevent nasty litigation from spilled Java."

"No thanks, I'll drink it now. Any discount for not using a lid?" she asked with a wink.

"Unfortunately, not. We'll apply the quarter-cent saving to our liability insurance policy. That'll be $2.50."

She paid him, and savored her first sip, thankful for the warmth. "You sound like you know something about the law."

"At one time, I had a rather significant shingle hanging over my door."

"What was your practice?"

He ignored her question. "Where did you say you were from?"

"I didn't. But if you want to know, I was born and raised here in Braxton. Now, how about answering my question? What kind of law did you practice?"

He paused, seeming to be swept away by a kaleidoscope of memories in distant places. A sparkle came into his eyes, and a glow appeared on his face. She wondered what adventure was playing in his head. Certainly, he had great stories to tell, if only she could tap the source. Then, as quickly as his mind took him somewhere else, he returned. She looked into eyes dulled by lost times in bars and hard times behind bars.

"My adventure in the jurisprudence system was many, many years ago," he said, "and best left in the past." He pointed to his coffee cart. "For now, this is the world I'm exploring. With apologies to Neal Armstrong, it's one small *sip* for me, one giant gulp for sobriety."

"Congratulations. Where's Mission Control?"

The man laughed and pointed to his head. "So far, Mission Control is right here. I've been sober for six weeks, a human reclamation project by Benjamin Green, who befriended me shortly after I washed into town."

"I'm Shelly Hinson. What's your name?"

"J. Oswald Theodore the Third, coffee salesman. You seem to specialize in questions. May I ask your profession?"

Shelly couldn't quite place it, but this mystery man was causing her to experience something different in her hometown. "Well, Mister Theodore—or can I call you by your first name? What do you go by— 'J' or J. Oswald?"

Theodore grinned. His once gleaming teeth looked more like the piano keyboard in a wild west saloon—yellow ivory with a few keys missing. "I haven't been called 'Mister,' in years. Actually, Ozzie will do just fine."

"I'm with *The Banner*, Ozzie, our local paper."

"What revelations can we expect in tomorrow's edition?"

"Oh, not too much, except how Braxton has handled the last six months." She handed him her empty cup. "Could I have a refill, please?"

"Certainly." He filled her cup. "And what have you found?"

As Shelly got out her money to pay him for the coffee, she realized what she was feeling. "You know, Ozzie, you're about the first person I've met in a long time who actually looks at me and doesn't see a dollar sign."

"Oh?"

"Yeah. Six months ago, before that article came out, before Braxton got too big for its britches—"

"Sorry to correct you, but the original word was *breeches*, as in 'too big for one's boots,' first credited to H.G. Wells at the turn of the century." Theodore seemed to be enjoying himself, perhaps pleased that his once photographic memory still held a few snapshots.

"I'm impressed," Shelly said with a smile. "Thanks for the lesson."

Theodore nodded. "Please continue. You were noting the change in attitude of the fine people of this once humble village."

"It's true. I grew up in this town. People used to have time to talk, like we're doing now. Folks would greet you on the street, shop owners made you feel welcome. Now, all they want is your money. Braxton had a community feel to it, a certain charm. Not anymore."

"In order to convict Braxton of misdemeanor greed, you need proof," he said. A woman approached the kiosk and ordered a cup of coffee and a sesame seed bagel. Theodore looked at Shelly. "Excuse me," he said, and turned to help the woman. He took her money, thanked her, and then a man came out of a nearby shop and ordered some coffee. While Ozzie poured it into a cup, he asked Shelly, "Do you have examples for your indictment?"

Shelly smiled. "Plenty, but now is not the time. And I'm taking you away from your business."

"I'll look forward to resuming the deposition another day," Ozzie said in a gravelly voice.

"Not any more than I, Mr. Theodore—" She stopped. Ozzie gave her a hard look at the word, mister. "Sorry—Ozzie."

The sparkle returned to his eyes.

CHAPTER 21

Assistant Police Chief Gina Wells knew about the car, a Porsche convertible, easily the most expensive set of wheels on the streets of Braxton. It was stopped in front of her now at Main and Lincoln, the radio blaring rock music loud enough for Gina to hear. The car's engine was revving up for what Wells figured would be another sprint to the next traffic signal. The Porsche's silver top was up, the afternoon apparently too cold for the young driver and his passenger. Gina reached for the buttons that controlled the two flashing lights on the front grill of her unmarked police car. She kept her finger on the toggle switch. *Peel rubber again, buster, and I'm going to light up your rearview mirror.*

Gina wasn't involved with traffic enforcement, but she'd heard the complaints from townsfolk about this particular car and its driver, who had arrived in town just three days ago. She recalled what she knew so far: the kid was the son of Pete Stanley—baseball legend, plenty of money, set for life, father might coach the high school team for free. Gina strained to see who was with the boy, but then the light turned green, and the car lurched forward. The screeching tires left lines of smoking rubber on the street as the wheels caught up to the engine's R.P.M.

Gina figured the car reached forty miles an hour in a few seconds. She watched in horror as it darted around a pickup, and closed in on Washington and Main. The traffic signal blinked yellow, then red.

A car suddenly entered the intersection from the right. *Oh Lord, please make them stop.* The driver slammed on his brakes as the Porsche whizzed past, missing him by inches. *Thank You, Jesus.* Gina flipped on her flashing lights, then turned on the car's siren. She was angry, and quickly maneuvered her car behind the Porsche.

When the Porsche pulled to the side of the street, she spotted an open space along the curb and headed for it. But before she could open her door, she heard a siren. A squad car, its bar lights on, screeched to a stop on the other side of the street. Blake Hesterman turned off his siren, but kept the lights flashing, as he charged out of his car and moved toward her.

"Chief, I've been watching these dirt bags all day. I saw what they did."

"I can take care of it, Hesterman. Go back to your car."

But, instead, he ran ahead to the Porsche. "We nailed you this time, punk!" he called out as he reached the driver's door.

Furious at Hesterman's unprofessional demeanor, Gina was seething when she reached the car. She peered in the driver's window and saw a good-looking kid with thick, curly red hair. He stared straight ahead.

"Chief, looky here," Hesterman sneered, "we not only got ourselves the rich kid, we got the slug he hangs around with."

Gina leaned over to see who was in the passenger seat. She recognized him—Rick Aguilara.

"I can't believe what I just saw," she said to the driver who continued to ignore her.

"He picked a bad time to do something stupid, officer," Rick said, and then pointed to Hesterman. "But tell me, what's with Deputy Doberman? Is he your new community relations officer?"

Hesterman leaned in the window. "Shut up!" he yelled and added a curse."

"No, you shut up!" Gina ordered. "I won't tolerate that language, no matter what. Understand?"

Twenty-One

Hesterman backed away, but bent down and spoke to Rick again. "You're riding in style, Aguilara. Where's your Harley? Someone finally push that noisy hog off a cliff?" He turned to Gina. "Him and that Harley of his have been trouble ever since he got here six months ago."

"Wrong, badge-breath," Rick cut in. "First, it's *he* and that Harley. Second, you're just bent because the ladies in town think I'm cute."

"Let me run 'em in, Chief," Hesterman begged.

Rick leaned over in his seat toward the driver's window. "Mother Law isn't impressed with your act, Officer Knot Head," he said.

"That's enough!" Gina ordered. She was actually enjoying the put-downs directed at Hesterman. She found Rick a likable oddball character, perhaps someone who could reach Brian Stanley. She turned to Hesterman. "Sergeant, get in your car and leave—now," she said with finality.

"You're on my list, Aguilara." Hesterman tapped the pistol in his holster as he walked away. "One of these days . . ."

Rick quickly opened his door, stood, and called across the roof. "Hey, Blakester, if I'm on your list, I haven't received my Christmas card yet."

Hesterman, without turning, raised his hand and made an obscene gesture.

Gina stifled a laugh. She would set things straight with Hesterman in private. Now, she motioned toward Brian, then looked at Rick over the roof. "I'm curious, where'd you meet?"

"Yesterday at the ARCO station. He liked my Harley, I liked his car. Any chance of giving him a warning?"

She leaned down and looked at Brian, who dropped his head. "Do you want a speeding ticket?"

Brian, still looking down, snickered. "Yeah, right."

"What's so funny?" Gina asked.

"Oh, this just reminds me of—like, when my dad used to get angry with me, he'd ask if I wanted a spanking."

Gina smiled. "Yeah, my parents did the same thing. Pretty dumb, huh?" But the boy didn't answer. Rick was now back in the passenger seat. Gina looked at him and asked, "Think you can get through to young Master Leadfoot?"

"I'll try."

"OK, Brian, this is our first meeting." He looked up at her finally. "Call this an early Christmas present. That stunt I just saw was not only stupid, you could have killed someone. No ticket today, but I expect to see you driving the speed limit from now on. Got it?"

Rick smacked the young man on the arm. "Thank her, you idiot!"

"Yeah, thanks," he mumbled.

"*Mother Law* says, you're welcome." She looked at Rick. "Good luck. He's in your custody."

Rick laughed. "No, you need the luck."

"Why?"

"You've got Officer Hesterman in your custody."

Gina winked. "I may want to trade you some day." She turned and walked to her car, feeling better about being in Braxton.

CHAPTER 22

Thursday December 22, 5:58 A.M.

Benny Green leaned back in his chair. He held his hands in a pensive pose, fingers touching, prayer-like, in front of his face, as he eyed the man standing in front of him. He had a good feeling about life lately. Actually, *good* wasn't the right word. Benny was just as tired now as when he ran his restaurant in Norfolk, but he liked his new surroundings. Business in Braxton was improving, and people were warming to him and his wife. No, the reason life seemed to have a deeper meaning was because of the person in his office. "How's our little experiment working out?" he asked.

"The pushcart or the person?"

Benny loved to joust verbally with what he called his "project," J. Oswald Theodore, III. The old man wore a green military fatigue jacket and held his familiar blue wool cap in his hand. Two white patches were sewn on the front of the coat; the one on the right, "Navy," was stitched in gold letters, the one on the left, "Jenkins," in black letters.

"Nice jacket, Lieutenant *Jenkins*. But I'm kinda partial to the air force. Is there a war surplus store in town?"

Theodore pulled down on his jacket, and smoothed the left sleeve. "Actually, I picked it up at one of the churches. They have a room full of good stuff for us world travelers. It gives me a more disciplined look, wouldn't you say?"

"Well, not exactly military reg., but it suits you fine." Benny paused. "Ozzie, forget the kiosk, the pushcart, the coffee—all of that doesn't mean a hill of beans." The old man smiled and pointed a finger at Benny to acknowledge his unintentional pun. "What I'm concerned about is you," Benny continued. "How are you doing, personally?"

"Can't say it's easy. When I was on booze, all my problems were fuzzy."

"You tell me," Benny said, "is our thing working?" The *thing* Benny had created was a way to help those who were down on their luck get back on track, but in an environment that wouldn't suffocate them. He'd had the idea in Norfolk, but never had the time to develop it. As his restaurant went up in Braxton, he had the opportunity, and in Ozzie Theodore, he had his first test case. And so Benny had bought himself a portable outdoor coffee stand and named it Casita de Coffee. Ozzie ran it for him, and was paid minimum wage plus a fifty/fifty split of the profits.

"I've been clean now for fifty-six days," Ozzie said. "I'm not sure what that means."

Benny motioned for him to sit down. "Ozzie, let me level with you. The kiosk is doing better than I expected, but what's important is the change I've seen in you."

"Still a lot of cobwebs to clear," Ozzie admitted.

"I know, I know." Benny rubbed his hand over his chin, more a nervous reaction than anything else. He wasn't sure how to say it, didn't want to rush things. "OK, listen. I've got a few ideas. How about, well, what would you think if you took on some more responsibility around here?"

"Like what?"

Benny held his breath. "Assistant manager for the restaurant."

Ozzie looked puzzled and Benny let out his breath. The old man stood up. "Are you serious? Me?"

"Couldn't imagine a better person," Benny said.

"When would this happen?"

"January first?"

Twenty-Two

Ozzie shook his head, but remained silent.

"Think about it," Benny urged.

Ozzie pulled his wool cap over his head. "I'll have to do a whole lot of thinking on that one," he said as he turned to go. "I've got to get to work—don't want to miss the morning merchants and clerks who depend on my caffeine." He turned back to face Benny. With a trace of bitterness in his voice, he said, "Never have understood the way people treat the alcoholic and the javaholic."

"How do you mean?"

"One person drinks on the job to *calm* his nerves and is an outcast. The other drinks on the job to *stimulate* his nerves and is accepted."

Benny watched Ozzie walk out of the room. The man was as much a mystery now as when he first came in.

CHAPTER 23

Leona Kyle dipped a tortilla chip into a bowl of salsa and looked at Cal Spencer sitting across the table from her. "How hot is this?" She held up the chip in her hand and wondered if Casa de Benny's house specialty was about to set her mouth on fire.

"It's not lethal, but not benign either," Cal said. "I've been here before. I think you'll like it."

"Are you sure?"

"Well, just as a precaution," he said, reaching for a water pitcher, "let me fill your water glass." Three ice cubes plunked into her glass, *one-two-three*, followed by a rush of water that flowed over the brim. "Oops, sorry. I'm making a wonderful impression." He mopped up the water with a napkin. "OK, your fire hydrant is ready if you need it."

Leona took a wary bite, knowing that with Mexican salsa, there was usually a delayed reaction. She waited a few seconds until it hit her. "Whew, not bad." She took a gulp of water. "Actually, that's very good."

"It's the best. The guy who owns the restaurant says his food is New Mexico style." Cal looked around the crowded room and spotted Benny Green talking with a couple a few feet away. "I never thought anyone could give Lolo's a run for their money, but Benny has and he's going to make a mint with this place."

Cal and Leona were doing well. She'd called him twice during the week she was getting settled, but this was their first time alone since she had literally exploded on the scene five days ago.

"Big weekend for you, right?" he asked, knowing the answer.

Leona took another chip, dipped deeper in the salsa, and crunched it into her mouth. "Yes, thanks to you. I pick up my car in the morning—got a Mustang demo. Thanks for calling the general manager. He gave me $300 for my Corolla—may it rest in peace—and they're even going to tow it away."

"I'm glad you got a good deal. I'm not the most popular guy in town with business people."

"So I'm told."

A Hispanic young man arrived at the table then with a tray of food. Leona read his name tag—Arturo. With great pride, he told them he had worked his way up from washing dishes in the kitchen. This was his first day as a waiter; until now, he had served tables under the supervision of someone else. "The plates are very hot," he warned, and with sombrero-shaped pot holders, placed their dishes in front of them. "The beef chimichanga for you," he said to Cal, "and the chicken enchilada supreme for the lady."

Leona and Cal eyed each other. She was about to say something, but Cal wrinkled his nose, shook his head, and held a finger to his mouth. Arturo stepped back and smiled broadly. "Please enjoy your meal," he said. "I'll be back to see if you need anything. You are my very first customers, and I consider it an honor to serve you." He turned and headed back to the kitchen. "Yes! I did it!" he exclaimed as he disappeared into the kitchen.

"OK, let's switch," Cal said, handing Leona his plate. "I had the enchilada, you had the chimichanga."

"That was sweet of you, Cal," Leona said with a smile, as she handed him her plate.

"Well, he was so proud of himself. This will give his confidence a boost."

"Do you know him?"

"Yeah, he's Reuben Francisco's boy—good kid, hard worker—not the greatest student. He left Braxton for a while. He's back, now that a few more jobs are available in town."

"And more to come, according to the mayor. Are you going to be at the big celebration on Monday?"

"Oh, I'll probably show up. Staying away would be more a pouting act than anything."

"How about going up in the hot air balloon?"

"Only if I can shove the mayor out of the basket."

Leona laughed loudly, while those at nearby tables glared at her with disapproving looks.

Cal leaned over. "Remember, you're with the town dissident," he whispered.

"That's their problem," she declared. "But come on, Cal. The festival sounds like fun. I haven't even been here a week, but everyone I've talked to is excited about it."

"All the mayor and his cronies want is more money. More tax revenue, a bigger school system, more tourists—it's all about dollars." An uncertain moment of silence ensued between them in the noisy room. "Let's change the subject to—you. Can I help you move Saturday morning?"

"Thanks, but I don't have that much. I lived a rather Spartan existence in San Diego. I'll be getting the heavy stuff later. I'm just glad the place comes with a refrigerator."

Cal nodded and sighed deeply. "An example of what Braxton was like before we became famous. I'm surprised your apartment owner still includes that. Most apartment owners have raised their rents and cut back on amenities."

"Well, I can't wait to get out of that crummy Motel 6. I thought you said it was a good place to stay."

"The night you rolled into town, you didn't hear the word I emphasized. I said it *was* a good place to stay—was, as in *used to be*."

"What happened?"

"A.D.," Cal answered with a smile.

"A.D.?"

"After *Destination*. That article changed a lot of things in Braxton."

CHAPTER 24

Saturday, December 24, Noon
Christmas Eve

"The tree looks nice, Pete."

Pete Stanley stood on the second rung of a stepladder and tried to straighten an electric angel that kept bending to the right. It sat atop an eight-foot blue spruce Christmas tree he and Beatrice had decorated that afternoon.

Pete's wife stood below him, her hands on her hips, admiring the tree. "Thanks for getting it," she said, "especially at the last moment. That was sweet of you."

He finally got the angel to cooperate and grunted approval. "No problem, I knew it was important—our first Christmas in our new home. I just wish the kids could have been here." He stepped off the ladder and folded the legs. He moved to a nearby table where two bowls sat—one filled with popcorn, the other with ruffled potato chips. Plates of homemade cookies and fudge surrounded the bowls, and a lazy Susan held an assortment of cheese, vegetables, and sour cream dip. Pete took a chip, and scooped up so much sour cream, the chip broke in his hand.

"Did Brian say when he might be home?" Beatrice asked.

Pete snorted. "Why should Christmas Eve be different from any other day? I not only don't know when he might be home, I have no idea where he is. Do you?" Pete scooped another chip through the dip and kept it in one piece. He popped it in his mouth, then walked to the fireplace.

Beatrice started placing empty ornament containers into a large box. "I asked him this morning if he could be with us for Christmas Eve."

"What did he say?"

"He and that Rick character were going to do something tonight."

"The motorcycle midget?" Pete grabbed a poker and began to break up a log in the fireplace.

"Uh huh."

"Wonderful. At least Brian's friends in Wilmette kept themselves on four wheels. Aguilara scares me with that Harley of his."

Beatrice shook her head and poured a cup of eggnog, then sprinkled nutmeg on top. "You know Brian drives it too?"

Pete sighed. "Yeah, I saw him ripping around town. What bothers me even more is Brian lets Aguilara use his Porsche. That dirt bag is going to wrap it around a pole."

"Have you talked with Rick?" she asked, as she gave a cup of eggnog to Pete.

"No, I've managed to avoid him." He took a sip and the foam stuck to his upper lip. "Have you?"

"Actually, yes. He's—well, he's different." Beatrice moved toward Pete and wiped the foam from his lip with a napkin. "You don't look good in a moustache."

Pete smiled. "What do you mean, he's different? He's a lot older, isn't he?"

Beatrice poured herself a cup of eggnog now. "Yes. I wondered about that. But I think, well—he hasn't known him long, but I think Brian kind of looks up to him as a big-brother figure."

"You mean, looks *down* at him, don't you?"

She giggled. "Yeah, there's nothing big about him. But as strange as it seems, Rick may be the kind of person who can help Brian."

"Where's Nicole?" Pete asked, changing the subject.

"Upstairs. We had an argument." Beatrice shrugged. "Says she hates me."

"Welcome to the club."

"She wants to go back home. Can't live without her boyfriend."

"Fernando, the hormonal maniac?"

She laughed. "Last time I checked, they were still on the phone. He's two thousand miles away, but his drool is seeping through the phone." Pete laughed as Beatrice sat down next to him on the couch. Logs popped sparks into the protective fireplace screen, and a CD blared out an upbeat version of "God Rest Ye Merry Gentlemen," cheering the air a bit.

Pete put his arm around Beatrice. It wasn't a forced gesture, he meant it. They'd only been in their new home a week, and problems with their children were worse than ever, yet Pete felt the new surroundings had somehow begun to return what was missing to their marriage. He pulled her close. "Hey, for once, forget the kids. Don't let them spoil things." He made a sweeping gesture across the room with his hand. "Look what we have. This was the best move of our lives. I think it's great—this house, the town . . ." He gave her a hug. "And you. When was the last time you and I were together like this, during an afternoon?"

"Forget the afternoon—try *ever*," she teased.

He felt the tension go out of her body, and kissed her full on the lips. She responded in a way he'd almost forgotten she could. "Merry Christmas, sweetheart," Pete said, and kissed her again.

2:32 P.M.

Ka-womp, ka-womp, ka-womp. Ozzie pushed his kiosk cart, with its hard rubber wheels, along Braxton's red brick sidewalk under a light rain. The afternoon temperature had dropped to forty-three degrees, and a breeze from the west had chased the few people on the street inside. Ozzie had finally decided to close for the day, thirty minutes earlier than normal.

He reached out to steady a stainless steel percolator and keep it from tipping over. He pulled his blue wool cap down over his ears and his green, government-issued foul weather jacket closer around him. The name tag still identified him as "Jenkins."

As he secured the kiosk to the side of a building with a padlock, he heard someone behind him. "It's about time you got out of this weather, Ozzie."

He didn't have to look to know who it was. He threw a gray canvas tarp over the kiosk, then turned to Maggie Green. "Don't tell the boss I quit early. *Ebeneezer* Green might make me work tomorrow."

Maggie laughed loudly. "No way that's going to happen. We're closed tomorrow, and you're coming to our home for Christmas dinner."

Ozzie looked at the woman's kind face. "You know, Mrs. Green, you've got to be careful with that twinkle in your eye."

She looked puzzled. "Oh? Why is that?"

"One of these days, you're going to make someone go blind."

She laughed again and came near him. "Don't call me Mrs. Green, you hear?" Her thick arm went around his shoulder. "How did the day go?" she asked. They began to walk toward the restaurant's side door.

"The day always *goes*, it never *stays*."

Maggie chuckled as they walked inside. "Ozzie, the sweet Lord blessed you with the gift of gab. Goodness!"

Ozzie handed her a purple pouch. "I haven't counted the receipts in this pathetic-looking container, but since I was able to zip it shut without difficulty, I'd say Green Limited probably lost some of its venture capital on me today."

"Oh, hush, you bag of wind," Maggie admonished him good-naturedly. "You've made Benny and me winners. And with the Lord's help, you're the one who's really winning. I pray for you every night, Ozzie."

"I know. It's been a long time since I've felt like this, Mrs. Green."

"Ozzie . . ." she warned.

"Sorry. I mean, Maggie."

"There, I like that much better," she said with a smile.

"I'm grateful for all you've done. My big words and pontificating seem to desert me when I try to tell you how much—well, how you— oh, blast!" He shrugged and dropped his head.

Maggie put her generous arms around him. "Your actions speak louder than any words. We're the ones who are blessed. Listen, here's an idea. Why don't you spend the night with us tonight? No use staying at that little place of yours." She held him at arm's length, and her eyes dared him to say no. "It's Christmas Eve. We've invited people by for an open house. Benny's been home all morning cooking up a storm. We can sit around the fire and talk. Will you come?"

Ozzie sensed the walls begin to close in. He'd forgotten the meaning of family a long time ago, and now it was making his gut turn flip-flops.

6:51 P.M.

"Joy to the world, the Lord has come."

The singers' puffy breath on Christmas Eve sent the genius of Handel's classic song into the crisp winter air. The First Baptist Church choir was making the rounds in Braxton, spreading peace on earth and good will toward men. While not always on-key, the message was loud, clear, and enthusiastic.

"Let earth receive her King!"

Cal Spencer kept his head down and nervously shifted his weight back and forth. He wasn't singing and he felt foolish even being there. He was doing this for one reason only, and she stood next to him. He'd just never met anyone like Leona Kyle. One of the church members had run into Leona at the grocery store and told her about the caroling. She had invited Cal to be her date. Cal listened to Leona's voice now as she sang.

"Let every heart, prepare Him room, and heaven and nature sing . . ."

He remembered enough of the song to join in and finish the verse. They glanced at each other and he smiled. She smiled back. Was she the woman he was searching for? *Don't push it*, he told himself. They'd only met last week and he'd seen her several times already since then. He didn't want to come on too strongly. But she could be the one.

Cal had arrived in town five years before, and the single scene had always been slim pickings. Bars and blind dates hadn't worked here or in Paso Robles and he wanted to forget what he'd tried before he moved to Braxton. He wasn't a churchgoing guy; he hadn't attended any church since as a kid, his parents had forced him to go. If he had to label himself, he would probably call himself an agnostic. Christmas caroling was definitely out of his comfort zone, but the new school teacher in town was worth it. Yes, she just might be the one.

The group of ten carolers stood on the cement walkway in front of Benny Green's house. The owner of Braxton's newest and most successful restaurant stood in the open doorway with his wife, Maggie. He wore a red Santa's cap and a yellow and orange African dashiki. Four or five people stood behind them. When the song ended, they all applauded.

"Merry Christmas!" the singers shouted.

"Merry Christmas to you!" Benny, Maggie, and the others returned.

"Come on inside," Benny invited, "we've got plenty to eat."

"Now you know why we picked your house, Benny," Cal called.

He took hold of Leona's hand and to his delight, she didn't discourage him. As they entered the Greens' home, Leona removed her baseball cap and shook her blonde ponytail loose, unaware that Cal loved what he was seeing. He helped her take off her leather jacket before he removed his own. Christmas music came from somewhere in the house.

"Just put all your coats on the sofa and follow me," Maggie said. "The food is in the family room."

Cal and Leona made their way down the carpeted hallway to the back of the house. Cal glanced into each room as they passed it. The home was orderly yet inviting, but what made the place irresistible was the aroma.

"Goodness, it smells like a bakery," Leona said. It was true: fresh, hot pastry wasn't far away.

"If my nose knows, there's also a table full of Mexican food," Cal added hopefully. He wasn't disappointed. "Wow, would you look at that?" In front of them was a spread that looked like a hotel brunch buffet—steam-heated platters of chicken, beef, and cheese enchiladas, soft beef and fish tacos, cheese quesadillas with green onions on top, homemade tortilla chips, and at least five different salsa and guacamole dips. Chile rellenos, tamales, taco salad, chimichangas—Cal couldn't believe his eyes. Desserts beckoned from another table—powdered-sugar churros, Spanish flan, and bananas Mexicana.

"With us being new in town, we weren't sure how many people would show up," Maggie said, shaking her head. "Benny started cooking this morning and when he gets going, he doesn't know when to quit. I told him to make a few things to nibble on, but look at this. There's enough food for an army."

"This is too good for the army," the retired air force sergeant said with a laugh as he entered the room. "Air force, maybe." Benny encouraged everyone to move to the table. "Dig in, everyone."

As Cal picked up a dinner plate he felt a tug on his arm. Leona nodded to her right. "Who's that sitting over in the corner?" she whispered.

Cal looked across the room and tried to place the man in the high-backed chair. He was dressed in a pair of stylish rust-colored slacks and a coordinated white golf shirt, and he was sipping a cup of coffee. "It's—yeah, it's Ozzie Theodore—I almost didn't recognize him. He's out of uniform."

"Who?"

"The guy who sells coffee from the kiosk in town."

Leona's eyes widened. "*That's* him?"

Cal was baffled too. But it wasn't just the clothes. There was something else. "Let me introduce you. He's kind of an odd duck, but you'll like him."

The two walked toward Ozzie who seemed to be studying the crowd milling around him. A layer of gentle conversation had started between the newcomers and those who had arrived earlier. Ozzie didn't see Cal and Leona approach.

"Hello, Ozzie," Cal said. The older man turned and quickly assessed Cal, then Leona. "I'd like to introduce Leona Kyle, our newest school teacher at the high school. She's been in town just a week. Leona, this is Ozzie Theodore—the *third*, I believe."

Leona extended her hand to Ozzie who remained seated, but reached up. "Pleased to meet you," she said with a smile and shook his hand. "Can't say I've ever met a *third* before."

Ozzie considered her comment, then chuckled. "Some people probably think I'm only a third of the man I used to be, but what's left of me believes it's nice to meet you too."

While Leona and Ozzie exchanged small talk, Cal stared at Ozzie. He'd always seen him on the sidewalk, his blue woolen cap pulled low to his eyes. Now, with the cap off, the old man's neatly combed silver mane hung just to his shoulders, giving him an almost senatorial look. Cal's hunger and the magnet-like aroma in the room turned his attention to the buffet table. He began loading his plate while Leona continued talking with Ozzie. Everything on the table looked good, and Cal quickly ran out of room on his plate.

"Excuse me, everyone," Benny interrupted, "could I have your attention?" The room gradually quieted. "Frosty the Snowman" played as Benny walked over to Ozzie's chair. Benny held two glasses of what looked like sparkling cider. "Thank you all for coming tonight. You've been good to us in the short time we've been in Braxton. We're honored you're here to help us celebrate Christmas, a time to remember Christ's birth and to renew His words that we help and love one another."

"Amen!" Maggie agreed.

Benny turned to his wife. "Thank you, Mother Maggie." A chuckle spread throughout the room. "We're still new in town," he continued, "but it has been a good move for us to come your way. Maybe the best move we've ever made." Benny then glanced at Ozzie. "This is a very special night in our lives and I hope for Ozzie too." Ozzie frowned slightly when Benny handed him the wine glass and motioned for him to stand. Reluctantly, Ozzie did. He gave Benny a suspicious look.

"Ladies and gentlemen," Benny beamed proudly, "it's my great pleasure to introduce to you, starting January 1, the new assistant manager of Casa de Benny's—Ozzie Theodore."

People glanced at each other with lifted eyebrows. Ozzie dropped his head, then looked at Benny. Was the old man angry, surprised, or just at a loss for words? Cal couldn't tell.

Benny put his arm around Ozzie's shoulder and looked directly at him. "I told Ozzie this was between the two of us, but—well, I'm too proud of him to keep it a secret." Benny held up his wine glass. "With this glass of *sparkling cider*," Benny paused and winked at Ozzie, "I toast

J. Oswald Theodore the third. Merry Christmas, Ozzie. May this be the start of a great new life for you."

Cal and the others echoed words of encouragement and lifted their glasses in unison.

Ozzie scanned the room, looked at his glass, and took a sip. Then he took a deep breath. "I'm not sure I'm ready to take on the job Mr. and Mrs. Green have for me—"

"Ozzie?" Maggie Green chided.

"Sorry," said Ozzie. "The job *Benny* and *Maggie* have for me."

"That's better," she harrumphed as everyone chuckled.

"The Greens took me in when I was at rock bottom." He looked around the room. "I was an unmitigated mess and still don't understand why I ended up in your town."

"It's now your town too," Maggie softly corrected, as she wiped a tear from her eye.

Ozzie seemed unconvinced. "Perhaps, but why the Greens took a chance on this old man defies reason. However, they did, giving me a place to sleep in their restaurant and a job running that coffee cart." He paused, and except for "Hark! the Herald Angels Sing" playing softly in the background, the room was hushed. "It wasn't easy. I can't tell you how many times I sneaked off in the middle of the . . ." Ozzie choked off a sob, ". . . middle of the night, only to come back. I'm grateful to all of you. I couldn't have blamed you for looking down at me, but you never did. I'm—well—" He couldn't continue.

"That's in the past," Benny said, coming to his rescue. "I have a feeling all of us may be looking at my future business partner."

Everyone joined in the celebration and congratulated Ozzie.

8:47 P.M.

The bone-chilling coastal mist sent a shiver through Shelly as she approached Benny Green's two-story house. She could hear muffled laughter and music, sounds that beamed warmth and good cheer from the lighted windows. Shelly needed something. Ever since the deaths of her parents and brother, she'd hated Christmas Eve, and Christmas Day was even worse. She'd decided at the last minute to go to Benny's open house after a disastrous phone call from her younger sister in Madison, Wisconsin. What began as good wishes for the coming year quickly deteriorated into petty bickering and then into a full-blown shouting match. As she climbed the steps to the house, she tried to recall what had started the argument. She'd probably lit the fuse when she asked why her sister sent Christmas cards with her name printed inside. It was so impersonal, Shelly had said. One snipe led to another and soon Shelly was left with the phone in her hand and a dial tone in her ear.

Shelly tried to put the squabble out of her mind. After all, it wasn't the first time. Her twenty-five-year-old sister had everything Shelly wanted—a husband and two small children. Shelly had begun to think she might never have a family.

Shelly stopped at the top of the steps. She didn't want to take her depression inside. Maybe she shouldn't go in. But then she spotted Cal's car parked under a street light. She smiled as she thought of the bearded teacher-councilman. Then Lance Milburn's face appeared in her mind. *Get real,* she told herself, *after my assignment is over, I'm history.*

Cal Spencer wasn't a bad-looking guy. Actually, he was the only eligible bachelor in town even worth considering.

Shelly rang the doorbell. The door opened and Maggie Green's smile made Shelly glad she hadn't turned around. "Hello, Shelly," Maggie gushed. She stepped back from the door to let Shelly enter. "We're so glad you could come. Let me take your coat."

Maggie made Shelly feel as if she were an old friend. In truth, Shelly hardly knew the woman, but the Greens had been accepted by most of the townsfolk. Some undercurrents of resentment toward them could still be felt here and there, but Shelly dismissed it as ignorance. Most likely, it wasn't so much bigotry as it was jealousy over the Greens' success. As Shelly caught a whiff of the food now, thoughts of prejudice were quickly replaced with the reminder that she was starving.

"I'm glad you got our invitation," Maggie told her. "We weren't sure who would come." Maggie laid Shelly's coat on a sofa, and they continued toward the sounds in the back of the house. "Benny appreciated the nice article you wrote about our restaurant."

"I only write the truth," Shelly said, and immediately realized the lie she'd just told.

Maggie led Shelly into the large family room and pointed to the buffet tables. "We've got more food than we'll ever eat. Please help yourself. And if you want to take some home with you, we'll load up a 'doggie bag.' You go ahead and mingle. I've got to check on something in the kitchen." With that Maggie left Shelly standing alone.

Shelly recognized nearly everyone in the room. She spotted Police Chief Talbot and his wife standing by the Christmas tree. Nearby was Gina Wells, Talbot's new assistant chief. Monopolizing the conversation with her was an animated Arnold "Moose" Montgomery, Braxton High School's flabby hulk of a football coach. Shelly had successfully fended off the advances of the three-time loser in marriage, each time while his divorce was still pending. "Moose" had achieved a small amount of fame in that he'd been invited to three NFL training camps as an offensive tackle. He'd never made it past the first cut, and none of his three wives had survived more than a year. Shelly thought the word "offensive" fit him better than his faded red golf shirt with the San Francisco 49ers logo on the front. Shelly figured Moose had swiped it after being cut from the team.

In another corner of the room Blake Hesterman talked loudly to one of Benny's newly hired waitresses, a slightly frumpy-looking woman in her mid-thirties who was a hard worker but painfully naive. She was probably listening to one of Hesterman's exaggerated tales of life on Braxton's thin blue line.

Marty Cavitt and his wife, Gini, stood at the buffet table. He nodded in Shelly's direction and she waved, but stood her ground. She wasn't in the mood to talk shop with *The Banner's* editor.

Standing apart from most of the activity were Pastor Nick Martinez and his wife, Karen. Shelly nodded in their direction when they noticed her, but she would keep her distance from them, at all costs. They were the last ones she wanted to talk with. Never get stuck with a minister at a party on Christmas Eve. Or, worse, his wife. Too easy for the conversation to turn to Jesus-talk. She shuddered just thinking about it.

Where was Cal Spencer? Shelly looked around the room just in time to see Moose Montgomery move to his right. He'd been blocking the one person she was looking for. When she saw Cal, her heart did an uncharacteristic flutter. Maybe it was the holidays, she wasn't sure. She did know she was fooling herself if she thought Lance Milburn would even give her the time of day after the *Destination* project was over. Her image of him popped like a soap bubble in the wind. It was time for reality and her target, Cal Spencer, was near the fireplace, talking with—she did a double-take and blinked her eyes. Ozzie Theodore? Benny Green had worked a miracle. Sober, stylish, and socially acceptable, Ozzie was a far cry from the bum who had showed up in Braxton's gutter seven months ago. But enough of Ozzie.

Shelly's eyes zeroed in on Cal, and she began walking toward him with a smile. *OK, Councilman Spencer, here comes your best constituent, lobbying for the two of us. I think our agenda dictates that we're going to have a great New Year together.*

Just as Shelly was about to call out Cal's name, her eyes were diverted to the woman standing beside him—Leona Kyle. Shelly felt as if someone had just socked her in the stomach. Cal and Leona were holding hands.

"Merry Christmas!" someone shouted, while another person followed with, "Happy New Year!"

Shelly Hinson slipped out of the room, found her coat, and left the house. She felt more lonely and depressed than when she had first arrived.

CHAPTER 25

Monday December 26, 9:30 A.M.

"Mario, you idiot, step on it, we're going to be late!" Heather Landis glanced at her watch, then at Mario Cedeno. "If we miss the ceremony, I'll kill you. So help me, if we don't get it on tape, you're a dead man. Do you hear me?"

"Loud, obnoxious, and clear, *Network*. We wouldn't be racing like crazy people if you had been on time for our early call." Cedeno was teamed again with Channel 6's resident beauty queen for a return visit to Braxton and the town's celebration festival.

Heather decided to ignore his comment. She opened a portable compact, and patted on some powder to take away the shine on her forehead and nose. "You know how important this story is to my career." Mario sniffed at that, then slowed for a yellow traffic signal. "Run it!" she ordered, snapping shut her compact. "You can make it— we're five minutes late!" The news car entered the intersection just as the light turned red. Cedeno gunned the engine and blew through undetected.

"OK, what does it say on your assignment sheet?" he asked. "Is this thing at the Town Square?"

Heather looked alarmed. "I wasn't supposed to bring directions— you're the cameraman. Don't you know?"

Cedeno slapped the steering wheel in frustration. "Great! Just great!" He motioned to the back seat. "Check the floor back there. I think I brought my copy." He watched Landis as she unbuckled her belt, kneeled in the seat, and leaned over the back. She was aware of his eyes on her skin-tight pumpkin-colored pants.

Heather rummaged through old newspapers, battery packs, and blank video tapes. "How do you ever find anything?" she mumbled. "As if I'm some sort of navigator."

"Forget it, there's something ahead. OK, I see it—it's a hot air balloon. It's next to the Wal-Mart parking lot."

Heather flopped back into her seat and reached for a folder. "You blew it, Mario." She opened the folder and took out a piece of paper. Her mood brightened. "The press release says they're having free hot air balloon rides. Can we go up in one?"

Mario nodded as he signaled right, and turned onto a dirt road that had recently been oiled. "I'll get you as close as I can and drop you off."

Heather groaned. "This is so embarrassing. I wonder if L.A. or San Francisco stations are here. Remember when NBC did a story after the magazine article came out?" Before Mario could answer, she said, "Mine was better."

"Did you shoot the story too?" he kidded.

"OK—ours was better," she grudgingly said.

Mario gunned the engine and drove toward an angry security guard, who was frantically waving for them to stop with one hand, and talking into a two-way radio with the other.

———◆———

The ground-breaking ceremonies were delayed, and Shelly Hinson was roasting. Weather forecasters had predicted slightly warmer than normal temperatures, but the day after Christmas had turned into a rare scorcher. Santa Ana conditions, with hot, dry winds, raced in from the eastern deserts. Blustery weather always messed up Shelly's hair, dried up her sinuses, and for some reason, usually made her grouchy. That was the case today as she headed to the media tent to get something cold to drink.

The blue-and-white-striped tent was set up on a grassy knoll, and as she hiked to the top, she looked back at Braxton's high school band, struggling to play the theme from *Rocky* on key. The musicians stood near a roped-off stage area and behind them towered a red, white, and blue hot air balloon, inflated with air heated by propane burners. The words written across the balloon read:

Best Small Town in America
Braxton, California

"Any Coke and crumbs for the local media?" Shelly asked as she approached the front of the tent. "I'm dying of thirst."

"Depends on what you write about my council district," Cal said with a grin.

"Then it looks like I go without my carbonation," she joked back. She suddenly felt better. "How come you're not down there with the *mucky-mucks*?"

"I prefer the company up here and your arrival makes it that much better." Shelly winked at Cal. At least Leona wasn't anywhere around. Standing nearby were Police Chief Talbot, the chief's wife, Courtney, who was in charge of the media tent, and Mayor Carter's seventeen-year-old son, Alan.

Shelly acknowledged each person. "Chief Talbot, Courtney, Alan." Her heart sank when she saw Leona walk out of the tent.

"Hi, Shelly," she said brightly, as she lifted her Diet Pepsi can to her lips.

"Mornin,' Leona—didn't see you."

"Well, I'm here," she said perkily. "Cal got me a VIP pass."

"How sweet," Shelly answered, coolly. She saw a catering crew inside the tent tending a variety of hors d'oeuvres in propane-heated containers. "Pretty impressive spread, Courtney," Shelly said to the chief's wife, as she opened a can of Diet Coke.

Courtney shook her head. "Thanks, but I'm really disappointed with the turnout. Channel 6 isn't even here. I guess times have changed from when I was in Dallas doing media relations. At least one TV station from LA showed up today, but no one from the Bay area."

Shelly turned to the mayor's son. "Are you here to scoop me?" she asked with a grin.

Young Carter was a physical reflection of his father—a nice face minus the pot belly and bald head. He wore his sandy hair in a ponytail, didn't talk much, but had a knack of manipulating people to get his way. "You'll see," he replied with confidence.

"Alan is our investigative reporter at the high school," Courtney quickly told Leona. "He's even written two free-lance articles for *The Braxton Banner*."

"Any plans to follow in your father's footsteps?" Leona asked.

"Not interested in elections, just exclusives, as in big stories."

"Any exposés on the town?" the police chief asked with a sparkle in his eye.

Alan cocked his head slightly as he looked at the chief and the councilman. "Actually, I'm working on one right now. It's a big one."

Courtney's face wrinkled with alarm. "Is it for the school paper, or *The Banner*?"

"*The Banner*."

"Well, that's a relief," she said, "I'm not ready for another brouhaha." She turned to Leona. "As you know, I teach journalism at the high school. Last year, without telling me, Alan slipped an article into our school paper about what time council members get to meetings."

"I kind of liked it," Cal said with a smile.

"Who was the biggest offender?" Leona asked the boy.

"My dad," Alan said matter-of-factly, and everyone laughed.

Shelly had seen Alan at the newspaper offices a few times over the past several weeks, working at a computer terminal. "Getting back to your latest story," she said, curious as to what the boy was working on, "when might we see it?"

"Pretty soon. I'm waiting for one more confirmation."

"Hope everything's OK with my department," Chief Talbot said in a tone that suggested he wasn't worried.

"It's about the festival," the boy volunteered.

"No kidding?" Cal said with raised eyebrows.

Just then, a horn, sounded in the distance. Everyone turned their attention to a car approaching wildly from the east. It was bouncing and fish-tailing on the dirt road, and the driver seemed unable to control it.

"Who in the world is that?" Shelly exclaimed.

"I'd say someone is either late, or about to make a grand entrance," Cal said, as the car came closer.

"Or both," Shelly said when she spotted Channel 6's logo in large block letters on the car's side. She turned to Courtney. "You spoke too soon about Channel 6. Could the *lovely* Heather Landis be about to grace us with her presence?"

Shelly noticed that people were now making their way to the roped-off area near the stage. Mayor Carter, three council members, and Pastor Nick Martinez were walking up the steps to the platform.

"Well, it looks like things are ready to start," Shelly said, as she walked out of the tent. "I'm going to get closer."

"Hold on, we'll go with you," Cal said, following her. To Shelly's dismay, Leona tagging along after him. Out of ear range of the others, Cal nudged both women. "Let's see which lifts off first, the hot air balloon or the mayor."

The three began to walk back down the grassy knoll, leaving Chief Talbot, his wife, and the mayor's son at the entrance to the media tent.

The news car was still making its entrance, careening now toward the roped-off area where the ceremony was about to take place. Its horn was sounding, and Shelly wondered if the driver planned on stopping.

The car did finally stop, sort of. It slid in loose silt for about twenty feet, knocked over a trash barrel, and sent a huge cloud of dust into the air. A gust of wind caught the silt, and dumped it on the crowd.

Photographers were cursing and desperately trying to cover their cameras. The band had stopped playing, and the musicians tried to protect their instruments.

Mayor Carter, the council members, and Pastor Martinez were spitting dirt out of their mouths. Suddenly Heather Landis jumped out of her car and shouted, "Wait! Don't start yet!"

"Ladies and gentlemen," the mayor began, "that was not a tornado that just blew in. I see that Channel 6 and Heather Landis have joined us."

Heather ran toward the roped-off area, waving her arms. "Hold it!" She motioned to her photographer. "Mario, come on!"

The mayor spit more dirt out of his mouth, then, "While we try to get ourselves dusted off, we'll give Miss Landis a few minutes to set up."

Like a movie star, Heather acknowledged the mayor, waved to the townsfolk, then gestured urgently to her cameraman who was struggling to set up his camera and tripod.

Shelly, Cal, and Leona reached the bleachers near the platform, while the mayor welcomed everyone to the event. Shelly followed Leona and Cal, counting eight steps as they climbed to a row with open seats. Trying not to step on anyone's toes, they excused themselves and shuffled sideways along the row until they could finally sit down. Leona sat on Cal's right, and Shelly sat on his left, trying to touch his arm with her shoulder.

The mayor reached under the podium and took out a large silver-plated pair of scissors. Off to his right, suspended in the air and attached to the edge of the stage, was a net full of small multi-colored helium balloons. Shelly knew that the balloons contained discount coupons redeemable at Braxton stores and would be released once the mayor and council members cut a foot-wide red ribbon. The hot air balloon would lift off the ground at the same time, marking the beginning of the festival.

Mayor Carter motioned for the council members to join him in front of the ribbon, then he spoke into the microphone. "Ladies and gentlemen, the junior council member from the second district, Cal Spencer, is not supporting our week of celebration."

The mayor's statement hung in the air. Everyone turned to look at Cal, who acknowledged their stares with raised eyebrows, pursed lips and a shrug. "Sorry, you ended up sitting with the leper," he said to Leona and Shelly out of the corner of his mouth.

"Is that tar I smell cooking?" Shelly asked, leaning closer to him.

Cal laughed. "No, it's probably my goose."

"Since Mr. Spencer chose not to stand with us," the mayor continued, "let me invite someone to take his place. She's a lady who has meant so much to Braxton." The crowd began to crane their necks and look around, wondering who the mayor was talking about. "Frances Hawthorne, the widow of our former mayor, and Braxton's town clerk, come join us, will you?"

Everyone applauded as the town clerk made her way down the steps of the grandstand, taking time along the way to shake hands.

"While Frances greets the entire town," the mayor paused, and the crowd laughed, "let me thank the news media for being here and remind them that we have press kits available. Courtney Talbot, our media coordinator and also the wife of our fine police chief, is in charge. I think Chief Talbot is with her at the tent." Carter looked toward the tent and waved.

"Yes, Chief Talbot is there, along with my son—fine boy, Alan Carter—who someday will be a great newspaper reporter."

"Better keep your desk locked at home, Mayor!" someone called out from the grandstand, which brought a laugh from the spectators and Mayor Carter too.

The town clerk now joined the group and stood next to the mayor. "The time has come," the mayor boomed. "Everyone, get your cameras ready."

Those on the stage gathered around the ribbon. A gust of wind swirled around them, creating a brief dust devil that threatened to rip the net full of balloons from the stage. The mayor reached out and kept them from blowing away.

"I'm going to ask the Reverend Nick Martinez to offer a prayer of dedication," the mayor said.

Martinez stepped to the microphone. "Let's pray," he said, and bowed his head. "Heavenly Father, we ask that our leaders seek Your direction in governing Braxton and do what's right." Shelly sneaked a look at Mayor Carter and saw him nodding in agreement. "We also pray that Your hand would be seen in a special way for our town. We ask this in Jesus' name. Amen." The mayor echoed a hearty "Amen" of his own.

Newspaper photographers fired off early shots, and television cameras rolled, while another gust of wind rustled the leaves in nearby trees.

Mayor Carter pointed a finger at the band, and a drum roll began. He nodded in the direction of the hot air balloon, and Shelly noticed that the older of the two men inside the balloon's gondola was smoking a cigar. The balloon started to lift off the ground.

"I now proclaim a week of celebration for Braxton, U.S.A.," the mayor announced, "the Best Small Town in America!"

On cue, trumpets blared, applause and cheers went up, but at the moment the ribbon was to be cut, a violent wind shear slammed into the area. A massive swirling cloud of silt rose into the air and over the grandstands. As the dust settled, everyone blinked and wiped dirt off their clothes. Then the crowd began to giggle. Shelly looked up front to see the mayor holding only one handle of the scissors in his hand. The scissors had broken, the ribbon had not been cut, and the net full of balloons, now airborne, hadn't opened. Instead, it was heading to the ocean. Everyone was laughing, including the mayor.

Then suddenly a woman screamed. Everyone lifted their heads to look at the hot air balloon. Several lines to the passenger basket had ripped loose, and the collapsing nylon balloon was plummeting to the ground. A flame from the propane burner flashed in the sky.

"The balloon's on fire!" Shelly shouted.

Horrified screams were heard as the fire ignited the gondola, and one of the men leaped from the basket.

"It's going to hit the tent!" Shelly cried and reached out to grab Cal.

CHAPTER 26

5:59 P.M.

Shelly Hinson stared numbly at her computer screen. The story she'd just written was not planned, nor was the special edition of *The Braxton Banner* now being frantically assembled in the newsroom. She heard editor Marty Cavitt nearby, but his voice seemed distant. Her eyes moved to a piece of wire copy she'd printed and reread.

URGENT URGENT URGENT
HOT AIR BALLOON CRASH
(BRAXTON, CA) SEVEN PEOPLE, INCLUDING THE CHIEF OF POLICE OF BRAXTON, CALIFORNIA AND HIS WIFE, COURTNEY, HAVE BEEN KILLED IN THE CRASH OF A HOT AIR BALLOON. CHIEF TREVOR TALBOT, 58, WAS STANDING IN A MEDIA TENT THAT EXPLODED WHEN HIT BY THE BALLOON.

ASSISTANT POLICE CHIEF GINA WELLS SAYS THE BALLOON WAS PART OF THE OPENING CEREMONIES FOR A WEEK-LONG CELEBRATION IN BRAXTON. TWO UNIDENTIFIED MEN IN THE BALLOON WERE KILLED, ALONG WITH THREE UNIDENTIFIED PEOPLE WORKING FOR A CATERING COMPANY. ALAN CARTER, 17, SON OF BRAXTON MAYOR ROGER CARTER, WAS PULLED FROM THE WRECKAGE WITH CRITICAL BURNS.

AP-URGENT-1135 PST 12-26

Shelly glanced back at her computer. The headline leaped off the screen and stabbed her like an accusatory finger.

SEVEN DEAD IN BALLOON CRASH!

Shelly stared at the words SEVEN DEAD and couldn't help but know that she was partly responsible. But before she could think more about it, a young man crossed the room to the television set, where he turned up the volume, just as KSBY-TV's production open, with visual effects and music, came to an end.

Throughout the day, Shelly and the rest of the staff had watched CNN and the other three networks, viewing the horrific tragedy over and over again with the rest of America. It played on regular speed, then in gruesome slow motion. TV and home video cameras at the ceremony had recorded the disaster from the first scream, to the balloonist's horrifying leap, to the fiery impact and explosion.

A local announcer breathlessly spoke into the camera, "Now, live from San Luis Obispo, News 6, the number one news team on California's Central Coast."

"Good evening," the male news anchor said, but his words had squeaked out. He glanced at his female co-anchor, shifted nervously, and cleared his throat. "Good evening," he repeated in a lower voice. "Seven people were killed this morning in the crash of a hot air balloon. It happened at the opening of a festival in Braxton."

At this point, his partner took a deep breath, and then, in a shaky voice, read her part off the TelePrompTer. "The dead are Braxton Police Chief Trevor Talbot, his wife, Courtney, two men in the balloon, and three food service workers."

Video from the ceremony began, footage that Shelly had not yet seen on any network newscast. Channel 6's camera had been close to the balloon, and now the tape zoomed in on the men in the ill-fated basket as the balloon began to rise.

"The most dramatic moment of the disaster," the young man went on, "involves a person we expected to have with us on the set tonight." A publicity photo of a smiling Heather Landis flashed on the screen. "Our reporter Heather Landis was at the crash scene. Heather and her cameraman, Mario Cedeno, were directly in the path of the plunging balloon when it crashed." Video of the balloon replaced Heather's photo, and Shelly heard once again those same screams that had pierced the air during the crash. The picture shook now and for a moment, the camera jerked toward the sky. Quickly, the video stabilized and focused on the balloon, now in flames and floating toward the camera.

"We warn you," the young woman said, "what you are about to see is very graphic." Shelly's coworkers moved closer to the television set. "Injured in the accident was Alan Carter, son of Braxton mayor, Roger Carter." Shelly gasped as she watched the burning gondola drift toward the media tent. The video bounced with each step of the cameraman, but the movement only made the pictures more realistic and terrifying. Alan Carter was shown at the tent's entrance, a terrified expression frozen on his face. Shelly found herself reliving every moment of the event again.

The pictures and sound told the story. Spectators in the grandstand were screaming, as with a flash and an explosion, the balloon landed on the rear of the tent and blew up. "At this moment," the anchor man said, "five people in the tent were instantly killed. Apparently, the flaming gondola ignited propane tanks used by a catering company."

The camera moved closer, showing the mayor's son on the ground, seriously burned, writhing in agony.

"Oh, no!" someone in the room shouted as the nylon tent collapsed in flames.

"What's she doing?" another person cried.

Shelly's mouth fell open as she watched Heather Landis rush to the burning entrance. A male voice, probably the cameraman, screamed,

"Heather, don't!" Ignoring the warning, Heather stepped inside the tent and grabbed hold of the boy. As she dragged him out, the tent collapsed in flames on her and the boy.

"She's on fire too!" a man in the room yelled.

"This is awful!" a woman exclaimed. "I can't watch."

There was a blur then, and someone grabbed Heather and the boy, pulling them out of the fire. In a bear hug, the three rolled on the ground to put out the flames. "The person you just saw is Braxton fire-fighter Ward Dayton," the anchor man said. And when another man appeared with a fire extinguisher, "He's joined by fellow firefighter Zeke Wallace, who can be seen dousing them with a fire extinguisher." And the video was over.

Shelly leaned back in her chair and closed her eyes. She heard the anchor man say, "We're joined by photographer Mario Cedeno who took that remarkable video." Shelly opened her eyes and saw Mario, still wearing the soiled clothes from the crash coverage. He sat stiffly in a chair, looking very much like a behind-the-scenes person.

"Mario, that was amazing video," the young woman said. "What was going through your mind?"

Cedeno was unshaven and hadn't combed his hair. He rubbed his hand across his face and paused a moment before answering. "I really don't remember much. Maybe because I was seeing most of it in black and white through my camera view finder. It didn't hit me then, like it did just now—" He swallowed hard. "Seeing that on the air." He struggled to keep his composure. "All I know is that Heather is a hero," he said in a choking voice.

"Yes, she is," the anchor man agreed. "The latest from the hospital is that Heather's in serious condition with second- and third-degree burns on much of her upper body. Alan Carter isn't doing very well either. He suffered first-, second-, and third-degree burns, and was hit by several pieces of flying metal."

Shelly got up from her chair, and in a daze walked out of the room, then down a hall. She opened the door to the restroom, went inside, dropped to her knees, and threw up.

CHAPTER 27

Braxton
9:00 P.M.

Shelly listened to the telephone ringing in her ear. It was midnight where she was calling: a new day had begun there. She wondered if somehow, once the connection was made, she could distance herself from the tragedy—if not emotionally, at least professionally.

Shortly after the accident, Shelly had telephoned Lance Milburn. At that time, he'd asked her to call again later with an update.

On the fourth ring, he finally picked up the phone. His "hello," told her he knew she was on the other end of the line.

"Hi, Lance."

"Are you any better?" he asked, but his voice wasn't particularly sympathetic.

"Not really." She felt defeated. The only solace was the silence of her apartment. If Lance wanted to talk, he could ask the questions.

"Thanks for passing along the eyewitness accounts. Great quotes, terrific emotion. We'll give them to the person assigned to the story."

"You're welcome," she said, but her voice was barely above a whisper, and she could care less who was assigned to the story.

"Shelly, thanks to you, we're kicking some serious butt on this story."

"Huh?"

"*Time, Newsweek*—you name it, they're all playing catch-up. No one else has someone on the *inside*."

"Lance," she said angrily, "seven people are dead because I'm on the inside. This didn't just happen, I mean, it's not a matter of—"

"Shelly, you're a reporter. You didn't cause that balloon to crash. You certainly aren't responsible. I won't accept you talking like that. I expect you to act like a professional—put your feelings aside."

Easy for you to say, Mr. Big Shot Publisher, Shelly thought. Out loud, she said, "OK, sorry. It's just that—"

"*It's just that* we're paying you to do a job," he said, finishing her sentence. "Now what did you find out?"

She took a deep breath. "The company—" She paused, then raised her voice. "The company that owned the balloon was under investigation by the Federal Aviation Administration."

"No kidding?" Lance said too cheerfully. "Tell me more."

"The town rented the balloon from Upper Limits of San Luis Obispo, a company the FAA had grounded. It looks like town officials knew they were grounded, but went ahead with the contract anyway."

"Very good, Shelly. No, that's excellent. Is this exclusive?"

"Sort of."

"Is it, or isn't it?"

"I got the story from the kid who was injured in the accident, Alan Carter, the mayor's son."

"Did you say the mayor's son?"

"Yeah."

"How did he know?"

"He hangs around the paper, wants to be a reporter. He mentioned something this morning, so tonight I looked in the desk we let him use here at the paper. I found a floppy disk in the back of a drawer. Some of the story was on it."

"Tell me more." Lance listened as Shelly read him Alan's article. When she finished, he asked, "You said the disk had just some of the story. Where's the rest?"

"I'm working on that."

Twenty-Seven

"Are you the only one who knows about this?"

"I'm not sure."

"OK, it doesn't matter. Everything's falling into place. We go to print tomorrow. For now, here's what I want you to do."

CHAPTER 28

Tuesday December 27, 7:30 A.M.

Shelly pulled the newspaper out of its plastic bag, but before opening to the front page, she reached for her coffee mug and took a sip. She walked across the stained, threadbare carpet to her crummy sofa, where she sat down and looked at the only evidence left of the holidays. With a roll of Scotch tape stolen from work, she'd attached thirty or so Christmas cards to her one apartment window. Five or six of them had come loose and dropped to the floor. She'd had no room, no money, and no desire to set up a Christmas tree.

Shelly pushed away the clutter on the glass top of her secondhand rattan coffee table, took another sip of coffee, then opened the paper.

SEVEN DEAD IN BALLOON CRASH!

Again. Shelly closed her eyes, and leaned back on the sofa. It was not supposed to be this way. What more was going to happen? The December 27th edition of Braxton's newspaper was to be a collector's edition, celebrating the town's success. For weeks, Shelly had helped plan the layout: there were to be photos of the opening ceremony, a history of the town, profiles of new businesses, predictions for the New Year, and interviews with some of the townsfolk. But in one horrifying moment all of that was scrapped. Instead, Editor Marty Cavitt and his staff had scrambled to chronicle a real-life tragedy that had literally blown up in their faces.

Shelly saw her byline on page one, but she knew the strongest part of her article belonged to Alan Carter. She had shown the contents on Alan's disk to Marty. The boy was correct when he spoke just before the accident; he'd uncovered an exclusive story. "They don't get much bigger than this," she said, nodding.

Shelly began to read her article.

BRAXTON—Last summer, the winds of fortune found their way to Braxton when it was named best small town in America. The town and its people wondered what this would mean. Yesterday, the wind, in one powerful gust, brought with it, tragedy. Seven people are dead, victims of a freak crash involving a hot air balloon during the opening ceremony for Braxton's festival week. The balloon was hit by a wind shear, then caught fire and crashed into a media tent near the ceremony. Killed in the accident were Braxton Police Chief Trevor Talbot and his wife, Courtney. Also dead were the pilot and owner of the balloon company, Tyrone Backus, fifty-six, his son, Rudy, twenty-three and three employees of Catering R Us, Sylvia Chavez, thirty-three, Magdalena Espinoza, twenty-six, and Hector Medina, Jr., fifty-five. Critically burned were Alan Carter, seventeen, the son of Braxton's mayor, and KSBY-TV reporter Heather Landis, twenty-five. Firefighter Ward Dayton suffered minor burns when he rescued Carter and Landis.

It wasn't until after the crash, that the staff of *The Braxton Banner* learned Alan Carter was working on an article that now has enormous implications on this event. Here is Carter's article, printed for the first time.

Balloon Company's Future Up in the Air
By Alan Carter
(Special to *The Banner*)

BRAXTON—An investigation by *The Braxton Banner* shows that Upper Limits of San Luis Obispo, a hot air balloon company, may soon be in violation of federal law. One of its balloons is scheduled to be flown Monday in the opening ceremony for Braxton's festival week, despite the company's grounding by the Federal Aviation Administration. According to records on file with the F.A.A., Upper Limits was suspended for ninety days, until December 29. The ground breaking ceremony is December 26.

Upper Limits was fined $5,000 and suspended September 30 for safety violations and improper maintenance records. When shown documents from the F.A.A., Upper Limits owner and chief balloon operator Tyrone Backus said, "I don't know where you got that. The papers I have show we can fly again on the 22nd." F.A.A. officials confirm the December 29 date.

Braxton Mayor Roger Carter said he knew nothing about the company's flying record. But two independent sources dispute that, saying the mayor went ahead with the contract because of his personal friendship with the owner of Upper Limits.

When asked about Upper Limits' intent to operate Monday, an F.A.A. spokesman said the agency could not investigate a violation that hadn't happened.

———————

Shelly's part of the story now continued.

Early findings in the accident suggest a spark, possibly from the cigar of balloonist Tyrone Backus, ignited leaking propane gas from one of the tanks. Eyewitnesses report seeing the gondola catch fire, then head directly into the media tent where it exploded.

A news conference is scheduled Tuesday morning at Braxton's town hall at which time—

Shelly had read enough. She peered into the kitchen at the digital clock on her microwave. It was 7:51. She didn't have time for any makeup. She laced up her tennis shoes, grabbed a baseball cap, and was out the door for the 8:00 A.M. news conference at the town hall. One of the benefits of living in a small town—she could get to any destination in minutes. She'd make it with time to spare.

Braxton Town Hall
8:05 A.M.

A light breeze was all that remained of the freak windstorm from the day before. An occasional flutter wasn't enough to ruffle the over-sized American flag that clung halfway up the pole atop Braxton's town hall. Cal Spencer looked at his watch, then out to the street. Mayor Carter was late. A car had just pulled up, but it belonged to Shelly Hinson, who was now running toward the covered walkway where Cal stood. He liked her in casual attire, always thought it suited her best. And she actually looked better with less makeup.

"Nice hat," he called.

She was breathing hard, but managed a smile as she hurried to his side.

"Up late last night—didn't feel like getting fancy this morning. Sorry, I look like a wreck."

"I think you look great," he replied.

She seemed surprised at his compliment. "Thanks, Cal, I needed that. Has the news conference started yet?"

"No, the mayor isn't here."

"What else is new, huh?" They began to walk down the outside passageway to the town hall's side door. Purple bougainvilleas hung on trellises on either side of them.

"Quite an article in the paper this morning," Cal said. "I guess that's what Alan was talking about yesterday."

"Should make for an interesting news conference," Shelly replied without enthusiasm. Cal thought that a bit strange.

They walked into the room set up for the media. A bank of television news cameras was set up on tripods, and photographers were making last minute adjustments with light stands. Still photographers, their cameras hanging over their shoulders, leaned against the wall. Reporters were scattered around the room, some seated, others standing, waiting for the mayor to arrive. Council members stood in the back of the room, but when Cal looked at them, they glanced away. He found a seat, but was confused when Shelly sat down beside him, away from the other reporters.

"Ladies and gentlemen, my apologies for the delay," the grim-faced mayor boomed as he entered the room from a side door. TV-types scrambled to start their cameras, while the sound of motor drives was heard from still photographers as they snapped off shots. The mayor was dressed in a long sleeve black western shirt and black cotton pants.

Assistant Police Chief Gina Wells followed him in a dark blue dress. Carter pulled out his folding chair, sat down, and motioned for Gina to take a seat. He then scooted closer to the table which had several microphones taped together on stands. Christmas decorations still hung on the wall behind the mayor, and a brightly decorated tree stood in the corner next to the window. Loops of silver and gold tinsel criss-crossed above the reporters and camera crews.

"Thanks for coming. For those who were not here yesterday, my name is Roger Carter. I'm the mayor of Braxton." He took a deep breath. "We're deeply saddened by the tragic deaths of seven people, including our police chief and his wife." Carter looked at Gina. "For now, Gina

Wells, his assistant, will be in charge of—"

"Mayor Carter," one of the television reporters interrupted. "Did you know the balloon—"

"If you don't mind, *Miss*," Carter said, cutting her off, "I'm not ready for questions yet."

"Well, too bad," the woman snapped. "We want answers. Your local paper says the balloon company was—"

"Would you shut up?" the mayor barked. Gasps could be heard around the room. "I realize you're a big-time news person from out of town, but when you're here, you'll act with a little respect. If you'll allow me, I want everyone to know the funeral for Chief Talbot and his wife will be at First Baptist, Thursday morning at ten. A motorcade and graveside services will follow at . . ."

Cal leaned over to Shelly. "Who's that TV reporter?" he whispered. "Wasn't she in town a few months back?"

"Name's Rosie Pender-Atkins, NBC News," Shelly answered. "She was here about six months ago, a real pain."

"When did she arrive?"

"Late yesterday. I guess NBC flew her up from LA by helicopter. She was making life miserable for us at the paper last night."

". . . We lost a great police chief," the mayor rambled on. "It's a personal loss that touches each citizen of—"

"Did you know the balloon company was grounded?" Rosie asked.

Carter glared at her. "I had no idea."

"Didn't your son tell you?" Shelly blurted.

The mayor looked surprised. "I told Alan that I knew nothing—"

"Sounds like he did a better job of checking than the town did," Rosie said.

The mayor squirmed in his seat. Cal felt a guilty pleasure as for once the tables seemed to have turned.

"What was done, and what wasn't done, will be addressed later by the N.T.S.B., F.A.A., and D.O.T.—"

"Forget the alphabet agencies, Mayor," one man called out. "What can you tell us?"

"It's too early to speculate. Captain Wells and her people are gathering facts. Right now, we're still in shock over the loss of life and those who were hurt."

"Roger, how's your son?" one council member asked from the back of the room.

"Is that you, Phil?" the mayor asked, shielding his eyes from the glare of the portable TV lights.

"Yes. How's Alan?"

"He's still critical, but stable. His mother and I are in debt to Channel 6 reporter Heather Landis and our fire department for saving Alan's life." The mayor again held his hand over his eyes. "Where is Channel 6's camera?"

"Over here, Mayor," a photographer called out with a wave of his right hand.

Carter looked directly into the camera. "Heather Landis is a very courageous woman," he said.

"What are your plans now, Mayor?" Rosie asked. "I mean, the festival and all?"

The mayor glanced at the council members in the back of the room. "We've canceled all events, except one."

"Which one?" several reporters asked at the same time.

"We're still planning to have the concert Saturday night."

"What in the world for?" Cal blurted before he could stop himself.

Everyone turned to look at him, and he saw Rosie Pender-Atkins nodding and smiling. Then they all turned back to the mayor, whose face was flushed with anger.

"This news conference is for the media, Mr. Spencer."

"You answered Councilman Prescott's question," Cal replied.

"How about it, Mayor?" Rosie asked.

"We've committed town funds for that, and I think after yesterday's tragedy, we need something to cheer us up."

"Just like the free hot air balloon rides?" Cal asked.

The mayor stood up. "The news conference is over," he said tensely. Then, without another word, he marched out of the room.

Cal watched the mayor leave, then turned to Shelly. He thought he saw tears in her eyes. "Are you OK?" he asked. Concerned, he reached out for her hand.

She glanced at him briefly, her lips pursed together. Then she shook her head and quickly left the room.

CHAPTER 29

It was the first time Mario had seen Heather since the accident. Bandages covered most of her face, and right now she appeared to be sleeping. He stood in the doorway for a moment listening to the *beep, beep, beep* that assured him his colleague was still alive. Tubes, lines, needles, and wires connected her to intravenous bottles, catheters, and monitors. Red numbers flashed on several screens, registering blood pressure, pulse, and oxygen levels. Other machines showed green radar-like scopes with squiggly lines that meant nothing to him. Mario had never seen the inside of an intensive care burn unit before, and this one at Braxton General Hospital smelled uncomfortably clean to him.

A nurse stood next to Heather's bed, writing whatever nurses write on hospital clipboards. "Be right with you," she said in a low voice that suggested she was a smoker. Her head dipped then, and she looked up and down her nose at him through bifocal glasses. She made an entry on her clipboard, then pulled a sliding cloth partition around Heather's bed for privacy. "Are you a family member?" she asked as she crossed the room to where he stood. She slid the clipboard into a wooden holder just outside the door.

Mario shifted the small gift-wrapped box he'd brought with him to his other arm. "No, I'm Mario Cedeno from Channel 6, Heather's cameraman. I was with her when—well, when she got hurt. Can I see her?"

"Normally, I'd say no, but her family is on the way from back east. Go on in, it'll do her good, but you can't stay long—five minutes, max."

"How's she doing?" he asked with hesitation, not having seen any movement from the bed. "Is she going to—will she make it?"

He knew she had first-, second-, and third-degree burns over fifteen percent of her body. Doctors had said the burns to her face were serious, and damage to her arms and back was massive. Of greatest concern, though, was possible blindness.

"With the kinds of burns she has, the first two weeks are critical, but she's a fighter." The nurse took Mario's hand and they walked to the bed. "Heather, you have a visitor," she said gently, then turned back to Mario. "I'll be back in a bit, OK?"

"Who is—" Heather coughed and grimaced. "Who is it?" she asked again, barely above a whisper.

Mario pulled a chair up to the side of her bed. "Hi, *Network*." He spoke the nickname for the first time with affection.

Her mouth formed a knowing smile. "Oh, Mario, it's you," she said in a squeaky voice. "How sweet."

"Hey, Heather, yesterday you made every network newscast."

"I did?"

"Yep. When you get better, you'll have all sorts of offers coming your way. You're a hero."

Heather's lips began to quiver. For a moment, the only sound in the room were the *beeps* from the electronic machines.

Mario suddenly remembered his gift. He placed it on a small table by Heather's bedside. "I brought you a present, *Network*. Uh, you can see it later."

She didn't respond to that. "I'm glad you're here," she said.

"The nurse says your folks should be here soon. You're going to be fine, Heather."

"Mario, I'm really scared," she said through trembling lips.

And his heart broke to hear it.

2:51 P.M.

"This won't take long." Gina Wells studied the thirty or so police officers before her. Most of them were seated, but some had positioned themselves in the back of the briefing room, their body language suggesting they weren't too thrilled about being there.

Gina glanced around the now familiar room. On the soiled, gray walls hung clipboards, photos of wanted suspects, work schedules, and several enlarged maps of the town with colored stick pins. A cork bulletin board held an invitation to join a credit union, a notice that Thursday's softball game had been postponed, and a card advertising a couch for sale.

"No speech, only something you all know," she said.

Two officers in the back of the room yawned. They stood next to a feeble Christmas tree, halfheartedly decorated with a few bulbs, a string of colored lights, and at the top, an angel that had somehow lost its head. Two pieces of wood nailed to the bottom held the tree upright. It had shed half its needles.

Gina cleared her throat. As acting police chief, she needed to make a few things clear to the other officers. This was the start of the swing shift; she'd already spoken to another group of officers that morning. "We have a job to do," she said and immediately was sorry she'd used the trite line again. Several in the room exchanged glances and raised their eyebrows. Two smirked, while a few exchanged words loudly enough to be heard, but not understood.

"Quiet!" Blake Hesterman barked. Using his authority as a sergeant, Hesterman seemed to be trying to impress Gina. Now, with the chief's passing, Hesterman had already put in his bid for a lieutenant's job. But as long as Gina was in charge, that would never happen. "Listen up!" he ordered now.

"All of you knew Chief Talbot better than I," Gina offered, "but I've been here long enough to know he was a good cop, a gentleman, and we'll miss him very much." Gina wore civilian clothes; as a captain, she only wore her uniform for formal occasions. Her first opportunity to do so would be on Thursday morning when Talbot and his wife were buried.

"I've given Sergeant Hesterman a revised list of those who will be working on Thursday." A few of the officers looked at each other and began to chatter.

"OK, knock it off," Hesterman ordered again. "The captain—er, the chief—isn't finished." Hesterman wore a knowing smile.

"I'm not the chief, Sergeant," Gina told him. "Let's keep things straight."

"Yes, sir—er, sorry. Yes, ma'am."

"We'll try to have as many officers as possible at the funeral," Gina continued. "It'll be on a seniority basis. Again, I'm very sorry and pledge that I'll try to carry on as the chief would want." She then yielded the troops to Hesterman. "It's all yours, Sergeant," she said.

"Connors, Phelan, Thorndike . . ." Gina returned to her office as Hesterman called out the names of officers and their assignments. She closed the door, hoping to muffle the sound of his bombastic voice. She sighed and sank into the chair behind her desk. Most likely, she would soon be named the town's chief of police. Her life had changed, and Miami suddenly seemed a million years ago. Was this what she wanted? Was this what *God* wanted for her? Could she hack it?

3:07 P.M.

Nick Martinez turned the ink-marked, coffee-stained pages of his Bible. He'd spent the past hour here in his makeshift study looking for words that would reach people, yet please the Lord. So far, he had found none. He stared blurry eyed at all of the wadded-up pieces of paper along the wall near his plastic wastebasket—failed attempts at what he wanted to say at Thursday's funeral. This was just a lousy way to end the old year.

"Here's something that may help." Karen appeared by his side with a steaming mug of cinnamon tea. She placed it on his desk. Actually, the desk was a wooden door that rested on two metal filing cabinets in their bedroom. He'd had to convert his study into a nursery for their baby, due any day. To Nick's right, brightly colored fish swam in slow motion on his computer monitor; the screen saver aquarium had bubbled for thirty minutes now.

He felt a rush of tenderness and reached for wife's hands, pulling them close to his chest. She nestled her chin on his shoulder. "What am I going to say, Karen? I've never had problems with funerals before."

"Have you prayed about it?"

"Yeah, but—well, it probably sounds silly, but it's like God has this look on His face."

"What kind of look?"

"A look that says, 'OK, Martinez, remember what you said before the balloon went up? You asked to see My hand. Be careful what you ask for.'"

Karen simply smiled.

———— ⋅•⋅ ————

6:19 P.M.

Mayor Roger Carter entered the elevator and pushed the button for the fourth floor. He had not visited his son since the night before, and he knew he would probably catch "what-for" from his wife. The doors opened to a nursing station. Carter stepped out of the elevator and watched the medical personnel on duty do a double-take—they looked at him, glanced back to what they were doing, then realized who he was. He enjoyed causing this kind of stir wherever he went around Braxton.

"Good evening, Mayor," said two young nurses in unison.

"Hello, ladies. How's Alan?"

"The doctor's with him now," one replied guardedly, and returned to her work.

Carter moved toward the intensive care unit. A male orderly came around the corner pushing an empty gurney on the shiny tile floor. Mayor Carter waited to see if the orderly would recognize him. They exchanged glances without a word, and no sign the man knew who he was. Disappointed, Carter continued down the hall. Through the open doors he could see the patients in their beds, while others had curtains drawn. He heard someone snoring and peered into one room to see an old woman asleep with her mouth wide open.

The mayor hated hospitals, hated everything about them—the gagging antiseptic smell, the drone-like pages over the intercom, and the clatter of food carts. He couldn't believe doctors and nurses were vitally interested in every patient. But what he detested more than anything else was visiting someone in a hospital. He was good for about thirty seconds, then he was ready to leave. He replayed a typical conversation in his mind:

"Hi, how are you feeling?"

"I'm getting better. Thanks for coming."

"You're welcome. How's the food?"

"It's OK."

Then what?

He was here to see his son, but he was also expecting a ration of abuse from his wife. He knew what she'd say: *"It's about time. Where have you been all day? Your own son, and you don't get here until now. Blah, blah, blah . . .* He could have written the tirade that awaited him.

He finally reached room 448 and stepped inside. There was Alan, wrapped in bandages, tubes leading in and out of—how many places? Carter cursed the operator of the hot air balloon, then moved to his son's bedside.

CHAPTER 30

Braxton
Thursday December 30, 11:40 A.M.

A fine mist swirled in the breeze and spattered the windshields of the procession of cars. Typical December weather had returned to central California on this painful day. Two motorcycle officers escorted the cortege at thirty miles an hour. The motorcade with its flashing red and blue lights snaked along Highway 46 for as far as the eye could see. Shelly Hinson, figuring she was somewhere in the middle, looked into her rearview mirror at the long line of headlights behind her. Never had she seen this many cops, F.B.I. agents, sheriff's deputies, highway patrol officers, D.E.A. agents—you name it. This was the last ride for Chief Trevor Talbot and his wife, Courtney.

Shelly drove alone in her beat-up Ford Escort. The only sound, outside of the rough running engine, was the scraping of her windshield wipers. The dried rubber blades were rock hard and did more to smear the water than clear it away. Today's funeral was the longest ninety minutes of her life. Mayor Carter had given a eulogy, as had many of Chief Talbot's former colleagues, including the State Attorney General. Talbot's younger brother, a lieutenant with the Dallas police department, had praised a man who had been his personal hero. Sadly, he admitted he'd never told his brother how he'd felt about him.

Braxton High School's a capella choir sang in honor of Courtney Talbot, the school's most popular teacher. The young people had stood bravely in their blue robes with white trim. But she doubted all would make it through their tribute and she was right. "When you walk through the storm hold your head up high . . ." Several students were overcome with grief as they sang. One by one, they dropped into their chairs, heads buried in their hands, consoled by friends while others continued singing. When the students reached the final crescendo, "You'll Never Walk Alone," Shelly broke down, but her tears came for a different reason.

———•—•———

11:52 A.M.

Nick Martinez, holding his Bible, stood under a green canopy near the freshly dug graves for Trevor and Courtney Talbot. Strips of AstroTurf were placed over the two mounds of dirt to lessen the obvious. A row of white folding chairs was lined up facing the couple's final resting place. Nick counted fifteen chairs reserved for the Talbot's children and the rest of their family.

Braxton's Memorial Park was a bleak chunk of land set on ten acres of rolling brown hills north of Highway 46 along Willow Creek Road. The sparse bits of grass here and there looked parched and full of cut weeds. The only green patches were next to a creek bed that angled through the cemetery. Recent rains had left a trickle of water visible from the bluff where Nick stood. Most of the grave markers lay even with the ground, although granite headstones were still in evidence. Nick wondered if any pastor who had ever stood on this ground felt more inadequate than he did now. He shivered, and it had nothing to do with the damp mist that blew in his face. He was embarrassed at how he'd stumbled and mumbled through the funeral service. His words had felt empty to him, and he doubted he'd been much comfort to anyone. He barely knew the chief and his wife and had no idea where they stood spiritually. They'd been to his church a couple of times, but they were taken so quickly, so violently . . .

Two men in dark suits caught Nick's attention now. They were frantically shuttling the floral wreaths and sprays from the funeral out of their van and arranging them around the graveside.

The funeral procession was now in sight and turning off Highway 46. Nick watched as the two hearses pulled up a few feet away. The doors opened and family members got out and began to walk his way. His heart was heavy for the Talbots' two sons, their daughter, and how many grandchildren? Six or seven? Nick prayed that his final words would comfort in a way they hadn't so far. There would be those present who needed to hear about a personal relationship with God through His Son, Jesus Christ. Would his words convince them of their need? Suddenly, panic gripped him. He quickly looked inside the front cover of his Bible. He turned to the back, then thumbed through the pages and shook the Bible, hoping something would drop out. It didn't. "Oh, Lord, this couldn't have happened," he said aloud with his eyes closed. He'd left his notes on his office desk. Nick looked up to see the pallbearers straining with the two caskets. Hundreds of people were walking toward him. "Dear Lord," he prayed quietly, "let Your Holy Spirit give me Your words—speak through me. I'm in big trouble."

12:46 P.M.

To Shelly's relief, the graveside service was brief. Unlike the memorial service at the church, with endless tributes, music, and the Reverend Nick Martinez droning on for a half hour, everything at the cemetery was over in less than ten minutes. The Talbots' daughter read a moving poem about her parents, and the chief's brother expressed his appreciation for kindness shown to the family. Shelly had expected another long sermon from Pastor Martinez, but she was wrong. He'd only spoken for about three minutes.

From her car, she watched everyone slowly leave, many of them seemingly hesitant to resume their lives. Some hugged, while others put their arms around family members and walked with them to their cars. Shelly knew their grief was compounded by the agonizing question: Why? Martinez had told them that only God knew the answer. But Shelly had niggling doubts. If it weren't for her magazine story . . . She shook her head. Nonsense. What was the old saying? If "ifs and buts were candy and nuts, we'd all have a Merry Christmas." Fate, not her story, had brought the balloon down.

Shelly took her notebook and began to write down her observations. She recorded her public impressions, reflections that would be printed in Thursday's *Banner*. They would also be useful six months from now for her grand finale article in *Destination*. Her private thoughts, though, were another matter. Inside the secret closet of her mind were hideous images that now included the grief-stricken family of those who were killed.

Shelly stared dully at her notebook. She reminded herself that she was at the funeral as a reporter first, and a friend of the Talbots second. So why had she written so little about the eulogies and so much about what Nick Martinez had said at the graveside?

She tried to erase those thoughts and turned her attention to bringing her Ford Escort to life. As she turned the ignition key, she gently coaxed the gas pedal. "Come on, honey, nap time is over." The engine sputtered reluctantly, then stopped. "Mommy still loves you." She tried again and the engine went, *ahraaa, ahraa, ahra.* "I promise, we'll visit the nice man at the garage—you just have to work a little harder. Come on, sweetie, come on." When the car began to die once more, she yelled, "Come on!" With that, the engine started and Shelly drove away.

Martinez's words echoed in her mind as she drove. Seven words: *To be undecided, is to be decided.* It was a thought that went counter to her idea about God. The pastor was saying that she'd already turned away from God. How dare he assume that? She still hadn't made up her mind about God and Jesus, heaven and hell, all that sort of stuff. How could she, after a so-called loving God had taken her parents, had caused them so much suffering? To be undecided, is to be decided. What gave him the right to say that? Shelly tried to remember a particular Bible verse he had read—something about believing in Jesus for eternal life. Shelly came to a stop sign, and the engine begin to sputter once more. Not wanting to take a chance, she revved the motor and rolled through the intersection. She flipped open her notebook to read something else Martinez had said that surprised her: *Everyone gets eternal life. Where to spend it?* She'd underlined the word, *Everyone.* Shelly switched off her radio to be alone with her thoughts. Were her parents in heaven? Were they in hell? What about Chief Talbot and Courtney? Did Shelly send them to hell before they had a chance to find God? Where would she herself spend eternity?

Shelly looked around her and realized she was only a short distance from where the hot air balloon had crashed. She hadn't intended to drive this way. What had brought her here? "The guilty person returns to the scene of the crime," she said aloud, and she knew she was dead serious.

She wondered if investigators were still on the accident scene and decided to check it out. Her thoughts returned to the funeral. Cal and Leona had sat together in church and then stood together at the cemetery. They seemed unusually close, and to Shelly, disgustingly familiar. Leona had only been in town for three weeks now, and it was as if their hands were already cemented together with Crazy Glue. What did Leona have that she didn't? She didn't know the new school teacher from San Diego that well, but from what she could tell, Shelly had her beat in all categories: looks, personality, smarts. But then, who cared what she thought?

Off in the distance, inside a chain link fence, Shelly spotted what looked like investigators at the balloon crash site. Thinking there might be some new material for her article, she continued driving toward the vacant lot. When she approached the T-shaped intersection, she decided not to risk her car stalling, and so she glanced quickly to her left, then rolled through the stop sign.

Suddenly, a motorcycle cut in front of her. The rider was desperately trying to keep control of his bike and avoid being run over. Horrified, Shelly slammed on her brakes. The bike and rider swerved to the left, then hard to the right. He was almost able to pull out of it, but then he skidded off the road into loose silt, crashing into the chain link fence. For a moment, the motorcycle and rider disappeared in a cloud of dust.

Shelly screeched to a stop, certain she had just killed someone. Where had he come from? She leaped from her car and ran into the dust cloud. "Are you OK?" she asked the person who lay crumpled under his motorcycle. Then Shelly's mouth dropped open—it was Rick Aguilara!

"What's wrong with you?" he screamed, pounding his fist into the ground. "Are you blind?"

"I'm sorry, I—I didn't see you."

"Duh—oh, really!" he mocked. "You stupid—" He turned away from Shelly and ran his right hand over his motorcycle. "If this bike is messed up, I swear, I'll kill you."

Shelly started to move toward Rick to help him, but instead, took two steps back. She watched as he pulled himself free from under the bike and rolled over on his side. "I, ah, are you . . . I can't believe—did I hit you?"

Rick yanked his helmet off and slung it into the fence. "Just shut up!" Blood poured from his nose. He began mumbling to himself as he set his motorcycle upright. "Stinking woman. First day here—she puts me down—now she nearly kills me."

"Is your bike wrecked?"

"I don't know," he said, as he touched a cut on his left cheek and studied his bike. "I'm so moved by your concern. You care more about my Harley than me."

"I'm so sorry." She took a cloth from his backpack. "Do you want to use this? You're cut."

Rick waved her away and wiped blood from his nose with his hand. "Stuff the sympathy." He straddled the Harley and with a deft kick of the starter, the motorcycle coughed once, then turned over and roared to life. A thrill shot through Shelly when she heard the sound. After revving the engine several times, Rick shut the motor off.

"Where were you going?" Shelly asked. "I mean, can I—"

Rick eyed her suspiciously. "What's it to you?"

Anger stabbed at Shelly. "Hey, give me a break, tough guy. This wasn't intentional, but maybe I should have run you over."

Rick raised his eyebrows. "Well, you didn't. If it matters, I'm looking for a job on the other side of town. In construction."

"I wouldn't imagine you have a whole lot of references on your résumé," she blurted before she could catch herself.

"Not like the ones that helped you get your job on *The Braxton Banner*," Rick shot back.

"Touché." Shelly smiled. "Want me to put in a good word for you?"

"Spare the favors. I'm already known by your local police."

Shelly had heard about Rick's encounter with Gina Wells and Blake Hesterman. "You were with the Stanley kid, right?"

Rick whistled. "No secrets around here, are there?"

"Not in a small town, especially when a loud hog and a hot Porsche are involved."

"The story has two sides," Rick said quietly.

"Care to tell me?"

"I'll think about it." His helmet in place, he started his Harley and roared away, leaving Shelly in a cloud of dust.

CHAPTER 31

Saturday December 31, 9:09 A.M.

For five days, Heather Landis' painful world consisted of beeps, pages, mysterious smells, and faceless voices. Doctors, nurses, orderlies, and the janitorial staff—they appeared at all hours, without warning and for different reasons. Occasionally, they announced their arrival with a gentle word, but most of the time they entered the room and simply went about their job. They fed, bathed, and helped her to the bathroom. They gave her pills and changed her dressings. All of this time, Heather would drift in and out of consciousness; sometimes she knew she was being moved about, other times she was only vaguely aware that something was happening. The scariest part for Heather was the recurring flashback—that one, awful flash of fire and heat that had plunged her into total darkness.

"Hey, *Network*, guess who?"

Heather smiled. "Mario, you are such a good friend."

Her parents, who had spent a few days in Braxton, were now returning home to their jobs in Washington. Besides her parents, Mario was the person who visited most often.

"Me, like Tonto—not Indian, but faithful Mexican cameraman. You, Lone Ranger-*kemosabe*, wear mask."

Heather giggled. Mario's presence lifted her spirits. "You nut. Thanks for coming. I wish I could see you."

"So, when . . ." He hesitated, then, "When do the bandages come off?"

"Not for another two weeks." Heather paused. She'd never talked about this with her cameraman before. "You know there's about a fifty-fifty chance I could lose part of my sight." She heard Mario gulp and clear his throat. Then she thought she heard him fidgeting in his chair. She was so much more sensitive to sound now.

"Well, I'll put my money on you. I say you'll be back on Channel 6 and getting job offers from the networks in no time."

Heather shifted her position and removed a blanket. "They keep this room so hot," she said, ignoring his prediction. He made it sound so simple. If he only knew how many hours she'd stayed awake wondering if she would ever see again. Would she be so scarred she could never appear on camera again? "What day is it, Mario?"

"Saturday."

"New Year's Eve?"

"Uh, huh."

"Do you know what *auld lang syne* means?"

"Something about the past?"

"It's Scottish and it means the good old days long past." Heather sighed. "For me, that was just five days ago."

———————

11:30 A.M.

Gina Wells spent the last day of the old year getting ready for the New Year. She carried two boxes of files over to the weathered oak desk and stacked them beside it. Her eyes were drawn to a loose-leaf desk calendar. The page was still turned to December 26, the day time had stopped for Chief Trevor Talbot. His neatly written note read: *Festival opening—9:30 a.m.*

On Tuesday, the town council had unanimously approved her permanent promotion to police chief, but out of respect for Talbot, Gina had held off moving into his office until now. The chief's family photos and other personal items had been removed, but the desk calendar remained. The open page reminded her of the fragility of life. She ripped December 26 from the calendar and was about to toss the rest of the year's pages in the trash can when she stopped. Hesitantly, she turned to December 19, where she found her name written on the page. It was the day she'd been hired. She smiled to see that the chief had drawn a large star beside her name, underlining it twice. After removing that page, she flipped back to October, curious about the day of her first interview. Gina could still picture Chief Talbot making notes on the calendar page while the two of them talked about her career and the job opening in Braxton. Tears welled in her eyes as she read his scribbled words: *G.W. High standards—Braxton too small—good cop—lucky if she even considers!*

Gina removed the page and placed it, along with the other two, in the back of the desk's middle drawer. *I'm the one who's blessed, Chief. I'm sorry we had so little time together.*

The police station was quiet. It would be another three hours before the extra officers reported for the swing shift on New Year's Eve.

"Hey, Chief, you don't have to impress no one no more," a male voice boomed behind her. "It's Saturday—New Year's Eve."

Gina cringed. She turned to look into the face of the last person she wanted to see on her day off. Sergeant Blake Hesterman stood in the doorway grinning from ear to ear. He motioned to someone in the hall. "Tell the guys I'll be right there, the chief's movin' in." He sauntered into her office and flopped down on the sofa, pushing several folders aside. He propped his black military-style boots on a coffee table, then, leaning back, he put both hands behind his head. "So, what's the word, boss?" he asked.

Gina glared at him. "Don't call me boss. And get your boots off that table."

Hesterman quickly swung his feet to the ground and sat up straight, his smirk replaced by a wary look. "Sorry 'bout that. I thought things would be a little looser off duty. Didn't expect to see you today."

"Well, I'm here and no matter what day it is, I expect you to address me the same way you did Chief Talbot. Understand?"

"Yes, ma'am."

"What's with the G.I. Joe outfit?" she asked, pointing to his long-sleeved camouflage shirt and matching pants.

Hesterman's eyes narrowed. "Do I need your approval for what I wear on my day off?"

"Not at all. I just get curious when one of my officers shows up at the police station looking like he's dressed for battle. Is that the uniform of the day for your buddies too?"

"Yes, it is, *Chief* Wells." Hesterman got to his feet. "Just to satisfy our lady leader's curiosity, here's what a few of Braxton's finest are doing on their own time." He walked closer to her and his jaw tightened. "We're going to look for illegal alien campsites, meth labs, and anything else that shouldn't be around here. You have a problem with that?"

Gina detested everything about Hesterman, from his chauvinistic bombast to his phony sense of duty. "Let's get one thing straight, Sergeant. What you do on your own time is your business. It only becomes a problem when you cross the line between being an off-duty cop and a vigilante."

"Any complaints on me?" he challenged.

Gina pointed to a pile of boxes. "Not on you or your commandos. But I have an old file of Chief Talbot's that I find a bit disturbing."

"What's in it?"

"Some ugly incidents around here over the past six months. Head bashing, extortion, at least one attempted rape."

Hesterman laughed. "You think I did it?"

"I don't know. It's just that I don't like what people keep finding outside the emergency entrance of our hospital."

"What's that?"

"Trails of blood from battered migrant workers."

Hesterman mumbled something Gina couldn't understand, then, "Chief or no chief, I don't have to take this." He began to leave.

"Sergeant, as long as I'm running this department you have two choices," Gina called after him. "You'll either take it, or you can leave your badge on this table and hit the road."

Hesterman stopped in the doorway. He turned to face her. "I thought our job was to cut crime," he said, his face growing red.

"No, our job is public safety. If you want to make the public feel safer, try solving some home break-ins." Gina pulled out a folder from a box on her desk. "Or find this week's five stolen cars." She tossed the file on the desk and reached for another folder. "Or see who's behind the rash of gang graffiti that's hit our town. Are these home-grown boys or have we imported this garbage?"

"So, I take it you're not interested in illegal aliens and drug labs?"

"Sure, I am. But let the border patrol, sheriff's department, and D.E.A. take care of that. We've got enough to worry about."

"You think you brought all the right answers from Miami, don't you, *Chief* Wells?"

Gina took a deep breath. "No one has all the answers. Not even you, Sergeant."

"Thanks for your confidence, Chief." Hesterman took two steps back into the office. "Let's cut through all the bull. I'll just kiss my chances of making lieutenant good-bye." He now moved closer and leaned toward her. "You were a hot shot with Miami Vice, but you've got a lot to learn about running this police department."

Gina studied the sergeant's face. His right cheek twitched once, twice, three times. "You're probably right," she replied in an even tone. "What should I work on, Sergeant?"

"A lot of us resent your rules." His twitch had stopped, and Gina sensed his cockiness returning.

"Like what?"

"Well, for starters, no swearing while on duty and removing the nude centerfold in the briefing room. We all know you're big into this Christian thing, but don't expect us to be your *Jesus* patrol. We're cops, not choir boys."

"So, does swearing and pornography make you tough?"

Hesterman jutted his jaw toward her. "Like I said, Chief, you've lost touch with the street. You have to talk the language of the scum you bust."

"Get out of here!" Gina exploded. "Your degenerate camouflage chums are waiting. But remember this, Sergeant, roaming canyons with a bunch of beer-drinking, redneck yahoos is not law enforcement."

Hesterman walked out the door and slammed it behind him.

Gina dropped into her chair. "Happy New Year, *Chief* Wells," she said.

11:46 A.M.

Shelly wished she'd worn tennis shoes. Her footsteps clicked on the glistening tile of Braxton Hospital's fourth floor. She followed the room numbers, 444, 446, and now 448, where Alan Carter was recovering. A nursing supervisor had given the OK to visit him, but said she could only stay five minutes, that Alan's family was expected soon.

She stood in the doorway and immediately heard a familiar voice—it belonged to someone she wanted to avoid. But before she could turn around or duck into another room, Pastor Nick Martinez spotted her.

"Shelly, come in." He looked to his right. "Alan, Braxton's star news reporter is here to see you." Nick waved for her to join them.

Unable to escape, Shelly entered the room.

"Hi, Alan," she said. "You're looking pretty good." It was true, the boy had made remarkable progress. He was still hooked up to an IV and monitors, but seemed greatly improved since she'd last seen him.

"I liked your—" Alan coughed. "I liked your story about the balloon crash," he said in a scratchy voice.

Shelly crossed the room to sit in a chair next to his bed. "Thanks, but you wrote the best part. We just printed it." Alan managed a weak grin. "When you get out of here," she went on, "we'll team up for more exclusives. What do you think?"

"Only if it's Carter and Hinson," he teased, "and not Hinson and Carter."

"Get out of this room!" someone yelled from the doorway. Shelly whirled to see the mayor and his wife. "Who said you could be here?"

"Mayor," Pastor Martinez said, "we're just visiting Alan until you and your wife—"

"We don't need it." The mayor then turned on Shelly. "And I don't want some two-bit reporter putting ideas in Alan's head." He walked closer. "You've got nerve, taking advantage of a young kid, half full of medication. Your publisher will hear about this." He pointed to the door. "Get out!"

Shelly winked at Alan as she got up to leave. "It's OK," she mouthed, as she and Nick walked toward the door. "Mrs. Carter, Mr. Mayor—goodnight to both of you," she said, wishing she could stay and learn more of what Alan had uncovered.

"Thanks for the visit, Alan," Nick said, and they were out the door.

"Whew," Shelly said once they were in the hall. "Imagine the words he would have used had you not been there."

"Sometimes the Lord allows me to be a buffer."

They walked together to the elevator. "I saw you at the funeral," Nick said, "but not the cemetery. Were you there?"

"Uh huh," she said, wishing she could shake herself of the pastor.

The elevator doors opened, and they stepped inside. To Shelly's dismay, they were alone. "Down?" he asked. Shelly nodded and the pastor pushed the button marked Lobby. "Actually, I've already made arrangements to go up when my time comes," he said with a tender smile. "How about you?"

Shelly felt trapped as the doors sealed them inside. Why did she know this was going to happen? She looked at the pastor and shrugged. The elevator quivered and began its snail-like descent. This had to be the slowest elevator Otis had ever built.

"Yes, I've decided Christ's death on the cross was for me. And you?"

"I'm undecided," she said with certainty. "Does that mean I'm going to hell?" The elevator groaned past the third floor.

Nick raised his eyebrows. "For now, that's the direction you've chosen," he said with resignation. The same anger she'd felt at the cemetery toward this man burned again. "But God allows a U-turn," Nick added.

The elevator now inched past the second floor. Shelly looked up at the plastic mesh ceiling, wishing she could escape. "You make it sound too simple," she said finally.

"It's not simple. What God did was so complicated, it defies human understanding. He loves you and wants to forgive your sin. All you have to do is believe that."

"What if someone is the worst person in the world? Someone who—well, how about someone who has lied and killed people?" Shelly waited, sure she'd stumped the pastor with this one.

Nick's words were feather-like. "Makes no difference, Shelly. The worst or the best, everyone's a sinner. That's where God's mercy is divine. He'll forgive us all, if we ask."

Disappointed she hadn't stumped him after all, Shelly was relieved when the elevator jolted to a stop and the doors slid open. "Thanks for the talk, Reverend—I gotta go." She stepped out, feeling as if she had escaped from something. Or was it to something?

"Happy New Year, Shelly," he called after her. "Whenever you're ready, let's talk about that U-turn, OK?"

Highway 46
5:39 P.M.

The silver Porsche sped west on the two-lane asphalt highway. Brian Stanley wore a white T-shirt, light blue slacks, and sunglasses clipped onto 1950-style frames. He was chain-smoking Chesterfields. At 5:40 P.M., he squinted as a spray of sunset loomed large on the horizon. His convertible streaked toward the intersection of Highways 46 and 41. He smiled as he looked ahead. A car was in sight. "That guy up there's gotta stop," he said. "He'll see us."

The low profile sports car moved faster. Brian jiggled the steering wheel left, then right. The car shuddered as it gripped the road. He felt like a road racer. He glanced at the speedometer—102 miles an hour.

Brian had made this trip before, but the timing was never exactly right. Seldom was anyone at the intersection precisely at 5:45 P.M. Now, a car sat there, waiting to turn. Brian floored his Porsche, aiming directly for the intersection. Would the other car cut in front of him? Brian looked at his digital watch—5:44:55. He gripped the leather-covered steering wheel as tight as he could. "Turn, turn, turn," he pleaded aloud. Life went into slow motion. He closed his eyes and readied himself for the inevitable head-on collision, but instead found himself zooming past the intersection. Half disappointed, half elated, his cigarette still dangling from his mouth, Brian Stanley called out, "Happy New Year, James Dean, wherever you are!"

5:45 P.M.

Beatrice Stanley lost her grip on the perfume bottle, and it tumbled in slow motion toward the oval-shaped porcelain sink. "Oh, no!" she screamed, and instantly reached out to catch the bottle with both hands before it landed.

Pete stood next to her, at another sink, shaving the cream from under his nose. "Hey, good hands! Hall of Fame catch. Too bad we don't have instant replay."

They were getting ready to go out to dinner, then to the Little Richard concert. Suddenly, Beatrice dropped onto a stool and slumped against the wall. Her face was ashen and she was shaking, as she tried with all her might to hold onto the perfume bottle. She looked up at him. Her mouth was open, but no words came out.

"What's wrong, honey?"

She swallowed once, then spoke in a shaky voice. "We nearly lost Brian."

6:18 P.M.

Cal was late and it was his fault. After he'd pulled out of his drive-way and driven two blocks, he turned around and went back home to change his clothes. Who was he kidding, wearing a pinstripe, three-piece suit and tie for his dinner date with Leona? He concluded he looked like a geek, felt like a phony, and smelled like a mothball. Now he was late, but at least it was Cal Spencer ringing Leona's doorbell.

When Leona came to the door, Cal blinked and whistled. "Hey, look at you."

Leona, who often wore her hair in a ponytail and under a baseball cap, was showing Cal a new side. She'd combed her blonde hair out full; it was frizzy on the sides, and she reminded Cal of a movie star at a theatrical premiere. She wore a dark patterned silk dress with three-quarter-length sleeves. The collar was full and buttoned at the top. Around her waist was a black leather belt, two-inches wide, with a sil-ver buckle. and on her left wrist she wore a silver watch and a strand of pearls. "Do I have the councilman's vote of approval," she teased, "or your usual dissenting opinion?"

Cal laughed. "I'm lucky you're still here."

"Why is that?" she asked as she closed and locked the door.

"If someone else had shown up on time, it would've served me right to spend New Year's Eve alone."

They walked down a stairway outside her garden apartment. "I thought you were one of those on-time-kind-of-guys. Didn't Alan Carter do a story once on town council members who were late to meetings?"

With all that had happened, Cal was impressed she remembered. "Yes, he did. You've got a good memory."

"The mayor got low marks. What about you?"

They crossed the parking lot to his car, a white Toyota 4Runner. "I try never to be late, but only because I don't trust those maniacs."

"Why is that?"

Cal opened the passenger door for Leona. "No telling what crazy schemes they'd pass if I wasn't there."

"Like the hot air balloon?"

"Not even I could stop that," he said and closed her door. He climbed into his side of the car, buckled his seatbelt, and turned to look at her. "OK, ready to close out the old year?"

"No."

"Why?" he asked, confused.

She smiled. "You haven't voted yet."

"On what?"

"On me, silly."

"A resounding, yes!" he said with relief. "You look terrific."

"Thank you, Councilman Spencer. I may vote for you in the next election."

"You don't live in my district."

She dismissed his comment with a wave of her hand. "Petty details."

Cal started the car and drove out of the parking lot and into the street. He was feeling good. He'd never met anyone like Leona in his life. She was—well, she was so real. "Any public comment on my attire?" he asked, looking straight ahead.

He felt her eyes giving him the once-over. After what seemed like a full minute, she said, "I'm glad you went casual."

"Well, that doesn't tell me much."

"Nice shirt, cool vest, OK pants. But you don't need that tiger tooth around your neck."

Cal reached for the chain, ripped it loose, and tossed it over his shoulder into the back seat. He looked at her and smiled. "Thanks. I thought it was dumb too."

"You didn't tell me where we were going for dinner," she said.

"I thought we'd return to where we had our first date."

"You mean where my car blew up?"

He laughed. "No, not Denny's. How about if we start the evening at Casa de Benny's and . . ." he paused, grinning sheepishly, "and end it with Little Richard?"

"Little Richard? I thought you were against the concert. Is this a double standard, Councilman Spencer?" she teased.

Cal gave her a guilty smile. "I have to support the town," he reasoned, "and besides, I can't wait to hear him."

Leona rubbed her hands together in glee. "Me too."

———— •◦• ————

6:32 P.M.

"I gotta save some room for the meal," Rick Aguilara said, as he dipped a tortilla chip into a bowl of red salsa. "But these are great." He bit into the chip with a loud crunch, then pushed the basket of chips away from his plate. "If I reach for any more, slap my hand, OK?"

Shelly studied Rick from across the table. Seven months ago, she was convinced he was the most obnoxious stump of a drifter she'd ever met. He was still a shrimp and not likely to settle down. After nearly running him over four days ago and the ensuing loud exchange, she figured the next time she saw him would be too soon. But, over the past two days, Shelly had seemed to run into him everywhere—at the supermarket, the gas station, and then in the offices of *The Banner*. They were either on the same path marked "coincidence," or Rick was following her. That morning, he'd asked her out, and now they were sharing tortilla chips and salsa. Shelly was fascinated at how quickly her feelings toward Rick had changed. She now regarded him in a new light. Instead of feeling repulsed, she felt alive just by being around him.

"Earth to Shelly Hinson."

"What?" she said, jarred back to the present.

Rick leaned over the table and waved his right hand in front of her face. "Earth to Shelly Hinson, please come in."

Shelly smiled. "Sorry, what did you say?"

"Never mind. It's time to eat."

Shelly looked up to see a young waitress standing next to their table wearing oven mitts and holding two large platters of food. "These are very hot," she said, placing the plates in front of Shelly and Rick. "Are you OK on iced tea?" When they both nodded, the woman said, "Enjoy your meals. I'll check back to see if everything is all right."

Rick had ordered nacho chips with generous amounts of melted cheddar cheese and carne asada on top. Shelly's selection was chicken and cheese enchiladas, refried beans, and Spanish rice.

"I guess you could say this is the last supper," Rick said, digging for a cheese-covered piece of steak.

"What's that supposed to mean?" Shelly asked with a start.

"Our final meal of the year," he answered with a sneaky smile.

She couldn't conceal her relief. "For a second, I thought perhaps you might be moving on."

"Not yet," he grunted while chewing on his food. "I kinda like this town." He motioned toward her with his head. "And, I might add, one particular young lady who looks better than a polished hog."

Shelly laughed. "From one Harley lover to another, I'll take that as the ultimate compliment." She nervously adjusted her blouse, the same one she'd worn months ago over lunch with Lance Milburn. She felt different with Rick. With Lance, she was on guard—always struggling for the right words. She never let her defenses down. But with Rick, even on their first date, she sensed no need to worry about what she said or having to put on a show. She could just be herself and she liked that.

Rick took a bite of his nachos, then winked at Shelly. "I'm also glad you don't have to spoon-feed me."

"Why would I do that?" she asked, wondering what Rick's latest off-the-wall comment meant.

"Four days ago, you almost turned me into road-kill."

Shelly shuddered at the memory of Rick suddenly flashing in front of her car, then skidding on his Harley into the chain link fence. An ugly purple and red abrasion still showed on his left cheek. "Well, at least you're in one piece. Did you ever get to where you were going?"

"Yep." Rick laughed. "They must have been desperate for construction workers, 'cause I looked like I'd just been in a fight. But the foreman hired me on the spot."

"You mean 'Biceps' Bidwell?"

Rick grinned. "Is that what you call him?"

Shelly nodded. "He's a weight-lifting nut I went to high school with. He's the mayor's cousin—handles most of 'Hiz Honor's' projects. Easier to keep track of money that comes under the table."

"Sounds like you've got the inside track on a lot of things," Rick said. He held out blistered palms, then smiled. "Well, he hired me. I'm working my fingers to the bone."

Shelly reached out to touch Rick's arm. "If you want to keep the bones on your fingers, just make sure you stay clear of my car."

As they were laughing, Shelly's attention was drawn to the front of the restaurant. Cal Spencer and Leona Kyle had just walked into the restaurant. The hostess pointed in Shelly's direction, then Cal and Leona were holding hands and following the hostess across the room.

Shelly watched Cal and Leona move through the crowded, noisy restaurant. Cal stopped and greeted people along the way. It was good politics, but it was also good manners. That's the way she remembered Cal before he ran for office; he hadn't changed after he was elected. Most people liked him and his sometimes quirky but always independent ways, even if he ruffled the feathers of some business leaders. Now, he was politely introducing Leona to his friends, his left hand touching her gently on the back of her dress and his right hand gesturing to the person she was meeting. Old pangs of jealousy briefly surfaced, then to her surprise, quickly retreated as she watched the man she'd targeted and missed. If she read Cal's body language correctly, he had fallen for the new school teacher. Let her have him, she decided.

When Cal was three booths away, Shelly looked up and their eyes met. He seemed surprised and glad to see her, smiling and nodding at the same time. Shelly returned his pleasantry while Rick worked on his nachos carne asada.

"Hello, Shelly," Cal said from afar. He seemed to be straining to see into the booth.

"Hi Cal, hello Leona," she greeted. "Happy New Year."

"You really look great tonight," Cal said, craning his neck to see her dinner partner. "I was wondering who your—" Cal's mouth dropped open when he saw Rick.

Rick peered around the booth. "How's it goin' Calsterino?" he asked with a sly grin.

Cal was obviously at a loss for words. "I, uh, well—I didn't expect you to be with—to be with Shelly."

"Well, shoot, Mr. Council Member," Rick quickly replied, "sometimes women just have to settle for the bottom of the barrel." He looked up at Leona. "Isn't that true, Miss Kyle?" Leona began to say something, but stopped herself.

Shelly put her hand over her mouth to suppress a giggle. Cal's eyes narrowed, and he glared at Rick, then gave Shelly a confused look. Without another word, Cal turned and half directed, half-pushed Leona to their booth.

Rick leaned across the table. Thankfully, the mariachi music in the restaurant was loud enough to keep others from hearing them. "Hey, what's his problem? Do I have salsa on my nose?"

Shelly laughed, but before she could respond, they were interrupted. "Is everything OK with your meal?"

She looked up into Ozzie Theodore's smiling face. "Hi Ozzie, everything's great." She gestured to Rick. "Have you met Rick before?"

Rick nodded at Ozzie who smiled and said, "Never actually met him, but I've heard him and his motorcycle."

"To hear me is to love me," Rick said in return. "Pleased to meet you."

Ozzie was dressed casually. A white name tag with red letters was pinned to his shirt: "Ozzie, Assistant Manager." She remembered Benny's announcement Christmas Eve and pointed to Ozzie's name tag. "Looks like your promotion came a day early. Congratulations, Assistant Manager, I'm impressed."

"Well, don't be. The name tag doesn't mean I can manage—it only tells people who to blame when something goes wrong."

Shelly and Rick laughed at Ozzie's honesty. She marveled at how he'd changed. He'd stumbled into town only six months ago, homeless and probably hopeless.

Just then, Benny approached their table and placed his arm around Ozzie's shoulders. "Well, folks, what do you think?" he asked beaming. "I'd say I found myself a pretty good right-hand man."

"That's not saying much, Benny," Ozzie retorted, winking at Shelly and Rick, "considering I'm left-handed."

Benny was caught off guard for a split second, then he bellowed in laughter, causing every person in the restaurant to look their way.

———— ·•· ————

An hour later, Shelly and Rick stood outside the restaurant, hand in hand. "It's not too cold," Shelly said. "We've still got some time before the concert. Mind if we walk?"

"Sure, as long as you let my Harley know it's nothing personal."

Shelly shook her head as they began strolling down the sidewalk. It was a few minutes before nine, and a light mist hung in the air—the promise of a foggy night. "Tell me, will you ever make it through a conversation without a joke?"

He thought for a moment. "I can think of at least once when that might happen."

"I'd like to be there. When might that be?"

Rick released her hand and put his arm around her shoulder. He squeezed her arm tenderly. "When I tell a woman I love her."

A shiver went through Shelly, and it wasn't from the coastal fog. She dared not look at him.

They walked in silence for a few moments, then he added, "It could be sooner than I ever imagined."

Shelly felt as if someone had lifted her off the ground.

That night, after the concert, Shelly and Rick shared a bowl of popcorn on the tattered sofa in Shelly's apartment. Outside, others in her apartment complex could be heard bringing in the New Year with raucous laughter, loud music, and booze.

There on the sofa, quietly, the two of them made a New Year's Eve resolution; they promised to get to know each other in the months to come. Rick seemed to share Shelly's search for a deeper meaning to life. They were both wanting to know more about their purpose on earth, and only Rick seemed to have an idea where God might fit in. It was a fuzzy memory, but during junior high school, a neighbor had taken an interest in him and paid for him to attend a church camp. He couldn't recall many details, but he remembered making some kind of a religious decision. After that, he didn't have time for church or the people who, as he put it, "dusted the pews every Sunday."

The two openly shared with one another their lives from early childhood, baring many secrets that had remained dormant until now. Some were intensely personal.

Shelly was amazed at how she seemed able to unlock closet after closet in her heart for Rick as she never had with anyone else before. He seemed touched by her willingness to trust him and in turn revealed much about himself.

Images of the past year replayed in her mind. She remembered her euphoria when she opened the letter from Lance Milburn approving her project. She recalled the day the article came out and how growth and prosperity had gradually come to Braxton. She saw in her mind's eye the faces of newcomers who had moved there. Then came the horror the day after Christmas—the balloon crash, the dead bodies, the funeral, and Nick Martinez' spiritual declaration: to be undecided, is to be decided. She saw Heather Landis' bandaged eyes and Alan Carter's painful smile—so many tears, so much—

Someone was calling to her from a distance. She wanted to tell the person to go away. Blinking twice, she saw Rick.

"Happy New Year, Shelly, it's midnight." He drew her near and gently kissed her on the lips. He held her cheeks with both hands and then kissed her again. She put her arms around his waist and pressed close to his body. Outside the apartment, Braxton's fireworks finale popped in the night.

Shelly snuggled in Rick's arms. "*Harley* New Year to you. I'm in hog heaven."

"Hey, I think I've met my match."

"What? No joke in return?" she teased.

"You know the woman I was talking about at dinner?"

"Uh-huh."

"I may have met her."

CHAPTER 32

MISS KYLE

Leona wrote her name in bold letters with a blue marker pen on a white board, underlined it, and turned to face her English class at Braxton High School. She took a deep breath to calm her nerves and summoned what she hoped would be a natural smile. "Good morning," she said to those students seated in front of her and the two who were now ambling through the door. Twenty-five faces stared back at her.

Leona walked from the white board to her desk. "My name is Leona Kyle, and I'm your new English teacher. For those of you who hadn't heard, Mrs. Aronson is going to have surgery next week, so it's you and me for the second semester." She looked at the notes on her desk and cleared her throat.

"Is she going to croak?" came the nasal voice of a student in the back. A few of the other students giggled.

Leona looked in the direction of the voice. She couldn't be sure who had spoken since she didn't know any of her students. "Thanks for your touching concern," she said. "I believe she'll be just fine."

"You sure dress better than Mrs. Aronson," one girl said with a smirk.

Leona had chosen a casual outfit for her first day—a soft khaki French linen shirt with oversized front flap pockets and black stirrup pants. She'd turned her collar up and pushed the shirt sleeves to her forearms.

"Thanks. I just hope I teach as well as Mrs. Aronson."

"It won't take much to do that." The nasal voice again and more giggles from the class.

Leona was not amused and traded her nervousness for a fleeting moment of panic. She'd looked forward to teaching in a small town, especially this small town, supposedly the best in America. However, the first few minutes with her new class were far less than what she'd anticipated.

Just then, she sensed a sudden movement to her right. She turned to see a can of Pepsi tumble to the hardwood floor, the liquid pouring out and foaming down the aisle.

"That was my drink, you idiot!" one girl screamed as she jumped up and let go a stream of obscenities at the boy in front of her.

"OK, enough," Leona ordered, trying to hide her shock. As tough as the junior high was in San Diego, she'd never heard an outburst of profanity like this in a classroom before. She pointed to the boy with the nasal voice, a pimply-faced punk with long greasy hair. "You, Mr. Wisenheimer, go to the bathroom, and get some paper towels." Leona stared hard at her students, silently daring any one of them to make the next move. "We haven't gotten off to a very good start," she said as the boy left the room. "In fact, I'd say it's as lousy a start as one could have." She began walking to the rear of the room. Most turned in their seats to watch her, some kept looking straight ahead, and Leona heard a few whispers. "Beginning right now, things are going to change. All of you have had your little laugh." Leona pointed to the girl who had cursed. She was slightly overweight with spiked purple hair and two rings in her nose. "What's your name?"

"Madonna." A few muffled laughs.

"That figures," Leona said, "your mouth is as filthy as hers. But can you sing?" A few students ooohed at her put-down. She waited for a smart comeback, but the girl said nothing. "Madonna here, or whatever her name is, gets an 'A' for giving us an example of the kind of language I never want to hear in this class again."

"Booorrring." One girl slouched down in her seat and gave a loud yawn.

Leona glanced briefly at the girl, decided she'd had enough of the students' insolence, and walked to the front of the room. The boy who had gone in search of paper towels now returned along with a smirk. "What do I do with these, *Leona*?"

"You can begin by calling me Miss Kyle. Then you can use a towel to wipe that smirk off your face and give the rest to toilet-tongued Madonna. She can clean up her mess."

"I didn't spill it!" the foul-mouthed girl protested.

"Tough," Leona answered. "You shouldn't have brought the can into the room. That's another rule you just taught the class—no food or drink in the classroom. Got it?"

The girl mumbled something and shoved a towel toward the spill.

"I'm going to call your names now in alphabetical order for assigned seats." Leona found a class roster tucked inside her grade book and began to call out names. "Curt Baker, Darlene Baldwin—" The students began to grumble, but she continued. "Baker, get your books and bring them up here." She pointed to where she wanted him to sit. "This is your desk." The boy slowly got to his feet. "Come on, we don't have all day. Connie, you're next."

"Mrs. Aronson let us sit anywhere we wanted," one boy whined.

"Oh, so now she wasn't so bad, huh?" Leona returned. "Well, until you start acting like high schoolers, you'll have assigned seats." She returned to her list. "Pablo Cortez, Jody Ecklund . . ."

For the next ten minutes, Leona directed her students to their new desks writing each person's name on a seating chart as she did so. She felt control shifting back her way.

Once everyone was settled, Leona passed out a syllabus that outlined the class schedule and assignments. She then told the class about her background and why she'd moved to Braxton. "I want to be here, and I hope that will be the same for you."

Several students grimaced. "Right," the boy directly in front of her mocked.

"No kidding. I want you to look forward to coming to this room every day."

"Dream on, teach," a surly looking boy toward the back of the room spoke up.

Leona stared at the thin young man with curly red hair. She glanced down at her seating chart. "Am I talking with Brian Stanley?"

"Yeah."

Brian wore a white crew neck T-shirt and a red windbreaker. Leona thought his tousled hair had a 1950's look to it. "I hear you're the son of Pete Stanley, the baseball Hall of Famer."

"No, he's the *father* of Brian Stanley." The class laughed, and this time Leona joined in. "Good way to look at it, Brian." She walked closer to his desk. "What would it take to make writing assignments in this class fun?" No one spoke. "Brian, your vocal chords are still warm—how about an answer?"

"If we wrote about cool people, maybe."

"And who would that be?"

"James Dean."

Leona returned to the front of the class. "OK, that's your first assignment. Write a paper—five pages, typewritten and double-spaced on James Dean."

"Cool," he said with a grin.

Leona scanned the other students. "For the rest of you, pick a 'cool' person and do the same. Put it on paper and have it on my desk one week from today."

A buzzer made Leona jump. She glanced at the clock and with a sigh of relief, realized she'd made it through her first class in one piece.

————•—•————

Mayor's office
9:05 A.M.

Shelly Hinson was already halfway through her twelve-month secret assignment for Lance Milburn and *Destination* magazine. Since her article was released more than six months earlier, she'd seen definite changes in her hometown. Some of these changes were positive ones, but she knew the story had brought tragedy, pain, and suffering. Several nagging questions wouldn't leave her alone. If she had never written the story, would the seven people killed in the hot air balloon crash still be alive? Had she put Alan Carter and Heather Landis in Braxton Hospital's burn unit? Would Heather lose her sight? Shelly didn't want to think about it. The images of the fiery balloon crash were a terrible memory that haunted her each day.

"Shelly, what do we gain by reporting this?" Mayor Roger Carter's words made her blink. He was seated behind his desk holding a ballpoint pen in his right hand, and nervously rolling it over and over. The latest crime statistics from the Braxton Police Department were spread out in front of him.

Shelly Hinson, at her editor's direction, was writing a story for Thursday's edition, an article similar to the one for *Destination* magazine. She fidgeted in her chair, sensing the mayor was trying to control the news as only Roger Carter could. But then who was she to talk about ethics? "The crime stats are public record," she said weakly. "Shouldn't the people know?"

The mayor tossed his pen on the paper. "Of course. We've got nothing to hide, but I'd just as soon let this remain on file. If someone wants to look it up, fine, but why get everyone all worked up over nothing?"

"Seems to me that a forty percent increase in crime over the last six months isn't exactly 'nothing.'"

Carter sniffed at the numbers. "Of course. Growth always means the import of a few bad apples. I think Chief Wells will get us back where we want to be—and a few months from now, you'll see this was nothing."

"And how is she going to get rid of those bad apples?" Shelly asked.

"Come on, Shelly," Mayor Carter said impatiently, "put a positive face on our hometown. Write about the new pride we feel, more jobs, new housing, new residents, new—"

"What about more traffic, noise, ripped up streets, inadequate sewage treatment, crowded classrooms, increased air pollution—"

"All part of progress." The mayor put on an earnest expression. "Some things have to be sacrificed."

"Like your son."

The mayor lurched forward. "What a rotten thing to say!"

Shelly bristled. "No more rotten than what Alan uncovered. It's been ten days now since the balloon crash. The information I have is this: You knew there were problems with the balloon company—but ignored it."

"Be careful where you're heading, Shelly. You're getting close to libel."

Shelly shook her head. "Forget me. Your son is the one who was close—but he was nearing the truth, not libel. We think he'd only scratched the surface with the article we printed."

"Don't you wish," the mayor pooh-poohed.

Shelly studied the mayor. Was his bravado real? "I believe Alan was ready to break this story and your administration wide open."

"Where's the beef?" the mayor said as he stood. "You haven't shown me proof." He pointed a stubby finger at her. "All that you and your two-bit paper have is one of Alan's computer disks. And you stumbled on that. He did some digging and found that the balloon company was

still under F.A.A. suspension. I'm proud of him, that's good reporting."
The mayor jutted his double chin toward Shelly. "You could learn a few
things from him. Why didn't you know the F.A.A. angle?"

"You're right, Mayor, I'd like to learn a lot more from him. We think
there were other disks, perhaps at home." She paused and waited for a
response. When none came, she asked, "I don't suppose you know
where they are, do you?"

A sly grin edged its way onto the mayor's face. "I haven't the slightest idea what you're talking about."

CHAPTER 33

Sunday, January 8, 6:59 P.M.

Pete Stanley propped two pillows against the arm of the sofa in his family room, then picked up the remote control and switched on the television. A Pine Mountain fire log burned neatly on its own in the fireplace and would do so for the next three hours. It was one of the concessions Pete had gladly made since coming to California. Firewood was a pain to get in Braxton, and he hated the hassle of keeping it burning. The log, made of wax, sawdust, and color crystals, wasn't nearly as romantic as a real chunk of wood, crackling, popping, and giving its best before turning to ashes, but it surely was easier. Beatrice walked into the room then, carrying some papers. She looked serious.

"Where's Brian?" she asked.

Pete sighed. "I have no idea. Hey, I want to watch '60 Minutes.' Can we talk about this later?" He turned back to the TV as the "60 Minutes" stopwatch started its familiar *tick, tick, tick, tick, tick, tick.*

"No," she said and pointed at the remote control in his hand. "Turn it off, please." She held up the paper. "I want you to read this."

Pete made an exaggerated gesture of pushing the power button. The screen went black. He held out his hand toward the paper. "OK, give it to me. What is it?"

"I took some clean laundry into Brian's room, and I saw this next to his computer. It's a report for one of his classes. I was curious to see how he's doing in school, so I read it. I think it's disturbing."

Pete's head jerked. "Disturbing? How can you say that? We should be thankful he did the assignment. Maybe he's beginning to turn things around."

Beatrice sat in a chair opposite Pete. "I thought so, too, until I read it. Go ahead, see what you think."

Pete looked at the title page:

> The Last Ride of James Dean
> by Brian Stanley

"I should have guessed," he said with a smile, then began reading.

James Dean was lucky. He never had to live in Braxton. He would have hated it. But his name will forever be linked to this area and this is why.

September 30, 1955, a silver Porsche 550 Spyder convertible sped west on Highway 466 (now called Highway 46). Two men were inside. The driver had purchased the seven-thousand-dollar car just eight days earlier. The number one hundred thirty was etched in black on the doors and front hood. LITTLE BASTARD was painted in red across the rear cowling. The driver wore a white T-shirt, light blue slacks, and sun glasses clipped on prescription lenses to correct nearsightedness. He was chain-smoking Chesterfields, and he had one minute to live.

At 5:44 P.M., the man at the wheel squinted as a spray of sunset loomed large on the horizon. His convertible streaked toward the intersection of Highway 466 and 41. "That guy up there's gotta stop," he said to his passenger. "He'll see us."

A blacktopped, white-hooded Ford sedan, heading east, was turning left from Highway 466 to Highway 41. The driver, twenty-three-year-old Donald Turnupseed (yes, that was his real name—he had to be a total nerd), was a college student at Cal Poly San Luis Obispo, and was driving home to see his parents. He later claimed he never saw the low profile sports car headed his way, until it was too late.

In the other car was an actor who, the day before, had completed filming his part in the movie *Giant*. Next to him sat twenty-eight-year-old Rolf Wutherich, his favorite mechanic from Competition Motors near Hollywood.

Was the driver testing his new Porsche for an upcoming racing event in Salinas, perhaps? No one will ever know.

Death would come at eighty-five to one-hundred-ten-miles an hour. It was 5:45 P.M., nine hundred yards east of the village of Cholame (pronounced "show-lamb," population sixty-five). The Ford turned, then tried to straighten out, but the wheels locked, and it slid thirty feet. The Porsche made a desperate attempt to swerve, and the cars crashed head-on into each other. Rolf Wutherich was ejected onto the highway, breaking his jaw, a leg, and suffering severe cuts and bruises. He survived.

For decades, the driver of the Porsche was blamed, but in 1997, an animated computer recreation of the accident suggested the Ford caused the crash.

Friends of the driver of the Porsche, following in another car, arrived on the scene and looked in horror at the mangled convertible off to the side of the road. They rushed to the car, their feet crunching through broken glass. The smell of gasoline, oil, rubber, and death was in the air.

Pete looked at his wife in amazement. "I didn't know Brian could write like this, did you?"

"Read on," she said, nodding.

The twenty-four-year-old driver was sprawled across the seat and slumped over the passenger door. His foot was pinned in the wreckage, mangled around the clutch and brake. Actor James Dean, his neck broken, had been killed instantly. One month earlier, while filming a highway safety commercial, he had said spoken these words: "Take it easy driving. The life you might save might be mine."

Donald Turnupseed suffered only cuts and bruises. He stumbled about the scene in shock, talked with investigators, then hitchhiked back home to Tulare.

Dean was taken by ambulance to Paso Robles War Memorial Hospital. He arrived at 6:20 P.M., and was pronounced dead on arrival. The cost for the ride was $56.14. James Dean had $33.03 in his pocket.

Less than one month later, Dean's film *Rebel Without a Cause* premiered, and on October 10, 1956, *Giant* opened in New York City. Found behind the seat of the crunched Porsche was Dean's red jacket, the same one worn in *Rebel*, the one he thought would bring him good luck.

Within a year after his death, James Dean, with two Academy Award nominations and just three films to his credit, became the biggest movie star in the world. His fans saw in him how they wanted to look, sound, act, and dress.

Rumors started circulating that Dean had escaped the fatal crash, but was so horribly disfigured, he went into hiding. They eventually fizzled out. He was dead, and when the wreckage of his Porsche was sent on a national tour, fans lined up, paying fifty cents apiece to sit behind the wheel of the car that crashed on Highway 466.

Today a small memorial sits just east of the intersection

where death came in a heartbeat. It was the dream of a Japanese man, Seita Ohnishi, who used fifteen thousand dollars of his own money to finance the project. The famed Hearst family donated the land for the monument. On a shaft of stainless steel, wrapped around the trunk of a tree, is a tribute to the late actor. The sculpture on the tree mirrors the bend in the road where James Dean was killed. A bronze plaque at the base of the monument reads: "Death in youth is life that glows eternal."

The tree on which the sculpture is mounted is native to China. It was planted in the 1880's during California's gold rush. Now it runs wild and is called a weed tree because it self-seeds. I like the tree's real name—Tree of Heaven.

James Dean was the coolest person who ever lived. No one else comes close. He died, but his spirit lives; every afternoon at sunset, it takes a ride on eastbound Highway 46. I know, because I've been with him.

Pete stared at the paper and tried to absorb what he had just read. "Amazing," was all he could say, still looking at the paper. "How could a kid write like this and be struggling with his classes?"

"Easy. He wrote about the most important thing in his life."

"Well, then there's no reason he can't do the same in his other classes." Beatrice looked at him and shook her head. "What?" he asked.

"You don't get it, do you?"

"Get what?"

Beatrice pointed to the paper. "Doesn't that scare you? Aren't you concerned about his little fantasy?"

Her incredulous, chilling suggestion boggled Pete's mind. "You think he's going to do the same? Come on."

"Buying that car was the worst thing you ever did for him, Pete."

She covered her face with her hands, then slid them down to reveal her eyes. "If you don't get rid of it . . ." But she couldn't finish. She got up and left the room.

CHAPTER 34

Thursday March 27
First day of spring, 12:15 P.M.

A fresh anticipation of spring blew in Shelly's face as she gripped Rick tightly around the waist. The Harley's seductive sound rumbled in her helmet. She didn't know much about the bike's mechanical refinements, only that Harleys were still the same basic rawboned, no-frills machines now as when they first hit the streets in 1957. On the back of a hog, clinging to Rick, roaring through her hometown—these were moments so intense, so personal—she knew Rick had no idea how cherished they were.

She'd met him at his job—the construction site of some new apartment buildings on the south side of town. The two of them would have lunch at Benny's. She'd left her car at the project site, welcoming the chance for a ride on Rick's hog. As they passed the infamous T-shaped intersection, where she'd nearly run him over, he pointed to it and with silent understanding, she grabbed him tighter around the waist. They couldn't talk freely on the Harley; the required helmets made it even more difficult. She hated the helmet—a forced imposition by do-good-er politicians who wouldn't be caught dead on a motorcycle. To Shelly, riding on a Harley was what living was all about.

To her left, Shelly could see the empty lot where the hot air balloon had crashed. Up on the grassy knoll, the media tent was long since removed, and weeds had grown up where fire had charred the hillside. Maybe it was just fate. Maybe those people would have been killed in another accident. Who could say she was to blame?

They rumbled by Braxton General Hospital. Shelly thought of Heather Landis, recovering on her own now in San Luis Obispo. Shelly had visited Heather a month earlier, ostensibly to do a follow-up story for *The Banner* and secretly for *Destination* magazine. But her real reason for visiting the news reporter was to check out in person the transformation she'd heard about from others.

A chill shot through her as she remembered knocking on Heather's apartment door that day. The door had opened slightly, and Heather had peered out through the six-inch opening. The woman, whose beauty was once so breathtaking, wore sun glasses, and bandages covered one entire side of her face. Her hair, burned off in the accident, had a long way to go before it could be styled.

"Hello, Shelly," Heather said with some degree of difficulty. "Please, come in."

Heather retreated to a dimly lit living room, leaving Shelly to open the door herself. "Thanks for letting me come," was all Shelly could think of to say as she stepped inside. "How are you doing?" she added.

Heather didn't answer, but walked to a sofa in the modestly furnished, dimly lit room and sat down, her legs curled under her. Heather wore a banana-colored, zip-front, nylon warmup with a stand-up collar. Her elastic waist pants had side pockets and zippered elastic ankles. All of these clothes made it impossible for Shelly to tell how badly burned she was. Heather picked up a cup and saucer from an end table and took a sip. "I'm sorry, how rude of me," she said. "May I get you some tea?"

It sounded good, but Shelly shook her head. She didn't want to make Heather move: even seated, it was obvious she was in pain. "That's nice of you, but I'll pass."

The women studied each other without speaking. Shelly didn't know where to begin: the guilt she felt for causing Heather's calamity was crushing.

"You asked how I'm doing," Heather said. "I often ask myself the same thing." She didn't sound at all like the egotistical, airhead Shelly had seen on Braxton's streets and in the town hall. "It's been three months since the—since the accident. Some days, I'd rather just forget."

"I noticed that you—well, you seem to be seeing OK," Shelly noted with some hesitation. "Can you—did they, ah—?"

Shelly was relieved when Heather stepped in. "Yes, the doctor's saved my sight." She motioned to the room. "I like to have the lights kept low. My eyes are still sensitive." Heather let out a tentative laugh, as if she knew the limit her emotion would allow without pain. "I know what you're thinking, and yes, being sensitive to light is not too good if you're hoping to be a TV news anchor."

"What are the chances of your resuming your career?" Heather didn't answer right away, and Shelly wondered if she'd been too blunt. But she had to know.

Heather considered the words, then, "My career?" She took a sip from her tea, then let out a sigh. "I've still got a lot of plastic surgery ahead of me. They've done some skin grafts, but that's only the beginning." She shrugged. "Who knows if I'll ever be able to go on the air again without breaking the camera." Shelly detected no bitterness in Heather.

"I'm sure you will," Shelly said.

"You're sure I'll break the camera?" Heather asked with a laugh.

"No, no—I meant you'll be able to—"

Heather waved a hand at her. "I know what you meant. I'm just teasing."

"Thanks, I feel like an idiot."

"Don't worry about it. I needed a good laugh."

"I'm not sure I could take this as well as you have," Shelly admitted.

"You never know until it happens to you," Heather said. "But as hideous as all of this has been, it's kind of a wake up call for me, Shelly. At one time, my career was the most important thing in my life. I never thought about the needs of others. I figured it was everyone for themselves. Well, that's not true. Without some very special people, I'd have never made it."

So, what others had told her about Heather was true. She was a different person—more beautiful on the inside than what she had ever been on the outside.

Heather's eyes fixed upon her, but Shelly glanced away, suddenly feeling the burden of guilt for what she'd done to her. "I told you that the doctor saved my eye. But thanks to a wonderful person, something more important has been saved through all of this."

"What was that?"

"I asked Jesus to come into my heart. He saved my soul."

Old, uncomfortable feelings replaced whatever sympathy Shelly felt and she only wanted to leave. Religion was the last thing she wanted to talk about with Heather. But her instinct as a reporter was piqued by curiosity. "Who was this *wonderful* person?"

"She visited me in the hospital and shared her faith with me when I came home." Heather pointed toward a Bible. "She showed me in the Bible how God promises peace and assurance." Heather's voice turned feathery. "I'm a Christian now, Shelly—my life has changed. This sounds crazy, but had the balloon not crashed, I'd still be lost."

Heather's words did nothing to take away Shelly's guilt, and she still wondered about the mystery woman. "So, who was it?"

"She's new in town. Her name is Leona Kyle." Heather reached for the Bible, then looked directly at Shelly. "Would you like to know how Jesus can give you peace?"

Rick's motorcycle accelerated through an intersection, bringing Shelly back to the present. They passed First Baptist Church, and she thought of Pastor Nick Martinez and his wife, Karen. In January, Karen had given birth to a boy—six pounds, eleven ounces. Cute as a bug, but a weird name—Caleb. Someone had told Shelly it was a biblical name. Then her warm thoughts of the baby turned to ice. *To be undecided, is to be decided.* She couldn't erase from her mind those seven words Nick Martinez had spoken at the cemetery on the morning of Chief Talbot's funeral. *To be undecided, is to be decided.* Shelly hated how Nick's words invaded her mind without warning. Apparently, Leona was one of those who had *decided* to be decided about Jesus. And now, Heather had made her decision to—how was it put—give her heart to Jesus? Shelly wondered what Rick would say about this.

Braxton's town hall came into view over Rick's shoulder, and Shelly remembered the mayor's son. Alan, critically injured when the hot air balloon crashed into the media tent, was making steady progress. The doctors believed he could return to school in two weeks.

Shelly had visited Alan frequently in the hospital and to a lesser extent once he'd gone home. While most people considered Alan's recovery a complete success, she knew otherwise. The teenager's mental scars went far deeper than any physical wounds. She wondered if it was because of what he'd uncovered on the balloon company, or what he knew about his father's involvement. But since the accident, the normally talkative, outgoing young man had become withdrawn and morose. And if there were more computer disks than the one she had found at *The Banner's* office, Alan wouldn't say.

Rick's motorcycle pulled to the curb of Casa de Benny's now. As usual, a line of people stood outside the restaurant. A few of the locals eyed the motorcycle and gave Shelly and Rick dirty looks. Shelly marveled how something that sounded so wonderful could make people so hostile. Rick waited for a moment before turning off the engine. He'd told her once that riders like the handlebars to shake when they're stopped so everyone can see it.

"Do we have time to eat and get you back to work on time?" Shelly shouted as she hopped off the back of the Harley.

Rick turned off the engine, removed his helmet, and shook his hair. Then he smoothed it back with his hand. "Yeah, we've got until 1:30—ever since Benny put Ozzie in charge, you get in and out of here a lot faster at lunch." Rick put the kickstand down. "I'm starved."

"You're illegally parked, biker-boy!" The amplified voice came over a loudspeaker. Shelly looked across the street to see Sergeant Blake Hesterman sitting in his squad car. "Move it out of the red zone," he continued, "or I'll have it towed."

Shelly and Rick looked at the curb—the Harley was a foot inside the red paint. She couldn't believe how petty Hesterman was acting. Suddenly Rick whirled to face Hesterman. He thrust out his right arm, clicked his boots together, and yelled at the top of his lungs, "*Sieg heil*, *Sieg heil*! Yes, *mein furher*!"

It was all Hesterman needed. The officer bolted from his squad car and, without looking, started across the street. A passing pickup skidded and swerved to miss him. The crowd outside the restaurant gasped as Hesterman jumped out of the way and fell hard to the pavement.

"You, dirt bag," Hesterman sneered as he picked himself up off the street. He brushed off his trousers, then took what looked like a traffic citation booklet from his shirt pocket as he approached the pair. "Let me see your driver's license, proof of insurance, and title to this pile of bolts."

Rick reached into his back pocket and pulled out his wallet. "Slow day at the Gestapo, *Herr* Hesterman?" he asked.

"Don't push me, Aguilara," the sergeant threatened. "And take the license out of your wallet."

Shelly sighed. "Blake, haven't you got anything better to do?"

"Stay out of it. What you see in this low-life, I'll never know."

Hesterman yanked the driver's license from Rick's hand. "OK, runt, where's your title and proof of insurance?"

"Probably at home, officer *pick-of-the-litter*."

"The law requires you to keep it on your person."

"*On your person*—very impressive, Barney Fyfe. You learn that in a correspondence course?" Guffaws of laughter from the crowd again. Even Shelly couldn't hold back a giggle.

Hesterman's face turned bright red. "You're under arrest!" He took hold of Rick's arm and tried to handcuff him.

"For what?" Rick protested, jerking his arm away.

"Unlawful operation of a motor vehicle, disturbing the peace—" Hesterman said, grabbing him with both hands. "Resisting arrest, threatening a peace officer—"

Suddenly everything turned chaotic as the two men began to scuffle. They somehow got their legs tangled, and as they fell to the ground, Hesterman began punching Rick in the head. Rick used his helmet to ward off the blows. Rick was on his back on the sidewalk, and Hesterman was on top of him, pinning his arms under his knees. Then he slugged Rick in the mouth. Rick managed to jerk one arm free, reach for his helmet, and swing it at the officer. Shelly watched in disbelief as the policeman unsnapped the holster of his service revolver. She turned to the crowd for help, but they were all just standing there, frozen in shock.

"Stop it, both of you!" Shelly yelled and then, *Boom!* Hesterman stared at his gun, and then in confusion at Rick. Rick's hands, gripped tightly on Hesterman's arms, now slid off and flopped to the sidewalk. Shelly screamed as she saw a widening circle of red forming on the front of Rick's T-shirt.

———— •◆• ————

12:55 P.M.

When Gina Wells found out one of her officers had shot someone, she didn't have to be told who it was. Blake Hesterman was the first name that came to mind.

As she arrived at the scene, the chief saw her patrol lieutenant walk up She knew a homicide detective would be close behind. Then she spotted Hesterman. His back was to her, and he was helping officers loop yellow tape between parking meters to cordon off the area. A crowd of about fifty curious onlookers talked animatedly and pointed to the victim. A body lay on the sidewalk—Rick Aguilara.

Gina walked closer and saw that the front of Aguilara's T-shirt was thick with blood. His eyes were open, seemingly fixed on the gray sky, and his lips were slightly parted, perhaps his last attempt at a word before he died.

"Chief, this dirt bag attacked me for no reason!" Hesterman said, getting up in Gina's face, waving his arms, and spilling his version of what happened. "It was self defense—" He pointed to the crowd. "I got witnesses. It wasn't—"

"Shut up, Hesterman!" Gina motioned with her head. "Get away from the crime scene. Now!" She stared dully at Aguilara's body, then at Hesterman. Gina could recall a number of confrontations between the two men. In most cases, Rick's sharp wit rendered Hesterman help-less and made him look like a buffoon in front of others. As far as Gina was concerned, Rick was just the opposite of the biker rebel image he projected. Instead, she considered him a carefree, spirited guy who made her laugh. He called her "Mother Law." He had used the term in a derogatory way at first, but when they got to know each other, the moniker stuck. In return, Gina called him, "Brother Outlaw." Now he was dead.

She motioned to an officer standing nearby. "Randall, take Hesterman inside the restaurant and stay with him." She turned back to Hesterman. "You're on administrative leave."

"But, Chief, you gotta hear what happened," the sergeant protested.

"I gave you an order." Gina pointed to the restaurant. "Find a table and wait inside." Gina turned to another officer standing by the body. "Get a plastic sheet, close his eyes, and cover him up."

Gina noticed Shelly seated on a bench. She returned Gina's look with a blank stare. "Did you see what happened?" the chief asked.

Shelly nodded.

"Has anyone questioned you yet?"

She shook her head.

Gina sighed, then directed officers to gather evidence, take photos, and confiscate Hesterman's .9 semi-automatic pistol. She motioned to Shelly, and the two went into Benny Green's restaurant.

Benny met the women as they walked inside. "Shelly, I'm really sorry about Rick. I know how special he was to you."

Shelly choked her thanks.

"Benny," Gina said, "we need a place that's private."

"Sure, use my office." Benny led them through the nearly empty restaurant.

Maggie stood at the door to Benny's office. She approached Shelly and took her hands. "I'm so sorry, Shelly," she said gently. "I'm praying that God will help you through this."

Shelly bristled and jerked her hands away from Maggie. "Don't talk to me about God, Maggie. I've had it up to here with . . ." She didn't finish, just shook her head.

Maggie stepped back, a look of understanding on her face. "That's OK, girl. I'm here any time you want—and, so's the Lord."

Once inside the office, Gina shut the door and chided herself for not supporting Maggie's attempt at spiritual comfort. Of course, it was unprofessional to mix religion with her job. But she could have said something—anything.

Shelly had taken a seat along the wall, next to some black metal filing cabinets. Gina pulled a folding chair up next to her. "Someone from homicide will be coming to talk with you. I just wanted to get you away from the scene, OK?"

Shelly nodded, then began pouring out the events that led to the confrontation. It wasn't normal procedure for a witness to do this, but Shelly was Gina's friend and talking about it seemed to help. Gina took notes on a pad as Shelly spoke, asking an occasional question or clarifying a point. There wasn't much to say.

"That's it. It happened so fast. Rick should have let Blake take him away, but Blake was way out of line. A lot of people will back me up."

"We'll talk with them," Gina promised.

"Rick never said a word—and I never told him I—" She broke down then. "I never told him how much I cared for him." She buried her head in her hands and wept.

Gina looked at her notebook. Investigators would question Shelly, and they would get Sergeant Hesterman's version. But knowing Blake Hesterman, Gina figured she'd just heard the most accurate explanation. "OK, Shelly, as I said, other people will talk with you." She pulled a Kleenex out of a box on Benny's desk and handed it to Shelly.

Shelly took the tissue. "So many horrible things have happened in our town," she said. "If only—"

"If only what?" Gina prodded.

Shelly shook her head. "Nothing."

CHAPTER 35

Cal's restaurant selection that evening struck Leona as odd: convenient, fast, easy on the budget, but not especially atmospheric. She put down the five-page cardboard menu and looked at Cal across the table. He was nervous, fidgety, with beads of sweat on his upper lip. He was dressed more formally than usual, wearing a brown tweed sport coat and an uncharacteristic necktie with a white buttoned-down shirt. One side of his collar was unbuttoned, but Leona liked him too much to point it out.

Cal raised his eyebrows and with a quick nod, gestured to the surroundings. "You probably wonder why I picked this place," he said in a low voice. "Not exactly a place for gastronomical delights."

Denny's was Braxton's only twenty-four-hour restaurant. "You're right," she said, wanting to put him at ease. She'd noticed he'd started curling the corners of his paper napkin. "No gastronomical delights, but I've had a few meals here that gave me gas."

Cal's laugh echoed out of the booth, causing a couple nearby to turn their way, then glance at each other, obviously not appreciating the raucous outburst. Her remark lightened the moment, but Leona chided herself for the crass comment, especially after Rick's Aguilara's shocking death just hours earlier.

"What's going to happen to Blake Hesterman?" she asked, hoping to bring the conversation back to a more serious tone.

"Officially, the investigation is ongoing—"

"And unofficially?"

"I think Hesterman is in big trouble. He may face criminal charges, and the word is that Chief Wells is ready to melt his badge."

"Good-bye, officer redneck?"

Cal nodded. *"Adieu."*

"Any word on how Shelly is doing?

"I called her just before I picked you up." He stroked his beard, then shook his head. "She's devastated."

"Rick's family?" Leona asked.

"Odd story," Cal answered. "Shelly told me Rick's father abandoned him after he was born, and he lost track of his mom years ago. Apparently, he had no relatives. Only person he was close to was Shelly."

"Funeral arrangements?"

"None. Shelly wants no service." Cal paused, then looked puzzled. "She told me something strange. She wants him buried as close to Chief Talbot and his wife as possible. Any idea why?" He waited for her to answer, but Leona had no idea what that was about.

Their waitress appeared then, pencil and order pad in hand. "Have you decided what you want?"

Cal ordered for both of them. Fish and chips for Leona, but she tilted her head in surprise when he chose Denny's high end of the menu, prime rib, for himself. Over the past several months, whenever they'd dined out, he always picked the cheapest entrees for himself, but encouraged her to do the opposite. Something was definitely going on.

Three months had passed since Leona and her sputtering, smoking Toyota rolled to a stop in Braxton. Cal Spencer was the first person she'd met that night, and she appreciated how kind and generous he had been to her since then. He had helped her find a new car, and an apartment, and had made her feel welcome in a town that did not eagerly embrace newcomers. He hadn't pushed for physical intimacy, although in recent weeks they'd enjoyed some passionate embraces. Once was at his apartment while watching, of all things, "The Simpsons." The other was during a picnic on the beach at Santa Maria.

They actually had many mutual interests. Each loved the intangible rewards of teaching young people in the classroom, and they shared a mutual appreciation of British pop musical groups from the '60s. They both liked to explore country back roads. Thanks to Cal, Leona figured she knew the surrounding area better than many of Braxton's natives.

The two of them spent most Saturdays together, discovering the wonders of California's central coast. One of Leona's favorite places was Harmony, a tiny town just southwest of Braxton on State Highway 1. Settled in 1869 by dairy farmers, for years it was a roadside stop where one could buy milk, butter, cream, and cheese.

Cal told Leona that growth had never come to Harmony. The town nearly lost its dot on the map in the '50s when the dairy operation shifted to San Luis Obispo. The cows, milking machines, and cheese factory, which had kept the place alive, moved twenty miles south, as did the town's fortunes. People struggled to make a go of what was left, but finally gave up. All that remained was Harmony's post office, a place Leona enjoyed taking letters for a postmark.

Cal and Leona returned often to Harmony. She loved the population sign as they entered town: 20. It was an artist's colony producing fine sculptures, pottery, and blown glass for sale. A small (everything in Harmony was small) family-owned winery produced seven wines, including Noel Vineyard's "Christmas Blush."

Cal and Leona looked forward to the short drive to Harmony. Once there, they would browse for hours in the shops, getting to know the artists. They would always eat at the same garden restaurant at the same patio table under an olive tree; this was where they took their time getting to know each other. It was here that he confirmed a rumor she'd heard—he had once been in the middle of fighting in Africa. Not as a soldier of fortune, but as a volunteer helping war refugees with a humanitarian group in Rwanda. At this point she'd asked him if he were a defrocked Roman Catholic priest. The question startled him so much, that he choked, spitting out his root beer. After he stopped himself from drowning, the answer was an emphatic no.

Leona found Cal a deeply sensitive and caring man who was neither motivated in life by fame nor fortune. For now, she truly believed him when he said his entry into local politics was strictly to serve the community he loved. He was reluctant to talk about his past, especially anything having to do with religion. She knew his parents had forced their Pentecostal beliefs on him, and he'd had some kind of a negative experience in college. He'd politely, but firmly declined all invitations to attend services with her at First Baptist Church. She prayed that Cal's heart would soften toward the Gospel, but other than going Christmas caroling with her, she saw no evidence of interest in spiritual matters.

Leona tried to rationalize that Cal was like most people who had a closet or two they wanted kept shut. When uncomfortable subjects came up, he simply shifted the attention to Leona. He was always at his best when he spoke about others. He was a remarkable storyteller and fascinated Leona with one particular tale about one of Harmony's most famous visitors. She could almost picture famed newspaper publisher, William Randolph Hearst, rumbling off of State Highway 1, driving down a small slope, and pulling his sleek roadster to a dusty stop. Twenty miles to the north, he had built his dream house on 127 acres atop a 1,600-foot mountain, overlooking San Simeon and the Pacific Ocean. It would become Hearst Castle. A month earlier, Cal had taken Leona to see it: the main house of 115 rooms, three magnificent guesthouses, pools, fountains, statuary, gardens, and millions of dollars' worth of Hearst's art collection and antiques.

Cal was intrigued with the magnet-like attraction Harmony had on the multimillionaire. While Hearst owned homes throughout the country and his art collection rivaled the most prestigious galleries, he enjoyed some pleasures that were simple, inexpensive, and personal.

For one thing, he would stop in Harmony to buy fresh dairy products. Leona imagined how the good folk of the town must have stirred with excitement when they saw Hearst coming their way. They never knew what famous person would be riding with the outspoken and controversial man. Many times, his traveling partner was actor Rudolph Valentino.

Leona felt the soft touch of a hand. Cal had reached across the table. "Welcome back to Denny's, traveler," he said with a warm smile. "You had the same expression on your face the night I first met you. That's why this place is special."

"So, three months later, we're back at the scene of the *grime*," she wisecracked.

Cal squeezed Leona's hand and slowly shook his head. "Queen of the one-liners comes up with another classic."

"Sometimes they work, sometimes I should keep my mouth closed."

While still holding her hand, Cal glanced down, then back up. "Well, for a few seconds, how about not saying anything?"

Leona feared what might be coming. She wanted to stop it, but she couldn't.

"I was going to wait until later, but I can't. Straight up-front—from the bottom of my heart, I love you, Leona."

It was worse than she'd expected. She looked around and took a deep breath. Where was the waitress? She prayed the power would go off. Something had to stop these words she didn't want to hear.

"You're unlike any woman I ever imagined existed," he continued. "We've spent a lot of time together—and have so much in common. The only way I could be happier would be if you and I could be together for the rest of our lives." Cal reached into his jacket on the bench next to him. He held up a small jewelry box, then gave it to her.

She knew what was inside. How could she keep from opening it?

"This looks serious," she said with a crooked grin.

"It is and so am I. Open it."

Leona thought back to her childhood, remembering how she'd anticipated the day a special man would ask her to marry him. *Will I cry? Will I laugh? What will love feel like? Will the ring fit?* But she felt none of these emotions as she flipped open the box. The light above their table reflected off the diamond engagement ring. It was no rock, but it was beautiful. It was the kind of ring she would expect from Cal. Now what should she say?

"The moratorium is over," Cal said with a twinkle in his eye that matched the diamond. I'm ready for a one-liner, but actually one word would be even better."

"What's that?" Leona asked, thankful for any delay.

"I hope you'll say 'yes.'"

She stared at the ring in the box, then back at Cal.

"Would you try it on?" he asked.

The smile on Cal's face disappeared, and his shoulders sagged when she snapped the box shut with a *pop*. "I think you're a wonderful man, and I'm touched by this, but I can't marry you—*now*, Cal." She placed the box on the table and pushed it back toward him.

Cal took a deep breath, held it, then exhaled through his mouth. "Hmmm," was all he said for a moment. "I didn't expect this," he finally spoke again. "Tell me how I could have read things so wrong."

The waitress arrived with their food then. Cal thanked her, then turned back to Leona. "Tell me why the ring isn't on your finger."

Leona prayed silently, then said, "Because of someone who isn't in your heart."

Cal slowly nodded. He seemed to understand.

Leona leaned toward him. "We talked about this before, Cal. I'm sorry, and I don't mean to hurt you. But this is the one thing—the most important thing we *don't* have in common. The man I marry must have

Christ in his heart." Cal's eyes hardened. She'd never seen him look like that before. "You told me before," she went on quietly, "you weren't interested in knowing Jesus."

"I know all I need to know about Jesus," he snapped. He took his knife, quickly cut into his prime rib, and stuffed a bite into his mouth. "I believe He lived," he said as he chewed, "He died and some say He rose again. Maybe, maybe not. One day, those who have been good enough in life, and I think that includes you and me, will know for certain." Cal pushed the jewelry box back across the table toward Leona. "Now that the Jesus-thing is settled, let's try again. Will you marry me?"

Leona picked up the jewelry box and held it, unopened, in her hand. "Cal, the *Jesus-thing*, as you call it, isn't settled, and you know it." She was angry with herself. "This is my fault. You wouldn't come to church with me, but I thought that by continuing to see you, you'd become a Christian. I wanted that, and still do, more than anything else."

"It's not going to happen." He tore open his baked potato and put an extra pat of butter inside. "I love you, but I'm not going to lie or be a hypocrite."

"Cal, I shouldn't have let our friendship go this far. You're a great guy, and you'll make some woman a wonderful husband and father. But unless the Holy Spirit changes your heart . . ." Leona didn't finish, but instead, set the jewelry box near Cal's plate.

Cal looked at the box, then at Leona. "Is that really the only reason you won't marry me?"

Leona's head dipped and then she looked back up at him. "I'd like to get to know you a little better. After, all, it's only been three months. But, yes, I'd say that's the main reason."

He sat back in his seat. "I don't get it. How can you let our relationship succeed or fail based on one thing?"

Leona began to cut into her fish, then stopped. "It's not one *thing.*

It's one *person*—Jesus Christ. My whole life centers on my faith in Him—and that must be true for the man I marry."

Cal's jaw tightened. "And so what happens now that you really know my life doesn't center on Jesus?"

"Then we'll just be friends, Cal," Leona said softly.

Cal picked up the jewelry box and slipped it into his pocket. They finished their meal in silence.

CHAPTER 36

Tuesday April 1, 3:39 P.M.

The motorcycle's rumble underneath her soothed Shelly in some strange way. It was one of the few things that comforted her and eased the ache in her heart since Rick's death five days before. She wondered if he'd had a premonition of what was to come. For only a month before he was killed, on Shelly's thirtieth birthday, he had added her name to the title on his motorcycle. His Harley was his prized possession; this action could only be described as offbeat and typically Rick.

She banked the Harley on a curve that passed the cemetery where Rick was laid to rest the day before. There had been no funeral, no graveside service. Pastor Nick Martinez had offered his comfort and the facilities of First Baptist Church, but Shelly wanted neither. What she wanted to avoid most of all was another *to be undecided, is to be decided* sermon.

Shelly had arranged for a burial plot about twenty yards from Chief Talbot and his wife Courtney's graves. She'd cleaned out the money she'd begun to save from the *Destination* magazine assignment and had gone back into debt to pay for the casket and burial plot. She wasn't sure why she'd wanted Rick buried that close to the victims of the balloon crash—it would always be a reminder of what she'd caused. If she'd never written the article, Rick would still be alive. But then, if she'd never written the article, she would have never met Rick Aguilara. And the last three months had been the happiest time of her life. If only Rick had picked another restaurant, if only Rick had parked his motorcycle differently, if only Blake Hesterman had been somewhere else—if, if, if. Each time Shelly replayed the scene in her mind, it ended the same. The person who meant more to her than anyone in the world was gone.

Shelly passed the high school and pulled up in front of the base-ball field. She was here to do a profile on Pete Stanley for *The Braxton Banner.* Marty Cavitt had given her the go-ahead after she'd told him the story would be more than a sports feature. She would offer a personal look at the Hall of Fame baseball player who was now Braxton's most famous citizen. In truth, however, most of the interview's content would be saved for the *Destination* magazine article, now six weeks away from publication. She'd almost completed her final draft of the story; the interview with Pete Stanley was all that remained. She felt good about the piece. It told the story of a town and its people that had changed dramatically in only one year. She kept trying to forget about the fact that it was based on a lie.

She acknowledged the waves now of several students walking home. "Rad bike," one young man commented as he walked by, and she smiled. She moved toward the chain link fence along the street, where she could see members of the baseball team inside. Some were playing catch, others were doing stretching exercises, and one player was at home plate taking batting practice. Ping! Ping! Ping! Shelly couldn't get used to the sound; she had always thought the *crack* of a bat against a ball was a romantic, defining sound of baseball. The bats these days were made out of aluminum rather than wood.

Shelly spotted Pete Stanley leaning on the metal brace of a portable batting cage set up behind home plate. She was drawn to his weather-beaten face. He wore gray sweat pants and a gray sweat shirt with BULLDOGS spelled out in Kelly green block letters across the front. His white baseball cap with green vertical stripes and a capital B over the bill, was pulled down over his eyes.

Stanley was watching a left-handed batter, taking his cuts against a pitching machine. Every five or six seconds, a baseball was propelled toward the batter.

Ping, pause. *Ping*, pause. *Ping*, pause. Shelly didn't know much about baseball, but she could tell the player in the cage was pretty good.

"Mr. Stanley?" she asked, as she moved through the gate to approach him.

Pete looked over his shoulder. "Hi. Are you Shelly?" He was chewing something, a large wad of gum, she hoped, rather than tobacco.

"Yes. I've seen you around town—but we've never met."

Just then, the batter lined a pitch deep to right field with a loud *ping*. The ball took two hops and bounced hard against a green, wooden fence, knocking out a slat. The tires continued spinning, as the player by the machine loaded more baseballs into it.

"Good hit," Stanley praised the batter. "Leave some of the fence standing, OK?" The player wore a green protective helmet with flaps that covered both ears. He didn't respond.

"Hit a few to left—go the other way," Pete ordered, blowing a bubble with his gum. When the next pitch came to the batter, he sent the ball on a high arc. It cleared the scoreboard by six feet, a prodigious blast to right field. "I said, *left*, not right!" Pete chided. The next hit rocketed just over first base and kicked up chalk on the right field foul line.

"Good hitter, bad sense of direction," Shelly observed.

"Good hitter, bad *attitude*," Pete corrected as he turned to smile at Shelly. "That's my son," he said with a hint of pride in his voice.

The batter sent another pitch on a line to right. He looked over at his father with an odd expression of contempt mixed with almost a plea for approval.

Pete waved a hand, then began to tell Shelly how Brian's presence on the diamond came about, how it was the result of a confrontation and clash of egos between father and son. Pete had asked Brian if he were interested in trying out for the team. Brian scoffed, saying there was no way he wanted his father, the "great" Pete Stanley, as his coach. Pete then challenged Brian, asking him if he thought he could make it past the first cut. At that point, Brian boasted that he could not only make the team, he would be the best player.

"Did you know he was this good?" Shelly asked as Brian tagged another pitch, this time directly off the scoreboard.

"I could tell he was a good athlete, but he pulled a fast one on me."

"How so?"

"About a month after we talked, I noticed he had a lot of blisters on his hands. He mumbled something about working on his car."

Shelly shrugged. "So—"

"He must have driven to San Luis Obispo every day and spent hours in the batting cages—just to prove me wrong." Pete turned back to Brian. "Hit one to left, son." Brian lined a pitch off the right field fence, knocking out another slat. "Next hitter!" Pete yelled in disgust.

"So, reverse psychology worked, huh?"

Pete shrugged. "Sort of—but there were other problems."

"Like what?"

"His grades back in Chicago and that ridiculous car I bought him."

"What's happened since you moved out here?" she asked.

"So far, the move has been good academically. He's kept himself eligible in class." He grunted. "Most likely, so he can play baseball and prove me wrong."

"And the car?"

Pete pointed to Brian now sauntering to third base. "He's still alive."

"Excuse my ignorance, but what position did you play with Chicago?"

Pete shook his head. "I played third base. But I never, never handled a glove like that when I was sixteen."

They watched as Brian deftly snagged ground balls rolling or bouncing to him from the batter in the cage. He ranged gracefully to his right now, backhanded a grounder behind the bag, then pretended he was going to throw the runner out at first. Instead, he rolled the ball toward a canvas bag near the pitching machine.

"So, will he make the first cut?" Shelly asked tongue in cheek.

"He already made the first cut, but to tell you the truth, I'm not sure he can make or stay on the team."

"How come?"

"Brian has great potential as a player, but he has no sense of comradery and so far, he won't be coached."

Just then, Brian backpedaled, as a fly ball was lifted to left field. The boy in left field moved quickly forward, clearly in the best position to catch the ball. The boy called out, "I got it, I got it." But Brian continued running toward the ball, and it looked as if the two were about to have a violent collision. Brian continued his pursuit, twisting his body at the last second to avoid the other player, finally making a miraculous, over-the-shoulder catch.

"Wow!" Shelly marveled, "what a play."

"No," Pete corrected, "what a *problem*."

He trotted toward his son, who was now laughing and taunting the player he'd nearly collided with. "Brian!" Pete called out, beckoning to him. "Come here!"

Brian looked at his father, but didn't move. Pete marched over to the boy then, and an animated conversation followed. Shelly could hear Pete's angry voice and Brian's loud protests. Suddenly, Brian threw his glove on the ground and stormed off the field.

CHAPTER 37

Thursday April 3, Midnight

The obedient laser jet printer had five more pages to process. Shelly pulled a completed page out of the tray and placed it, face down, on a pile to the right. Rolling her head slightly, she felt her neck crackle from the hours of sitting. She was tired, but her project was done. An amber light on the printer let her know it was out of paper. After taking a sip of coffee, she grabbed several sheets of paper from her last ream and loaded them into the tray. Soon, the printer came back to life with a *whirring* sound, completing its assignment.

Shelly placed the last page on top of the pile, then turned it over, and held the manuscript in both hands. A year's work. She looked at the front page:

Braxton: From Best to Bust
How America's Best Small Town Was Spoiled by Success
By Shelly Hinson

Braxton, California
Everyone dreams of being the best. What happens when it comes true? The people of Braxton, a small town of 15,000 residents in coastal central California, found out the hard way. I know, because I live there.

First, a confession. A year ago, *Destination* magazine picked Braxton as the Best Small Town in America—at my suggestion. Braxton was neither the best nor the worst; it was not unlike thousands of other small towns across the nation. But I wondered if national recognition alone would help or hurt a town. So, the award was made, and my article was written under the ghost name Bernardo Javier. For the past twelve months, unbeknownst to my neighbors, I've recorded the town's fortunes and failures as it tried to be something that never existed in the first place. This was a journalistic experiment, a "study" rather than a story—an odyssey of exhilarating highs and crushing lows.

You know you live in the sticks when you learn from outsiders that your town was selected best in America. That's what happened in June of last year. The news was first on radio, then television, and two days later we read the article in *Destination* magazine. Talk about a bombshell! I was born here thirty years ago, and nothing, believe me, nothing any bigger in the town's history had ever happened that rivaled the news that Braxton was number one.

Shelly sighed and ran her hand over her face. She hoped when Lance Milburn read her story, he would agree she'd knocked one out of the park. The article read like a made-for-TV-movie—it had both heroes and villains, triumph and tragedy. For some, the decision to move to Braxton was one that enriched their lives; for others, like Rick, it was one that caused loss of life. Technically, the piece was the best work she'd ever done. Ethically, it was probably the worst. In the morning, she would take the manuscript into town and send it Federal Express to New York. She began reading page two:

The day the June issue of *Destination* arrived was the day Braxton's charm was run out of town. Actually, it wasn't run out—it left on its own.

The article went on to explain the change of attitude in those she'd grown up with. She watched consideration for the good of the community turn into individual greed. Smiles of trust turned into sneers of suspicion. Her words captured the frantic scramble of merchants to stockpile food, goods, and souvenirs that first Friday night as the town prepared for a wave of visitors. She reported the giddy, goose bump anticipation that swept the town Saturday morning on Main Street. Her story then shoved the reader off a cliff as she wrote of the town's bitter humiliation when no visitors showed up the first weekend. Even though Shelly knew the outcome, her spirits soared now as she read her story. Would Lance feel the same? Would the magazine's readers?

Then, miraculously, the story went on, from the depths of despair came redemption. The following Friday, people by the hundreds drove in from out of town and jammed the streets of Braxton, curious to see if Utopia really existed, as the magazine article implied. This was Shelly's most difficult challenge—who to write about. Hundreds of people liked what they saw, and proceeded to move to Braxton, thinking it was the best small town in America. Was it wishful thinking on their part? Were people this desperate for happiness? What went through their minds when they took their first look at Main Street? But move, they did, and for some, it was their best move. The article profiled people like Benny and Maggie Green, who had built a prospering restaurant. She wrote about Nick and Karen Martinez, who now had a baby boy and a new church. There was J. Oswald Theodore, III, the Greens' human reclamation project who was seemingly on the road to full recovery. Gina Wells was now Braxton's chief of police, Leona Kyle was nearing the end of her first semester as a high school English teacher, and Pete Stanley seemed to be reestablishing his connection with his family.

Yet for some, the move to Braxton was their last. Shelly shivered when she remembered Rick Aguilara and the way his life had ended on a sidewalk outside Benny Green's restaurant one week ago. It seemed longer than that to her. Sweet reflections of Rick were forced out by the mental image of his killer, Blake Hesterman. At the very least, investigators were considering charging him with assault under the color of authority. However, there was talk that Chief Gina Wells wanted involuntary manslaughter charges brought against the police sergeant. One way or the other, he was going to jail. He faced a minimum sentence of one year in the county jail and a $10,000 fine. If it were up to Shelly, Hesterman would be locked up for second degree murder. She continued reading her story

The day after Christmas in Braxton dawned warm and dry, but the winds of fortune that seemingly had swept into town six months earlier were about to shift tragically. At Mayor Roger Carter's urging, the town council voted 3-1 to celebrate the town's success with a year-end festival. The gala, complete with parades, contests, games, special sales, and a carnival would last six days, culminating with a concert and fireworks show on New Year's Eve.

Opening ceremonies Monday morning were held on a vacant lot at the far end of town. Members of Braxton's high school band played the theme from *Rocky* as townsfolk gathered in bleachers set up near a platform. A hot air balloon sat off to one side; it would lift off, symbolizing the festival's beginning. Later, free rides would be given. Speeches were memorized, food was ready, and while the band was off-key, it didn't seem to matter; everyone saw how hard the kids were trying and besides, the band members were the sons and daughters of the townsfolk. For this one day, at least, everyone could remember what Braxton used to be.

Unfortunately, the ceremony was also buffeted by a Santa Ana, a hot, dry wind that carries the name of a canyon near Los Angeles through which it often blows. The powerful blast rushes down from desert plateaus and is heated by compression. When it arrives, the wind can change people's moods, making them testy and irritable. The mystery-story writer Raymond Chandler once wrote, "Meek little wives feel the edge of the carving knife and study their husband's necks." In Braxton, one enormous gust of wind plunged the town into hell.

Shelly's story then recounted the hot air balloon's fiery crash into the media tent, and the deaths of the police chief, his wife, the two men in the balloon, and the three catering workers inside the tent. She imagined how the article would look laid out and accompanied by photos of the crash which were taken by still photographers at the ceremony. A photo of Heather Landis would accompany the story of her heroism—how she pulled the mayor's son out of the burning tent. And then, the follow-up story of Heather's life since the accident. They were able to save her eyesight, but could do nothing to restore the beauty to her face. She would carry the severe physical scars for the rest of her life; her career as a television news reporter was over.

Shelly put the article down. She briskly rubbed her hands together, then looked at her palms. Why had she just done that? She knew the answer—because she had the blood of others on her hands. Manslaughter charges were being brought against Blake Hesterman—why not against her?

Shelly picked up the first page of her article again and looked at the disclaimers—"study, not story," and "journalistic experiment." Those were Lance Milburn's words, not hers. Confused, tired, and frustrated, she shook her head. Maybe she was too close to this. Maybe Lance was right when he said that every new form of journalism seemed unacceptable. What if she'd broken new ground? She couldn't give up now.

Shelly flipped through the rest of the article. There were stories of Braxton's development, with new housing and new businesses. The town's population was now close to twenty thousand, and the increase meant critical new demands not yet being met. Police and fire protection were stretched past the limits of acceptable response time. Potholes were getting wider and deeper, and the wind brought constant reminders of inadequate sewage treatment. Shelly chronicled a fiscal crisis that had lowered the town's credit rating. Cal Spencer had told her that the council was secretly considering increasing the town's sales tax by two percent.

Mayor Roger Carter was also in serious trouble. The families of those killed in the hot air balloon crash had filed wrongful death suits against the town and its mayor. Carter was being investigated for alleged bribery connected to the contract with Upper Limits, the owner of the hot air balloon. Shelly began to replay the *what-ifs* in her mind. What if a different hot air balloon company had been hired? There would have been no crash, Chief Talbot would still be alive, Gina Wells wouldn't be the police chief, Hesterman would have been on another assignment, and Rick wouldn't be dead. But what-ifs never come true, she reminded herself.

Shelly glanced at the clock and winced when she saw it was 2:03 A.M. She'd proofread her manuscript so many times she had it memorized. She slipped out of her jeans and T-shirt, brushed her teeth, found a cotton nightie in a chair, and climbed into bed. In four hours she'd get up and drive to San Luis Obispo, where she'd send her manuscript Federal Express to Lance Milburn in New York City. The fifty-mile round trip was a drag, but she couldn't risk someone in Braxton spotting the package and making note of its destination.

CHAPTER 38

Braxton
Friday April 4, 6:46 P.M.

It was easy for host Alex Trebek to look so smart on "Jeopardy," Shelly thought. He clutched the answers to every single question in his little hand. Not that she would have hit the buzzer that many times tonight—her mind was elsewhere. The TV show was on, but she was barely paying any attention. She was too intent on waiting for her telephone to ring. Lance had the manuscript by now. What did he think of it? Why hadn't he called yet?

Shelly jumped off the sofa when the phone finally did ring. She reached for it, then held back, not wanting to seem too eager. It rang again. Was it him? She watched the phone as it called out to her again. She would wait for one more ring. There! She picked it up and forced herself to slowly bring it to her ear. "Hello?" she said calmly.

"Shelly?" Marty Cavitt said with a touch of urgency.

Her heart sank. "Yeah, what's up?"

"Head out 46 east—the other side of Paso Robles. There's been a bad wreck. I've already got a photog. on his way."

"Anyone we know?"

"Yes. Brian Stanley. About an hour ago. He put his Porsche into the grill of a Mack truck."

"That's awful. What happened?" Shelly recalled the last time she'd seen the curly-headed boy on the baseball field.

"I don't know—that's your job. The police called me. But one story going around is that his father kicked him off the baseball team."

The sound of emergency radio traffic echoed in the night as Shelly approached the accident scene on foot. Two fire trucks from Paso Robles and one from Braxton were parked at the curb. She marveled at the brightness of the highway patrol vehicles' headlights. Although it was dark, the lights lit up the area to the point where it seemed like day. Hissing red flares were spread along the highway, and the smell of gasoline, oil, rubber, and death hung in the air. She watched as a CHP officer ignited another flare, while a fellow officer directed traffic around a small detour. The semi was still in the left turn lane; the turn signal was blinking from the rear of the trailer.

Shelly flashed her *Banner* press card to an officer and was allowed to walk to the front of the truck. She caught her breath, and her eyes widened, when she saw the mangled Porsche. What was left of the car seemed imbedded in the truck's grill. As she glanced to her right, she saw a sheet of yellow plastic covering a body on the street—Brian Stanley. Two feet protruded from the plastic cover; one revealed a white blood-soaked sock, the other a black loafer with a penny tucked in the top flap.

Shelly flashed back thirteen years to the memory that would always haunt her: three white sheets covering her father's, mother's, and brother's lifeless forms on another part of Highway 46. Shelly was seventeen then, nearly the same age as Brian. She stared numbly at the yellow plastic covered body. It was surrounded by crumpled metal, broken glass, and leaking oil. Brian was surely killed instantly, but Shelly knew his fate was sealed when she'd started writing her article. How many people had died now because of her story? Seven in the balloon crash, then Rick, and now Brian Stanley. Nine lives!

She turned from the carnage, then spotted Brian's parents in the back of a highway patrol car, talking with an officer. Her reporter's instinct told her to walk over and talk with them. But the sickening guilt she felt made her turn back to her car. Just then, she felt her shoe kick something on the shoulder of the road. The black object spun and slid along the ground, then came to a stop. When she stepped closer, she could see that she'd tripped over a handheld audio tape recorder. It was scratched and dirty, but looked to be in one piece. After checking to see that no one was watching, she bent down, picked up the recorder, and quickly slipped it into the pocket of her jacket.

She knew she should give the recorder to investigators. She was removing possible evidence from an accident scene. But the temptation to listen to the tape was too strong. She would listen to it, then give it to an officer. After all, she'd shaded the truth up until now. How much more harm could she do?

Shelly returned to her car, but rather than listen to the tape at the scene, she drove just down the road to the Jack Ranch Cafe. The restaurant was only a few strides from the James Dean Memorial. She parked her car in the lot behind the Tree of Heaven and its stainless steel sculpture. Then she removed the tape recorder from her pocket. Taking a deep breath, she pushed "Play." There was no sound. Just as well. Now she could just go back to the scene and give the tape to investigators. Go back! That was it! Shelly pushed the "Reverse" button, felt the tape rewind, then stop. She hit "Play" once more and immediately heard the sound of a car's engine.

"Highway 46," a young male's voice said, "Friday, April 4, 5:39 P.M. I'm speeding west on a two-lane asphalt highway in a silver Porsche convertible. The number '130' is secured with black electrical tape on the doors and front hood. 'Little Bastard' is spray-painted in red across the rear cowling."

Shelly swallowed hard and turned the recorder off. She looked around to see if anyone was nearby. She was still alone. She switched the machine back on, though she turned the volume down a bit.

"I'm wearing a white T-shirt, light blue slacks, and sunglasses clipped on non-prescription lenses. I'm chain-smoking Chesterfields. It's 5:44 P.M., and I'm squinting as a spray of sunset looms on the horizon. My convertible streaks toward the intersection of Highways 46 and 41. With my eyes straight ahead, I say, 'That guy up there's gotta stop. He'll see us.'"

Shelly's heart was pounding as she pushed the stop button on the recorder once more. She didn't want to continue, but knew she had to. She had learned at the accident scene that the Mack semi-truck trailer, heading east, had stopped before he turned left from Highway 46 to Highway 41. He claimed to have followed the low profile sports car right up to the point of impact. She pushed "Play" for the last time, knowing the end was seconds away.

"Death is traveling at eighty-five miles an hour," Brian calmly said. "It's now 5:44 P.M., one mile east of the village of Cholame. At the intersection, I see a 1955 blacktopped, white-hooded Ford sedan waiting to turn left. Inside the car is twenty-three-year-old Donald Turnupseed, a college student at Cal Poly San Luis Obispo, on his way home to see his parents."

Shelly held her breath when she heard Brian order in a low voice, "Turn." Two seconds passed and he repeated, "Turn!" Then he declared, "This day, this minute, this second."

Shelly thought she could hear the Porsche accelerate, and then Brian shouted, "I've got your $33.03!" Immediately, the over modulated sound of an explosion was heard. It lasted only a split second and was followed by a *whish* of air. Then came the sound of metal or plastic scraping and bouncing on a hard surface.

And silence.

CHAPTER 39

Sunday April 6, 5:50 A.M.

The telephone broke the night but not the darkness. Shelly lay motionless in bed, confused and semiconscious. *Ring, ring, ring.* She was paralyzed with slumber, then bolted upright in bed. *Lance?* She fumbled for the phone just as her answering machine began its greeting. "Hello, hello?" The recording stopped. "Hello?" she repeated.

"Shelly, this is Lance."

Shelly reached for her nightstand lamp and turned the switch. "Sorry, I was asleep," she mumbled and flopped back on the bed.

"Oh, yeah. Sorry. Listen, I got your article late yesterday."

Holding her breath, she waited.

"We passed it around—everyone got a chance to read it." Shelly's heart began to race, and her hands began to shake. There was silence on the line. Why wasn't Lance saying something? What did he think of it? It was agonizing. She sat up straight on the edge of the bed. "It's better than I ever hoped for," he said finally. Goose bumps rocketed up and down her spine. Chilled with excitement, she slipped back under the covers. "I'm only going to make one one change," he went on. "It's minor."

A swarm of butterflies scattered in Shelly's stomach. *Minor?* "What are you changing?" she asked.

"We're not going to reveal that the award was a hoax. Everything else is perfect."

Shelly swallowed hard. She closed her eyes and felt the room spin. "Lance, I can't tell you how troubled I am with that change."

"Oh?" he asked in surprise. "How so?"

"I think it's absolutely wrong not to reveal it was made up. Please, don't edit that out."

His voice hardened. "Your story is strong enough on its own. The piece doesn't need it, Shelly."

"But our readers need to know the truth."

After a pause, Lance said, "For our protection and yours—trust me, this is best."

"Why? What do you mean—for my protection?"

"Lawsuits, Shelly. If we admit we made this up—we're asking for the same lawsuits the town is facing."

"But Lance—"

"No more discussion," he snapped. "You've written a spectacular piece. It's in our hands now."

Shelly knew any effort at argument was futile, but she still made one last plea. "It's wrong, Lance. It's very wrong."

"Leave that to us, Shelly. We've finished the layout. The only thing left is some artwork, a few changes on two photos, and your boxed profile on Mayor Carter." Shelly didn't respond until Lance finally asked, "Shelly? You still there?"

"Yes," she answered quietly.

"OK, we're right on track. Anything new out your way?"

She sighed. "Brian Stanley was killed Friday night."

"Pete Stanley's boy?" he asked with shock.

"Uh huh. He ran his Porsche into a semi."

"Wow. You wrote about him—he's the kid who's—who was the James Dean freak, right?"

Shelly knew where Lance was heading. "Yeah, and he died near where Dean was killed."

"Great! Unbelievable." Lance exclaimed. "Develop that. Put something together, then Fed-Ex it. Your story just keeps getting better."

"I found out—I know exactly how it happened."

"Sure, sure—get it all from the police report," he said impatiently.

Anger replaced Shelly's apprehension. She held back telling him about the tape recorder. "Lance?"

"What?"

She summoned up her courage and took a deep breath. "I insist we tell the truth about the award," she said, "the hoax, and everything."

Silence on the line again, then, "Don't push me on this." Lance's words came in a rush. "The story's going to be done the way I want—you have no say in it."

"But—"

"This is a dead issue, Shelly." He paused. "And your future with us may be too. It's been under wraps, but we've been thinking about bringing you on full time." Shelly's lips went dry. She licked them and wondered if she'd blown her big chance. "Now," he went on, "after hearing a side of you that's very disappointing, I'm wondering whether we should reconsider."

"I only want to do what's right."

"Talk to me about right and wrong when the awards start coming your way."

"Well, I had to tell you how I felt," she said, giving up.

"And I respect you for it," Lance said quickly. "This is revolutionary stuff in journalism, and I feel privileged to be part of it. OK?"

"Yeah, I guess. We'll see."

"Trust me," he said. "Get the Brian Stanley story to me, OK?"

"Good-bye, Lance."

———•◦•———

Noon

The two women looked across the table at each other. Shelly surveyed the room which was about half full. "I hope you don't mind meeting here," she said. They were in a booth at Benny's.

Leona shook her head. "Not at all. But it's got to be tough, with what happened to . . ." She glanced down, then back at Shelly. "Well, you know."

Shelly thought it kind of Leona to say something. It was her feeling too. "You're right. This is the first time I've been inside Benny's since Rick was killed." She gently ran her hand over the table. "But this place, this table, is where we had some good times. You remember New Year's Eve?"

Leona laughed. "How could I forget? That was the night Rick knocked the stiffness out of the Honorable Calvin Spencer."

Shelly grinned and felt warm inside. "It was one of his best moments. Sorry that you and Cal split up."

Leona just shrugged.

"I've heard that he asked you to marry him. Is that right?"

"Is this for publication, gossip, or just between us girls?" Leona asked.

Shelly blushed when she realized how tacky her question was. "Sorry, I had no right to ask. It's just that no one thought Cal would ever consider marriage."

"It wasn't meant to be," Leona said, "or should I say, the Lord didn't mean it to be."

"How did God know? Did He tell you that?"

"He surely did. God lets us know what He thinks through the Bible. It's His letter to us—and the Bible is clear that believers and non-believers are not to be married. Cal wasn't a Christian, didn't have any intention of being one—so, that was it."

Shelly shifted nervously in her seat, smoothing down her Boston Proper cropped sweat shirt with its oversized sleeves. The last thing she wanted to talk about was religion. "I'll have to tell you, I didn't expect you to be calling me, especially after our New Year's Eve encounter."

"And I didn't think you'd meet me," Leona admitted. "I'm still embarrassed after what I did to you the night I rolled into town."

Shelly laughed as she remembered her snit at Denny's when Cal left to buy Leona midnight breakfast. "Yes, I didn't know who I was more upset with, you or Cal."

Leona nodded and tugged on the collar of her gray sheared chenille jumpsuit. "The next day I thought about what happened and felt pretty dumb. You had every right to leave—it was incredibly rude of Cal."

Shelly dismissed her confession with a wave of her hand and felt a new liking for Leona.

"And what would Braxton's double tandem of brains and beauty like for lunch?" Ozzie Theodore had arrived unnoticed at their table.

"My goodness," Leona said, feigning wonder, "the assistant manager is here to take our order."

"Say, Ozzie, whatever happened to your young waiters?" Shelly cracked. "Why else do you think we came?"

He turned and pointed toward the kitchen. "They're cowering behind that door—afraid of being intimidated by your beauty."

Shelly laughed. "Well, I'm glad you're not overwhelmed by what you see."

"Actually, they called in sick," Ozzie dryly countered. "I'm the only one here. What would you piranhas like for lunch?"

"Watch your step, old man," Leona kidded. "Beautiful women can be bad tippers."

Shelly ordered taco salad, while Leona asked for two cheese enchiladas. Each ordered iced tea.

"Any more libelous comments about my age," Ozzie said with a straight face, "and you'll wear the house salsa."

As Shelly watched Ozzie return to the kitchen, she recalled her first conversation with him at his coffee kiosk that cold December morning on Main Street. At least here was one person who had not met with disaster because of her article. She focused on Leona once again. "When you called me this morning, you said you had something of Brian Stanley's. What is it?"

Leona opened her purse and removed a letter-sized envelope. She took out two sheets of paper and placed them on the table. "I know you're writing a story on Brian's death for *The Banner*. I called his parents, and they gave me permission to show you this."

"What is it?" Shelly asked without picking up the papers.

"It's a report Brian wrote for my class. You should read it, but I'll warn you, it's scary." She slid the papers across the table.

As Shelly read the first few lines of Brian's essay, a chill raised goose bumps on her arms. She looked up at Leona. "Do the cops have this?"

"Not yet. I wasn't sure what to do with it. Read the rest."

Shelly felt sick as she read the same self-fulfilling prophecy she had heard on tape the night before. She remembered the twisted mass of nothing that was Brian's car. She recalled his blood-soaked sock, protruding from the yellow plastic sheet, and then her mind shut off. She didn't want to think of how the rest of his body looked. Was it right to use his last words in her story? And did she dare reveal the audio tape? To Leona? To the police? His school essay would be strong material, but his exact words—that would be overwhelming. It may even clinch her job with the magazine. "What would you do with this?" Shelly asked.

"I don't know—you're the journalist. It's just that—well, I thought you might want to put it in your article . . ."

"If you could write it, what would you say?"

Leona looked confused for a moment, then, "I'd tell people that Brian had marvelous writing skills, but destroyed himself with obsessive, compulsive behavior."

Leona's words hit Shelly full in the face. "An unusual combination?" she asked. Without knowing it, Leona had just described Shelly.

Leona nodded. "When you consider that he apparently killed himself over it—I'd say, yes—very unusual."

"What would you say if I told you it wasn't an unusual combination?"

Ozzie arrived with their food then, and to Shelly's relief, quickly left after telling Leona her plate was hot. Shelly was about to take a bite of her taco salad when Leona asked, "Would you feel uncomfortable if I prayed for the food?"

Shelly put her fork down. "Not at all—please, go ahead."

"Dear, Heavenly Father," Leona prayed, "thank You, for the food we're about to eat. We remember Brian Stanley's family—please comfort them by sending someone into their life who knows Your Son. Thanks for this time with Shelly—You know why we were brought together. I ask this in Jesus' name, amen."

"Amen," Shelly said, surprising herself.

"This looks great." Leona began to cut into her enchilada with her fork.

"You just said something I don't understand."

"What—that this looks great?" Leona smiled.

Shelly smiled too, then grew serious. "How can Brian's parents be comforted by someone who—how did you put it—knows Jesus?"

"Well, someone who knows the Lord would have peace in his heart. That peace can be shared during difficult times."

"Peace that takes away guilt?" Shelly asked hopefully. She was remembering her talk with Pete Stanley and his regret at buying Brian the Porsche. But she also was asking for herself; directly or indirectly, her article had led to the deaths of nine people.

"The Bible says that it's a peace that goes beyond all understanding." Leona smiled. "I'd say that covers it all, wouldn't you?"

Shelly suddenly felt a sensation, unlike any other, and in a place that seemed odd—not in her heart or in her stomach, but deep within her sternum. It was an odd, uncomfortable feeling, yet she almost felt relief, as if something had begun to melt within her—*soul*? "What did you and Heather Landis talk about?"

The question seemed to catch Leona off guard and in the middle of a bite of her steaming enchilada. She fanned her mouth and took a sip from her water glass. "Sorry," she said. "Did you say, Heather? I thought we were talking about Brian."

"Well, it's all kind of tied together. She told me you helped her find peace in her life How did that happen?"

CHAPTER 40

2 P.M.

The computer screen showed the beginning of what Shelly thought could be her ticket out of Braxton. But the words were slow to come. She'd returned to her apartment a short time ago after meeting Leona, and now she struggled with how to weave the story of Brian Stanley's sudden, violent, and tragic death into her magazine article. Brian's essay, a graphic account of James Dean's death on Highway 46, turned out to be a preview of his suicide, verified on the audio tape she still had in her possession. She knew it was exactly what Lance Milburn wanted, so that her article would have a dramatic conclusion. It also was something she could not write until she made a phone call.

She reached for the phone and dialed Lance's number. It was a little after five there, and she hoped he was home. The phone rang once, twice, three times, and after the fourth, an answering machine kicked in. Disappointed, Shelly decided to hang up. No, she would leave a message. She waited for the beep. "Hi, this is Shelly. It's important—please call me back. I'll be home for the—"

"Shelly?"

"Lance, you're home—thanks for answering—"

"Yeah, yeah—what's going on? Was I right on that kid's death and the tie-in with James Dean?"

"More than you can imagine. He wrote an essay for his high school English class where he predicted the crash and foretold his own death."

"Really?" Lance asked with a laugh of wonder.

"Uh, huh. The CHP isn't sure, but I know Brian killed himself by running into a truck at the same intersection where James Dean died."

"That's incredible. Is that in the essay?"

"Not completely. Let's just say that I know for certain."

"Well, then you've got to use it—no matter what his parents say."

Suddenly Lance repulsed her, and she was sickened with herself, as well. She'd let him drag her into something worse than sleaze. "Your compassion is heartwarming," she answered, surprised at her boldness. "In this case, his parents already gave their permission."

"Shelly, that is terrific! I'm sending you a thousand-dollar bonus as soon as we get your story."

"Before I do that, we need to get something settled," she said.

"Like what?" Lance asked uncertainly.

For the first time in her life, Shelly threw up a silent prayer for help. *Dear Lord, please give me the right words* "Unless you change your mind and let me clearly state that the award was made up, I can't send you anything more."

"I can't do that, Shelly."

O Lord, what now? "But that was a condition of my doing the story."

"I have nothing on paper about that," Lance said coldly. "Send me what you have on Brian Stanley. Everything."

"No."

Lance sighed. "OK, Shelly—do you want this to be your last piece for us? I have an eight-page contract in my office, an offer for you to come to work with us, starting at $65,000 a year. Do I get the Brian Stanley story?"

Lord, what should I say?

"I'm waiting."

"I'm sorry, I can't do this, unless we tell the truth."

"Why is this so important to you?"

Shelly felt the same sensation in her sternum that she'd experienced just hours earlier with Leona. But now, instead of discomfort, there was a glorious feeling of peace. "Lance, it's important because as of a few hours ago, I have a new editor in my life. I answer to Him."

"What's his name?"

"Jesus Christ," she said softly.

"Oh, come off it, Shelly. When did you—with the unbuttoned blouse—get *religion*?"

Shelly was startled that he remembered how she looked so many months ago over one lunch. "It's not *religion*, but a *relationship* with Jesus Christ."

"I could care less—whatever *relationship* turns you on," Lance said flippantly. "But what does that have to do with the article?"

Shelly remembered Leona's words, still fresh on her mind, as she explained the plan of salvation to Lance. "This is kind of new for me, Lance, but Jesus is not only my Savior, He's my Lord."

"OK, Jesus saves. So what?"

"He's also the Lord of my life. That means I have to be honest in what I do—and it begins with telling the truth about the article. Unless that happens, you won't get Brian's story."

"Who do you think you are," Lance snarled, "telling me how to run this magazine? There will be no change in the article, Shelly." He paused for a moment. "Jesus may have saved you," he said quietly, "but He's not going to save your job. That contract I mentioned? It goes in the shredder on Monday."

The words, although not unexpected, still pierced the dreams Shelly had had since she was a child. "Thanks for almost hiring me," she said gently, not knowing where the words had come from. Her pattern was to lash out in anger. No, in this case, she would have given in and compromised herself.

"You've told me enough on Brian Stanley to complete the article," Lance said. "All I can say is you blew it, Shelly. When this is printed and the awards come out, think what might have been for you."

"I don't care about awards, Lance, only doing what's right. And that's what's going to happen," Shelly promised.

"How?"

"You'll find out."

"Go public with this and the only thing you'll ever get published is a help wanted ad in your local fish wrap."

She felt God give her confidence. "I'm not impressed with your threats. The Lord is on my side."

"And the *law* is on my side. We'll sue you," Lance countered. "You've got no defense."

"Yes, I do. It's called the truth."

And the telephone slammed down in her ear.

Shelly replaced the receiver as slowly as she'd lifted it. What an emotional roller coaster. Then she laughed out loud. This was positively, weird. She had just turned down the chance of a lifetime and she was laughing. The laughter came again, from deep within—she felt as if an enormous weight had just been lifted from her shoulders.

She walked over to her computer and sat down. Then, taking a deep breath, she began to create a new document. Unlike before, the words now flowed freely.

CHAPTER 41

Braxton
Monday April 7, 9 A.M.

Shelly reached out from her chair and swung the door closed. It slammed shut, causing the room to shake and startling Marty Cavitt, who sat across from her.

"Sorry," she said.

The kindly and respected editor of *The Braxton Banner* studied her from behind his desk. When Shelly had arrived at the newspaper that morning, she'd asked to meet with him in private. She genuinely liked and admired Marty, which made her task doubly difficult.

"We've never had a closed door meeting," he said now with a grin, "and after that door-rattling, I'm not sure I want another."

Shelly's mouth was parched; she tried to lick her lips, but they felt like gauze. Her breath was short and her dread of Marty's reaction made it hard for her to look him in the eye. She silently asked God for help, but this time she didn't feel the peace she'd experienced while talking with Lance Milburn.

"I'm not sure how to put this," she said finally.

Marty tilted his head a little to the left, and he looked at her with concern. "Personal or professional?" he asked.

"A little of both." Shelly's eyes welled with tears.

"Hmm. Let's start with what's most important. Give me the personal, first."

"I've been living a lie."

"OK, now what about the professional?"

She felt a tear roll down her cheek. "I've betrayed your trust," she whispered hoarsely.

Marty leaned back in his chair, folded his arms, then put his right hand under his chin. "What kind of lie?" he asked carefully. "What kind of trust?"

Shelly could tell he really didn't want to know. She took a deep breath and began to tell him about the query letter she'd sent to *Destination* magazine. She told of the trumped-up award and her agreement to work secretly for the magazine while covering Braxton for *The Banner.* Then she confessed to writing the first article and using false information to make the town look better than it was. She also admitted withholding her best material for the magazine's follow-up story. With painstaking detail, and sometimes in tears, she revealed the entire hoax for what it was and what it had become. As she spoke, she kept expecting Marty to react. At times, she even wanted him to yell, scream, or berate her, but he only listened, stone-faced and silent. Finally, she brought him up to the present; she told him about her last conversation with Lance Milburn and his refusal to acknowledge the hoax.

"The worst part of all, Marty—" she choked back a sob and reached in her purse for a Kleenex, "and what I'll never forgive myself for is the deaths of nine innocent people—because of my article. Seven in the balloon crash, Rick, and now Brian Stanley." Shelly leaned forward in her chair, her voice now faltering with regret. "Without the story, they'd all be alive. No hot air balloon, no crash—and Rick and Brian would never have come to Braxton." She leaned back in her chair and braced herself for the worst.

Marty hesitated for only a moment. "Shelly, there's nothing I could say that would make you feel worse than how you feel right now. This was difficult to tell—it took a lot of courage and I thank you." Shelly smiled slightly. Was he going to spare her what she deserved?

"However, I can't let it go at that," he continued. "As your coworker, your boss—but most of all, your friend—I must tell you that I am disappointed beyond words."

"I'm sorry, Marty. . . ."

Marty rose from his chair and walked to the window that looked down on Main Street. "Why are you telling me this now?" he asked.

Shelly reached down beside her chair for a folder. "I hoped you would let me set the record straight and apologize to the town."

Marty turned from the window. "And how do you suggest I do that?"

"By printing this," she said placing the folder on his desk.

He eyed the folder from the window. "What is it?"

"The truth about what I did and what happened to this town. I finished it last night. I'd like for you to put it in this week's paper."

"Why should I believe you now?" he asked, returning to his desk chair and picking up the folder.

"Because I've changed."

Marty opened the folder, read for a moment, then looked back at Shelly. "I'm shocked at what you pulled, Shelly—but now I'm getting angry." He read her suggested headline out loud: "'Braxton's Small Town Award Is Big Time Hoax, by Shelly Hinson.'" Then, as he read the story to himself, Shelly did the same.

Braxton's Small Town Award Is Big Time Hoax
by Shelly Hinson

Braxton—For nearly a year, I've lived a lie and betrayed the trust of the people of Braxton. It's not as if I came from out of town to lead a life of deceit. I was born and raised here.

I went to school in Braxton. My father was a teacher and my mother was a principal. But what I'm about to reveal, what I perpetrated, was nothing I learned from them. The shame I feel and the guilt I carry cannot be described. This story is my confession to my friends and neighbors, to let everyone know how sorry I am.

It began with an idea, a wild, radical, give-it-a-shot chance. I thought to myself, all they can do is say, "no." But to my amazement, they said, "yes." *Destination* magazine agreed to name Braxton as the Best Small Town in America. But the award was nothing more than a sham, a phony honor given to see how the town, its people, and those who moved here would change over the course of a year.

I wrote the original article under the ghost name, Bernardo Javier. Many of the facts and figures used for that story were false. I created a town that wasn't real.

To my surprise, most of the people in Braxton accepted the distinction without question. Maybe they loved our town so much, that in their hearts, they truly believed Braxton was best. Others, like Mayor Roger Carter, ignored reality and plunged the town into debt for perceived economic benefits that never fully happened. Council member Cal Spencer was the only elected official to oppose the mayor.

Mayor Carter pushed for, and got, a festival to celebrate Braxton's six-month "reign" as Best Small Town in America. On December 26, at the festival's opening ceremony, a hot air balloon crashed into a media tent, killing seven people, including Police Chief Trevor Talbot and his wife, Courtney. The mayor's son, Alan, and KSBY-TV reporter Heather Landis were severely burned in the accident. Shortly after the crash, it was discovered that Upper Limits, the company operating the balloon, was under a suspension by the

F.A.A., a fact Mayor Carter knew before the balloon lifted off.

After my article was printed in *Destination* magazine, hundreds of people moved to Braxton. They did little or no research and based their decision solely on the article's claims about Braxton. For some, it was their best move; for Rick Aguilara and Brian Stanley, it was their last move.

One person I regret using in all of this, is *The Banner's* editor, Marty Cavitt. My actions will reflect poorly on the credibility of the newspaper, and for that, I am profoundly—

"This stuff about me is garbage," Marty said, breaking the silence.

"I had to write what I felt," Shelly replied. "Will you print it?" She smiled weakly. "Please?"

Marty quickly leafed through the rest of the story. "I'll print it—but understand one thing."

Shelly's eyes brightened. "What's that?"

"It'll be the last story you write for this paper," he said firmly. "You're fired."

Shelly slowly nodded. "I understand. I expected that."

Marty cocked head to the right. "Earlier, you said you've changed. I can see a difference. It's on your face and in your voice. What happened—what made you stand up to Lance Milburn?"

"I told him I have a new editor," she said with a smile.

Marty flinched. "Huh?"

"You may have heard of Him. His name is Jesus Christ."

CHAPTER 42

San Luis Obispo
4:34 P.M.

After meeting with Marty, Shelly made some corrections to her story and then printed two copies—one for *The Banner* and one for herself. She began cleaning out her desk, but finally decided there was nothing she wanted, so most of the desk's contents went into the trash. The next person to sit at this desk could decide the value of anything that remained.

Shelly couldn't bring herself to say good-bye to anyone. She slipped out a side door and walked quickly to the street, where she climbed on her Harley. As she fastened her helmet under her chin, she noticed that a coastal fog had begun to roll into town.

She sighed, started her Harley, and in a style Rick would have been proud of, she rumbled up Main Street. She had one more person to talk to in private before her soul would be bared in public on the front page of Thursday's *Banner.* She passed Benny's restaurant, the grassy knoll where the balloon had crashed, the intersection where she nearly ran over Rick, the cemetery. *Oh, Lord, please let me see Rick in heaven some day,* she prayed. She remembered back to their talk on New Year's Eve, when Rick had spoken of a decision he'd made once at a junior high church camp. If only she knew for sure.

Shelly then headed east on Highway 46, eventually passing the spot where her parents and brother were killed. She roared off in the direction of the ocean, continuing on until she finally rode into San Luis Obispo and pulled up in front of Heather's apartment.

Heather opened the door, and the two women stared at each other. "I love your sweater," Shelly said, admiring Heather's short-sleeve, fluffy, fur-blend, pink top with its slightly cropped collar. She followed Heather into the living room where they sat down on opposite ends of the plush sofa.

"Thanks. It's as soft as it looks," she said with a smile.

It had been two months since her last visit, and Shelly noticed that Heather's reddish, clay-colored hair, burned in the accident, was beginning to take shape once again. And she didn't seem to be in as much pain. All the bandages were removed, but Shelly's heart broke when she saw the scars fully visible now.

"I've never forgotten what you asked me the last time I was here," Shelly said.

Heather's eyebrows shot up. "I'm not exactly Miss Quotable. What did I say?"

"You asked me if I wanted to have peace in my life."

Heather nodded. "Oh, yes. What did you do about it?"

Shelly recalled her reaction the last time Heather had brought up religion. Now, instead of recoiling from any discussion, she welcomed the chance to share the change in her life and the part Heather had played in it.

"I met with Leona Kyle on Saturday." Heather's eyes lit up at that, and she smiled in anticipation. "We had lunch together and I prayed to have Jesus come into my heart."

"Looks like God sent Leona to Braxton to reach both of us," Heather said brightly.

Heather's words seemed heavensent. "You know, up until now, I hadn't thought of that," Shelly said. "But you're right. You have no idea how much that means to me."

"It's great that you're a Christian, but you could have told me this over the phone. Did you come all the way here just for that?"

The warmth of the moment disappeared as Shelly's eyes moved from Heather's smile to the ugly, crinkled scar on her face. "No, the main reason I'm here is to ask your forgiveness."

Heather's mouth opened in surprise. "Why?"

"You'll probably hear or read about this on Thursday, but indirectly, I caused your accident."

Heather looked even more confused. "Sorry, I don't get it."

"The whole story about Braxton being the best small town in America was a fake."

"Who would do that?"

Shelly prayed silently for the right words. "Me. I wrote the magazine article. It was a big lie."

Heather thought for a moment, then frowned. "What did that have to do with my accident?"

"Don't you see?" Shelly pleaded. "Because of my story, you were there when the balloon crashed. Since I wrote that article, nine people in Braxton have been killed and you and Alan Carter were—" she faltered, "you were—hurt. You need to know how sorry I am. I hope you can someday forgive me."

Heather nodded slightly, then absentmindedly traced the scar on her face with her finger. "You're a Christian now, right?"

"A brand new believer with a ton of questions," Shelly agreed.

"Well, so am I. But from what I read in the Bible, there's no way you need to carry the guilt of my accident, or the deaths of anyone."

"Thanks for being nice—but I know the truth."

Heather reached across the sofa to take Shelly's hand. "You're wrong. I've asked myself a million times why this happened. Have you any idea how many answers I've gotten?"

Shelly shook her head.

"A million *I-don't-knows*, that's how many. God is in control, Shelly, and allows things to happen in this world."

"But the article brought you to the accident scene . . ."

"And I could have been killed driving to work that day," Heather shot back. "Would you have been responsible for that?"

Shelly was silent.

"You can't take the blame for this. I don't know all that much about the Bible, but I can tell you that Christians are supposed to be set free from guilt." She reached for her Bible and pulled a piece of paper from the inside flap. "When I had my time with Leona, I wrote some stuff down. Here, listen to this: God forgave you and He forgave me from all our sins, past, present, and future. There's nothing for me to forgive. God took care of that. But if it will make you feel better, here goes." Heather feigned a serious look and in an official sounding voice, proclaimed, "I, Heather Landis, now exonerate Shelly Hinson from any and all guilt in the hot air balloon crash on December 26." She winked. "There—are you happy?"

Shelly felt tears streaming down her face. "Very." They both rose from the sofa then and hugged. "Thank you, Heather. Thank you so much."

Heather stepped back. "Now it's my turn to ask some questions," she said. "What's going to happen to you after your story is printed?"

Shelly shook her head. "I have no idea. Marty Cavitt did what he had to do—he fired me. I'm sure after my story is printed, word will get to the wires and then to Lance back in New York."

"What will he do?"

"I'm not sure. It takes part of his thunder away. The June issue isn't due out for another four or five weeks."

"You'll probably be interviewed on radio and TV," Heather warned. "Maybe even some of those TV tabloid shows."

"I thought about that—but it'll be a chance to share my faith."

"How about if I give the TV exclusive to Channel 6? I'll call Mario after *The Banner* comes out."

Shelly smiled. "I can see that you're recovering. You're thinking news again—but who's Mario?" Quickly, Shelly remembered. "Wait, he's the cameraman who was with you when . . ."

Heather reflected a moment and nodded. "Yes, he was my cameraman that day. He's a great guy, Shelly. He doesn't care what I look like. Let me just say he's very, very special."

Shelly recognized that look in Heather's eyes; it was the same one people remarked about whenever she would talk about Rick. She turned her attention back to the *Destination* project. "Heather, it's weird, but Lance thought the article was going to win all sorts of awards."

Heather held up a finger of caution. "It may still do that, only not with the magazine."

Now it was Shelly's turn to be confused. "OK, fill Miss Density in on that one."

"If it's as good as I think it is, what you've admitted to and written for your local paper just might win *The Banner* a Pulitzer."

Shelly laughed out loud for the first time since Rick's death. "I'd pay to see Lance's face if that happened," she said and looked at her watch. "Before I go, what about you? Can I help with anything?"

"No, I'm doing fine," Heather replied. "Mario checks in all the time. The TV station's insurance and worker's comp. are getting me by for now. I may go back to work as a writer or on the assignment desk— but it's too early to think about that. I've hired an attorney who thinks I can recover damages from the balloon company and perhaps Braxton and its *not-so-honorable* mayor."

"Should I expect a summons too?" Shelly asked.

Heather laughed. "Are you kidding? I saw you when you arrived. And now, after hearing your story, the only thing you'll have that's worth anything is that hog parked out front."

"On that note, I'm leaving." She hugged Heather, then moved toward the door. "Thanks again for being so special."

"I'm not so sure about that. I can't believe the way I acted when I was the local TV news queen."

"At least you didn't hide what you were," Shelly said with a grimace.

"Hey," Heather chided, "don't get off on another guilt trip, you hear?"

"OK," Shelly agreed, "but let's keep in touch—you, Leona, and myself."

"The three believers, right?"

"Two believers and a confessed deceiver." Shelly opened the door and walked down the steps.

She looked over her shoulder to see Heather shaking her finger in mock disapproval. "Yeah, Leona's the teacher, you and that hog are the screecher, and I'm the scary creature."

Shelly's laugh echoed in the apartment complex.

Selected Bibliography

Cameron, Kevin. "Once & Future World." *Cycle World*, (Fall 1995) Interview with Harley Davidson's Vice President of Engineering, Earl Werner.

Funk, Charles Earle. *A Hog On Ice*. New York: Harper & Row Publishers, 1948.

Hyams, Joe with Jay Hyams. *James Dean Little Boy Lost*. New York: Warner Books, Inc., 1992.

Riese, Randall. *The Unabridged James Dean*. Chicago: Contemporary Books, 1991.

The New Encyclopedia Britannica, Volumes 5 and 23. Chicago, 1988.

"Whole Hog!" *Road and Track*, February 15, 1995.

And these great titles,
from Chariot Victor Publishing,
by popular author Jack Cavanaugh. . .

THE VICTORS
Jack Cavanaugh

The seventh book in the popular adult fiction series, "An American Family Portrait," *The Victors* follows the path of a new generation of the Morgan family. Four siblings are caught up in the events of World War II, and each will handle the challenge differently. Nat, Walt, Alex and Lily must face life's worst before they find out what it really means to be "the victors."

ISBN: 1-56476-589-X
PACKAGING: PAPERBACK
SIZE: 5½" X 8½" • 463 PAGES
AVAILABLE NOW

The Peacemakers

Jack Cavanaugh

Into the volatile backdrop of cultural and political turmoil of the '60s, the author sets the final chapter of this popular series. How will the thirteenth generation of the Morgan family in America tackle the challenges of the Vietnam War, hippies, social protest and assassinations? Will their faith in God, symbolized by the passing of the family Bible from generation to generation, remain strong and vibrant?

ISBN: 1-56476-681-0
PACKAGING: PAPERBACK
SIZE: 5½" x 8½" • 512 PAGES
RELEASE: OCTOBER 1998

Jack Cavanaugh is a full-time free-lance writer and public speaker. He lives with his wife and their three children in San Diego, California. Jack's other books in this series have appeared on the ECPA best-sellers list, and the first book, *The Puritans*, was a Gold Medallion finalist.